ADVANCE PRAISE FOR *JUST MY TYPE*

"With its sharp writing, hilarious banter, and delightful characters, *Just My Type* is an absolutely perfect romantic comedy. I only wish I could read it again for the first time!"

—Lacie Waldon, author of *From the Jump* and *The Layover*

"Falon Ballard delivers a page-turning second-chance romance bursting with crackling banter and delightful characters, anchored by a layered, emotional, and sexy love story at the center. I couldn't put it down!"

—Ava Wilder, author of *How to Fake It in Hollywood*

"*Just My Type* sparks with enemies-to-lovers wit and dazzles with Los Angeles flair. A fabulous, banterrific workplace rom-com, and just our type of romance."

—Emily Wibberley & Austin Siegemund-Broka, authors of *The Roughest Draft*

"Everything about Falon Ballard's writing cuts straight to the heart. With supremely relatable characters, sparkling wit, and a second-chance rivals-to-lovers romance to die for, *Just My Type* is an unputdownable showstopper! Ballard's fresh and affirming voice reminds readers what it's like to fall in love, and what it means to love yourself most of all. An auto-buy author guaranteed to skyrocket straight to the top of TBRs everywhere!"

—Courtney Kae, author of *In the Event of Love*

"*Just My Type* is a must read. With the perfect swirl of lovable characters, sizzling chemistry, and perfectly crafted humor, Ballard's sophomore novel is a story you won't want to put down. Falon Ballard is an auto-buy author for me and she always delivers stories that take up residence in my heart—this new story is no exception!"

—Denise Williams, author of *Do You Take This Man* and *The Fastest Way to Fall*

PRAISE FOR *LEASE ON LOVE*

"[A] fun and light read . . . Ballard intersperses the book with text conversations (emojis and all) between Sadie and Jack, as well as her group conversation with her friends, that make readers feel like they're really part of the story. When Sadie's and Jack's feelings for each other are finally realized, you can't help but celebrate alongside the characters."

—*USA Today*

"Laugh-out-loud banter, smart characters, and heartfelt charm . . . this rom-com has it all!" —*Woman's World*

"[A] cozy romance." —*PopSugar*

"[A] quirky, heartwarming contemporary romance . . . Ballard's snappy prose and unconventional couple charm, and she gets some good chuckles out of skewering the New beautiful love story about finding something precious that seems out of reach. *Lease on Love* is one of my new favorite romance novels!"

—Denise Williams, author of *Do You Take This Man* and *The Fastest Way to Fall*

"A hopeful, heartwarming debut. With a relatable disaster of a protagonist and an adorably nerdy hero, this opposites-attract, roommates-to-lovers romance is a true delight."

—Rachel Lynn Solomon, author of *Weather Girl* and *The Ex Talk*

"Sadie is a firecracker of a protagonist who's very aware of her flaws, and Jack is her perfect counterpart, embracing all of her rough edges with softness and understanding. *Lease on Love* warmly and wittily underscores that none of us are perfect, but we are all worthy, we are all enough; we all deserve to be loved, not just by others, but by ourselves too."

—Sarah Hogle, author of *Just Like Magic* and *Twice Shy*

"*Lease on Love* is a crackling, compulsively readable debut about forging new career and romantic paths, finding strength in found family, and discovering what it truly means to be 'home.' I enjoyed every minute of it!"

—Suzanne Park, author of *Loathe at First Sight* and *So We Meet Again*

York City real estate market. Meanwhile, stellar supporting characters (especially Sadie's besties, Gemma, Nick, and Harley) provide a solid underpinning to this enjoyable tale. This is a treat." —*Publishers Weekly*

"Ballard's debut novel, a fantastic read for fans of *The Flatshare* (2019), is a sharply funny roommates-to-lovers, opposites-attract rom-com. . . . With profound sensitivity, Ballard shows how therapy and each other's company help Jack deal with his grief and Sadie with her low self-esteem and negative self-image." —*Booklist*

"This charming story of new beginnings and emotional growth has a sassy and likable narrator in Sadie, and the novel keeps a light tone despite touching on difficult subjects like toxic families and grief. . . . Readers who enjoy female entrepreneurs, found family, and gentle romantic leads will enjoy." —*Library Journ*

"The romantic beats and the slow-burning attraction tween [Sadie and Jack] are things to savor. . . . Ballard sw explores the ways they complement one another ar how they hope to reinvent themselves following cata personal changes." —*Kirku*

"*Lease on Love* is a delight on every level. Ballar soft, sweet story with enough shadows to mak ever after feel that much more earned. Jack gether are real in the best ways, and the c shows the abiding love of friends and foun

ALSO BY FALON BALLARD

Lease on Love

someone to be happy with long term 10. Learn to be okay with being alone Lana's List

Lana 1. Get actual furniture and household items (i. e. linens and towels) 1. Go on a

wardrobe 2. Go to therapy 3. Set up a dating profile on a relationship seeking app/

something that's new to you 4. Go to therapy 4. Play tourist in LA for a day 5. Delete

call numbers from phone 5. Kiss a stranger 6. Get and care for a pet 6. Go speed dating

three dates with the same person 7. Volunteer 8. Keep a plant alive for the duration of the

guy's number Have a one-night stand 9. No sex for the entire ten weeks 9. Take a vaca

Falon Ballard

G. P. PUTNAM'S SONS
New York

PUTNAM
— EST. 1838 —
G. P. PUTNAM'S SONS
Publishers Since 1838
An imprint of Penguin Random House LLC
penguinrandomhouse.com

ISBN (trade paperback) 9780593419939
ISBN (ebook) 9780593419946

Printed in the United States of America
1st Printing

Book design by Ashley Tucker

To all the moms—you're doing a great job;
and especially to my mom, who has
always done the best job

JUST *my* TYPE

1

They invite you to a place that
has special meaning to the two of you.

—Lana Parker, "Ten Signs Your Partner Might Be About to Propose"

I'M HAVING AN ELLE WOODS MOMENT.

And not a "wearing a pink power suit, getting into Harvard Law, smashing the patriarchy" Elle Woods moment.

More like a "hysterically crying in a public place because instead of being proposed to I'm getting dumped" Elle Woods moment.

The good news is I haven't actually started to cry yet. Which is a relief because my mouth is hanging open in complete and utter shock, and adding heaving sobs to the mix would make for a huge, snotty mess. A literal one, not just the figurative one my life has become.

"I'm sorry, what did you just say to me?"

"I said, I think we should break up."

I stare at the stupid, stupid man sitting across from me. I don't want to see Evan's stupid, stupid face for even one second longer, but I can't seem to look away, my face frozen in a mixture of horror and WTF-ery. I force my eyes shut, hoping against hope that when I reopen them, all of this will have been some kind of sick joke.

But it's not.

When I open my eyes—eyes Evan once told me weren't just brown but *brown with flecks of gold*—he's still there. Still watching me with a gaze full of pity.

I wish I could channel a Real Housewife and throw my dirty martini in his face, but that would require a level of motor function I don't seem to have. Also, something tells me I'm going to need the liquid courage to survive the rest of this night.

Finally, after several minutes of painful silence, Evan reaches over and pats my hand. Like I'm some grandma he helped across the street and not the woman he's been dating the last four years.

"I know this isn't what you were expecting, Lana Banana." His stupid, stupid mouth curls up in a condescending hint of a smile.

I always hated that nickname. *Lana* doesn't even rhyme with *banana*.

Stupid. Stupid.

I'm so fucking stupid.

I yank my hand out from under his, the mere touch of his skin on mine enough to give me the icks. "I thought you brought me here to propose." I mean for it to come out accusatory, but instead my voice hitches with a tinge of whine.

A proposal is a reasonable assumption when the man you've been in a committed relationship with for four years plans dinner at the restaurant where you had your first date. Assuming the man isn't a stupid, stupid asshole.

Evan's face scrunches up like the very thought of marrying me is painful. "Oh." He nods slowly, in a way he probably thinks is wise and sage and Gandalf-esque. "I can see now how you might've misinterpreted this."

"How *I* might have misinterpreted this?" My voice screeches and several patrons at surrounding tables subtly—and not so subtly—turn our way. I reach for my martini and for a second really consider how good it would feel to watch the olive-green-tinted liquid drip down his self-tanned face.

But then I wouldn't get to drink it. I chug the remainder of the cocktail before holding my empty glass in the air.

A server rushes over and removes the glass from my hand, as if he's been waiting for me to chuck it at someone.

"Hi, yes, more of these please." When the server gives me a wary look, I point across the table. "This motherfucker thought it was appropriate to bring me—his girlfriend of four years—to our first-date spot to break up with me."

He winces sympathetically. "I'll just keep them coming then?"

I salute him with my invisible glass. "Good man."

The keeper of the martinis, a.k.a. my new best friend, scampers off.

Leaving us with a silence that now doesn't feel painful as much as it does heavy. The longer we sit and stare at each other, the more my ire flattens into defeat.

"Can I ask why?" I try to remove any anger from the question so he knows that I mean it, that I really want to know. Even though I'm not totally sure myself.

He sighs and picks up my hand again, but this time the gesture is one of comfort, as if there's a chance we might actually walk away from this still friends. "Lana, you don't want to be with me any more than I want to be with you. You know the two of us aren't actually right for each other."

"Then why have we been together for so long, Evan?" I might as well be asking myself that question since I know he's right; the two of us *don't* belong together. We shouldn't be dating, let alone thinking about getting married.

His grip on my hand tightens. "Do you want the real, honest answer?"

I purse my lips, nodding, even though only half of me—the sadistic half—wants the truth.

"Every girl I dated before you hated my mother, and I liked how you two clicked. I get that she and I have a relationship that might be closer than most, but I never thought it'd be an issue in my dating life. But all my old girlfriends complained about her and how much time she and I spent together, and how much I shared with her." A hint of an apology darkens his eyes, also brown, though with zero flecks of gold.

"Until me."

"You know, sometimes I think you like her better than me," he grumbles under his breath.

I don't refute his comment, which he takes for the confirmation it is. Judy is one kick-ass woman—was I not supposed to hang out with her when she asked?

"It was a nice change for a while, but then I realized I don't think I want to be married to someone who's got Olympic-level mommy issues." He crosses his arms over his chest and an actual pout forms on his thin lips. How quickly we've moved from a semi-rational conversation to throwing barbs.

"Oh, is that the newest Olympic event? Damn, I can't believe I missed the trials." I slip back into sarcasm like it's my favorite old Princess Leia T-shirt, comforting and safe.

"Lana—"

"Look, Evan"—two can play the condescending game, and I drip it into my voice like I'm pouring salted caramel on a sundae—"I really have nothing left to say to you other than you better drop some serious cash on this table before you leave. I'm going to be drinking on your tab for the rest of the night." I happily accept a fresh martini from our server—already thankful I like them light on the vodka and heavy on the olive juice—who glares at Evan before retreating to the bar, where a small crowd of employees are pretending not to watch the reality TV drama unfolding right before their eyes.

This is LA though, so chances are pretty good they've seen *actual* reality TV play out in front of them. In fact, I'm sure the cast of *Vanderpump Rules* has filmed here more than once, so they've most definitely seen top-tier cocktail tossing.

I take a long sip of my fresh drink as Evan clearly doesn't get the hint. "I'm sorry, why are you still here?"

"I'm not just going to leave you alone when you're well on your way to being drunk. I may not love you, but I'm not that much of a dick."

I channel my inner Thor, tilting my head to the side and scrunching up my face. "Aren't you though?" Another quarter of my drink goes down, chilling my throat and numbing my feelings. I know that once those feelings return, my inevitable sobs will make Elle Woods's look downright peaceful. Therefore, numb they must stay. "Also, I won't be alone for long. May is already on her way."

He sits back in his seat, frowning. "Seriously? Do you guys have some kind of Bat-Signal?"

"Yeah, it's called a cell phone, dipshit. I texted her while you were in the middle of your it's-not-you-it's-me speech." I stab an olive, imagining staking the toothpick right through his eyeball. I can't believe that for half a second I thought we might be able to get through this breakup like mature adults. Now I'm taking solace in the image of a plastic cocktail skewer burying itself in his pupil. Anger, keep the anger flowing. It's far better than sadness. "For the record, I'd like to make it clear that you are one hundred percent right about that. It is most definitely you."

His pout transforms into a scowl. "Why am I not surprised? You can't even make it through one breakup conversation without needing someone to lean on."

I cross my arms over my chest. "What the fuck is that supposed to mean?"

"You're incapable of being alone, Lana. And frankly, it's exhausting."

"Your face is exhausting." Ouch. That not-quite-a-comeback slips out before I can stop it.

"Are you sure you want me to leave? I wouldn't want you to be by yourself for five whole minutes." At least the maturity level has dropped across the board.

"I've literally never been more sure of anything in my life." I swig the rest of my martini, and before I even set down the empty glass, another full one is sitting in its spot. Someone is getting a very large tip tonight. "And if I were you, I'd blow this joint before May arrives." Unlike myself, my best friend would never hesitate to throw a drink, and there's a fifty-fifty chance she might also throw a punch.

The skin beneath his spray tan pales. He reaches into his wallet and throws three hundreds down on the table. He pushes his chair back and stands, lingering for just a second too long. The quips and the insults fade away, leaving space for memories of the good times we managed to have over the last four years. "I really am sorry, Lana."

Yeah, well, me too.

I expected to be leaving this restaurant engaged, our arms wrapped around each other, both of us happily buzzed on the complimentary champagne that would've accompanied my giant rock of a ring.

A ring that probably wouldn't have looked anything like the hundreds I have pinned to my public wedding board, which I've conveniently left open on my laptop any time Evan has been at my house over the course of the last year.

But I would've grown to love it.

Just as we would've grown to hate each other.

"Bye, Evan," I say, only to find he's already left and I'm talking to my martini glass.

My empty martini glass.

But never fear, a new one filled to the brim floats in front of my face. I turn to thank the server, only to find the glass is being proffered by my best friend, May. The server is right behind her, a plate of fried pickles in one hand and a giant piece of cheesecake in the other.

He drops the goods on the table while May slides into Evan's now empty seat. She flashes the server one of her knockout smiles and he's only momentarily stunned, scurrying away a second later.

"Is it too soon to say how much I will not miss that guy?" May dips a pickle in ranch and hands it to me.

Mmm. Pickles and a dirty martini. I can practically feel my blood pressure rising due to the salt intake, but that doesn't stop me from shoveling one after another into my mouth. Plus, the breading will help soak up the alcohol already sloshing around in my stomach, so really, I'm making the healthy, sensible choice.

"You've never exactly been shy about your feelings when it comes to Evan. No need to start now." To be fair,

I've never exactly been shy about my feelings when it comes to Evan either. Perfect partner the man is not—was not.

She softens her voice, reaching over and squeezing my hand. "Want to talk about it?"

I gulp down half of my drink. "I thought he was going to propose and instead he dumped me, I think that's about all there is to say."

"He's lucky he left before I got here." May inches a glass of water in my direction, but I ignore it.

"That wasn't a coincidence." I give her a look dripping in drunken, sappy love. "You're terrifying when you go all mama bear."

May flashes me a gentle smile, and that's when my eyes fill with tears. Tears that only seconds later rush down my cheeks like that really big waterfall in Yosemite, though not nearly as picturesque, I'm sure. It doesn't even take a breath before I'm enveloped in a hug, May's spicy citrus scent wrapping around me like my old security blanket.

I'd never try to claim the thick black tracks of mascara streaming down my face are due to genuine sadness at the loss of my relationship. I'm not bereft at the thought of no longer being with Evan. Even now, less than an hour after listening to him tell me it's over, I know deep down we were never right for each other in the first place. I know in a day or two, relief will wash over me like a cleansing ocean wave sweeping across the shore.

And that's all well and good and positive-vibes and look-on-the-bright-side kind of shit.

But for tonight, I just got dumped. I just got dumped in

public when I was mostly expecting a proposal. I just got dumped by a man I thought I was going to spend the rest of my life with. It's embarrassing, to say the least.

And the truly terrible part is it's not the first time this has happened to me. Or the second. Or even the third.

Stupid, stupid asshole-face Evan is the fourth man I thought was "the one." The fourth man whose parents took me in as one of their own. And the fourth man to very clearly not want to make me a permanent member of the family.

I pull away from May and dab at my eyes with my napkin. "I'm an idiot," I say, my voice so quiet she has to lean in to hear me.

"We're not going to do that tonight." May moves the pickles out of the way, making room for the slice of cheesecake, which is the size of my head. "We can talk about your terrible relationship decisions tomorrow, LP."

"Gee, thanks."

She shrugs, helping herself to a bite of cheesecake. "You know I'm right. But as I said, we're not going to talk about that tonight. Tonight, we will eat and drink until we feel like puking, and then go crawl into that big-ass bed of yours and watch whatever chick flicks your little romance-loving heart desires." May's voice takes on a serious tone, one that's rare for her. "I'm sorry that little shithead broke your heart, my friend, but I can say with one hundred percent certainty that you are better off without him."

"I'm not saying you're wrong—"

"I'm never wrong."

I roll my eyes but pair it with a tiny smile. "I'm not saying you're wrong. About Evan. But I need some time to process all of this before I can just learn a lesson and move on, knowing he taught me something or whatever."

May snorts into her wine.

"I know it's cliché, but you know what I mean, May." I chug half a glass of water before reaching for my martini glass in a silent request for another cocktail. Then I think better of it and go back to the water.

"The snort was about you taking time to process." She taps her watchless wrist. "You'll be in a new, long-term, fully committed relationship within twenty-one days."

"That is both precise and insulting."

She grins, showing off a smile of straight white teeth framed by perfectly lined red lips. "You're incapable of being single, LP."

"Am not," I bite back, though I do appear to be incapable of being mature this evening. Which may or may not have something to do with the fact that May is basically echoing Evan's words. And the only thing worse than hearing your faults listed by your ex in the middle of a breakup is having them confirmed by your very best friend.

"Are too. But, again, we don't have to talk about that tonight." She holds her glass up to the center of the table. "To my darling bestie. You're the sister I never wanted and the partner I never knew I needed. Any man who can't hold on to you is a complete fucking moron and we hate him."

"That was beautiful." I clink my glass to hers before taking a long swallow. "Now let's get smashed."

TWO OR THREE or four—who has the ability to keep count at this point?—hours later, May and I stumble out of our Lyft and up the stone walkway to the front door of my house.

I love my house. Were I in a sober state of mind, I'd probably spend a minute appreciating its beauty and acknowledging the generational wealth and impeccable timing that afforded me the opportunity to buy this prime piece of Los Angeles real estate. Located in the super-trendy neighborhood of Atwater Village (though it was more up-and-coming and less hipster haven when I bought this place), the small Spanish-style abode has everything I need. Two bedrooms, one fully remodeled bathroom, air-conditioning, a parking space, a small backyard, and it's walking distance to multiple coffee shops and bars. Yes, I know how lucky I am.

But tonight I don't care about any of that. I care that I'm able to get my key in the front door and get it unlocked without either of us puking in my lovingly tended front garden.

Together we stumble down the hallway to my bedroom, and I think we manage to discard our shoes and purses before we collapse on my bed, which is a major win at this point.

"I want to watch a movie that's going to make me cry." I pull myself up for just long enough to turn on the TV that's mounted over my dresser.

"Does that seem like the best idea right now?" May's voice is muffled by the pillow she's face-planted on.

"Yes. This is what you do after getting dumped. Step one, get drunk."

"Check!"

"Step two, watch rom-coms. Step three, eat ice cream." I scooch off the bed with the intent of heading to the kitchen to grab the emergency pint of Ben & Jerry's I keep stashed in my freezer. However, the spinning room throws me off balance and I have to steady myself on the edge of the bed.

May turns her face to me. "What's step four?"

"Step four of what?"

She tries to throw a pillow at me but can't seem to launch it farther than a few inches. "Step four of the post-breakup plan?"

"Oh." I flash her a grin. "Find a new man, of course." Finally steady enough to walk comfortably, I leave May to groan into my pillows as I make my way to the kitchen.

Wisely, I decide I should chug a glass of water before I do anything else. And then I swig a second just to be safe. I grab the pint of Tonight Dough and two spoons and start back toward my bedroom. My purse is dropped about halfway down the hallway, and I reach in and pull out my phone, pretty impressed with my foresight.

May is passed out diagonally across my bed when I get back to my room, snoring in a loud and deep-throated way that tells me she's clearly no longer conscious. I nudge myself in next to her, tucking myself under the covers and turning on *While You Were Sleeping*. After taking down the whole pint of ice cream, I reach for my phone to set my alarm so I don't sleep away the entire next day. I have to squint to make the words and numbers on-screen come into focus, but I'm able to make out the fact that I have an Instagram DM. From a username I only see when I really lose my grip and deep-dive on an ex-stalking binge. Something I haven't done in at least a year. Okay, six months.

I tap in my passcode and navigate over to the app, ignoring all other notifications in favor of plunging directly into my messages.

@SethCarson: Hey. I've been trying to call you but every time I get sent straight to voicemail, so you're either ignoring me or you blocked me. We need to talk. Call me when you can, sooner rather than later.

Okay.

Wow.

First of all, the nerve of him to think that his number wouldn't be blocked. Obviously, I have no desire to talk to him ever again. The *only* reason he isn't blocked on social media is because I like to check in occasionally and make sure he is still alone and miserable. As he should be.

Second, I am in no shape to consider any and all implications of this message. "We need to talk"? "Call me"? What the fuck could the two of us possibly have to talk about?

Because I'm heartbroken and still slightly, if not mostly, drunk, I click on his profile. Seth rarely posts photos of himself, his feed instead full of pictures of his travels. For the past however many years, he's been a roving reporter, traversing the country and sometimes the world for his stories, which are mostly investigative, serious-type pieces. He's an in-demand freelancer, so he's never in one place for very long. When we were still young and naïve, we thought we'd be journalists together at the same newspaper, him covering news and politics, me reviewing books and the arts.

I scoff into my empty pint of ice cream. Neither of us ended up where we thought we'd be.

I squeeze my eyes shut because suddenly all my brain wants to do is replay the first of my catastrophic breakups. The worst one. The one that started it all and has yet to be beat, even by tonight's should've-been-a-proposal. But despite sobering up somewhat thanks to the ice cream and water and probably the jags of crying, I know I'm in no position—physically or emotionally—to be able to handle a DM from an ex, especially not *the* ex.

I need reinforcements. "May." I poke her repeatedly until she finally murmurs something that sounds somewhat conscious. "I just got a DM from Seth."

"Oh shit."

At least I think that's what she says since she hasn't removed her face from the pillow.

"I need another drink." I'm sort of joking, because lord knows I've imbibed enough alcohol over the past few hours to last me a lifetime, but if this situation doesn't call for excessive drinking, then I don't know what does.

And when May actually rises from the bed and joins me in the kitchen, my decision is validated.

"Wanna talk about it?" May clinks her shot glass full of tequila against mine, asking me the question for the second time that night.

"Nope. How many shots do I need until I black out?" I down the liquid from my glass, wincing as it burns my throat.

Turns out, just the one.

2

My cure for getting over a breakup?
Move on to the next person!

—Lana Parker, "So You Got Dumped, Now What?"

AN EVIL BRIGHT LIGHT FORCES MY EYES OPEN THE NEXT morning. It's either the ass crack of dawn, or my drinking caught up with me and I'm being beamed up—or down, jury's still out.

I have to literally pry my eyelids apart as they seem to be caked in some kind of black gunk that I really hope is the remnants of last night's proposal-worthy makeup look. Once I finally manage to unstick them, I'm forced to survey my surroundings. Which immediately makes me want to close my eyes again.

I managed to make it into a pajama shirt at least, an old one from high school, hanging off one shoulder and frayed at the bottom. Something warm is wrapped around my thigh. A minuscule lift of my head—one that sets my brain spinning—lets me know it's just May, our legs both intertwined and also splayed across the bed in some sort of drunk feat of physics. When I thunk my head back down, May grunts, because said thunkage lands on her right boob, which has apparently been acting as my pillow.

"Are you going to puke again?" she mutters, none too gently pushing my head onto a real pillow.

"Not sure." I hold my head as still as possible, not ready to find out.

"We are way too old for this shit."

"Think we can Postmates Gatorade?" I shift my head a fraction of an inch and the room doesn't rotate. Progress.

"And will they bring it directly to this bed? Because I do not plan to get up for at least twenty-four hours." Her voice is now muffled by my quilt, which she has wrapped around her entire body, presumably to hide from the light and the sound of my voice.

There's no reasonable explanation for why this is the moment I get the giggles, but one escapes my parched lips, and before I can control it, an avalanche of laughter spills forth.

"Oh my god, shut up." May tries to throw a pillow at me, missing entirely

But my giggles are contagious, and once I get going, she can't help but join. Before long, we're curled up in tight cannonballs, hysterically laughing and, thankfully, not puking.

"Oh my god," I choke out when I can finally form words. "I got dumped last night!"

The declaration sparks another wave of laughter. I clutch at my stomach, both as a way to continue to remain puke-free and because this is the most intense ab workout I've gotten in years.

"I thought I was going to marry him, and instead I got dumped!" My cackling continues for several seconds before I realize I'm the only one still laughing.

May manages to push herself into a sitting position, though the quilt is still wrapped around her like she's a mummy. She brings herself too close to my face and stares dead-on into my eyes. "You are too good for that milque-toast motherfucker."

I swallow down another laugh, which is on its way to morphing into another bout of tears, tears that I do not want to shed. Tears that wouldn't so much be for Evan or our relationship, but for what this breakup means in the bigger picture of my life. "Good word."

"I know." She pulls her head free from the quilt. "I'm going to get in the shower. Then you are getting in the shower. Then we're calling in sick and going for brunch."

The word *brunch* makes my stomach turn. "No booze."

"No booze. Coffee and carbs."

A magic combination that's enough to perk me up, just a tad.

May shucks the rest of her blanket cocoon, shimmying until she is sitting next to me, both of us leaning against my natural wood headboard.

"How are you really?"

"Mostly, I just feel like a total dumbass." I don't bother to lie to her; she'd be able to hear it in my voice. "It's not the sadness, not really. I just can't believe I let myself waste four years on him."

She picks up my hand in hers, lacing our fingers together and squeezing.

I wait for her to argue with me, to tell me all relationships teach us something or happen for a reason or some other Hallmark-level bullshit platitude. But instead we just sit in the silence, my head resting on her shoulder, until I gently nudge her. "Go shower. I need caffeine."

She basically falls off the bed but still manages to do it gracefully. A minute later the shower in my en suite bathroom turns on and I hear her groan of relief even over the rush of the water.

I let my head fall back against the headboard as I attempt to process everything that went down last night. Not just the breakup, but Evan's accusation, that I'm incapable of being alone. And May's assertion that I'll find myself in a new relationship before the dust of this one even settles. My brain isn't functioning well enough to puzzle it all out, but I know it's something I shouldn't ignore this time, as much as I want to.

May emerges from my bathroom looking almost like a human being. She steps into my closet, no doubt helping herself to whatever items she wants from my wardrobe. Not that any of them are up to her standards. "Are you feeling sorry for yourself yet?"

"Yes." Again, there's no point in lying. Even from the closet she'd be able to hear the deception in my voice. Perhaps I should think about brushing up on my fibbing skills now that I no longer have a serious boyfriend to occupy my time.

"Cut it out."

"It's been less than twenty-four hours, May. I think I'm allowed to wallow a little."

She emerges from the closet outfitted in one of my simple coral sundresses. Of course, since she's a good four inches taller and four cups bustier than I am, it hits a little differently on her than it does on me. She points to my Spider-Man alarm clock. "You may wallow for five more minutes. And then you're cut off."

"You're so bossy."

"Duh." May is one of that rare breed of Californians who not only were born and raised in LA but are third generation. Her great-grandparents immigrated from Mexico decades ago and her entire family has stayed local, meaning holidays at her grandparents' house are the best, and you can count on her to throw "duh" or "dude" into most any conversation.

She and I were roommates our freshman year at USC, and luckily she took my Connecticut-born ass under her wing, schooling me on the unwritten rules of the freeways and ridiculous traffic, and helping me pop all my LA cherries, everything from my first In-N-Out burger to my first Dodgers game. I honestly don't know how I would have survived freshman year, let alone college, without her—both her Los Angeles tutelage and her quick wit at the times when I needed laughter the most.

If only my supreme luck in friends could extend even the slightest bit into some kind of romantic good fortune.

Ha.

R2-D2's telltale chirp beeps at me from across the room, alerting me to a text message and pulling me out of my haze of self-pity. And of course I left my phone an insurmountable six feet away from where I am currently plastered to my bed.

Beep boop beep bop.

"Oh my god, shut that thing up," May calls from the kitchen, where hopefully she's pouring me water or making me coffee. She has very little patience for my intense love of all things nerdy.

"I can't. He's too far away." I try scooting down to the foot of the bed in some sort of backward army crawl, but I don't make it more than a few inches.

When the blasted droid keeps chirping, I attempt a busted barrel roll to get myself out of bed without having to engage my core muscles. I manage to make it over to my dresser, where drunk me casually tossed my phone on top of my jewelry tray. I squint to force the alerts on the screen to come into something resembling focus.

"Shit. Shit shit shit."

"Please tell me you did not just actually take a shit." May returns to my bedroom and hands me a glass of water and some aspirin, along with a grimace.

I groan, stumbling over to my nightstand to plug my almost-dead phone into its charger. "No, I did not. Gross."

"Then what's the problem?" She seems to have fully returned to functioning human, which is really just not fair.

"I forgot that Natasha scheduled a meeting for today. Apparently she has some big announcement and we're all expected in the office even though most of us work from home on Fridays. Shit." I head directly for the bathroom, wishing I had time for an actual shower. Instead, I splash cold water on my face before sticking my mouth under the tap and drinking like we aren't in a permanent drought.

May follows me into the bathroom, leaning against the counter, removing a nonexistent smudge from under her eye. "Are you going to be late?"

"Not if I leave in five minutes." I wipe the final trail of mascara from my cheeks and don't bother putting on any fresh makeup. I head for my closet, throwing on leggings and an old USC T-shirt—not my best look, but it will have to do. I pull my long auburn hair into the messiest of buns and unplug my phone. Thank god for car chargers. "Can you lock up?"

May emerges from the bathroom just in time to give my outfit a sneering look. "I would be fired if I stepped into my office looking like that."

"I'm a writer, this is me in my natural state. Thanks, love you, bye!" I don't bother waiting for her response, striding as fast as my queasy stomach will allow out the door and to my car. When I hook up my phone to my charger, two things happen: Britney blares from my speakers at an unholy level, causing me to recoil backward. And I notice the DM notification still on my screen from last night.

And the second half of my fucktacular evening comes rushing back to me.

Seth's name on my screen and the memory of his cryptic message are enough to make my stomach churn again. The last thing I need in my current state is any sort of communication from him. I clear the notification and decide to deal with it later. Or never. He can't actually be expecting me to call him, right?

Before I can even put the car in reverse, my phone rings, right as I'm vowing to never dial Seth Carson's number for as long as I live. I physically jump in my seat.

It's not Seth calling, but I'd almost rather it were.

I click *Accept Call* and switch the audio to my car's Bluetooth. "Hi, Mom."

"Hello, Lana." My mother always calls me by my name. Never "sweetie" or "dear" or anything showing even a smidge of affection.

"This isn't a great time, I'm on my way to work." At least I have a legitimate excuse to stay on this call for as short as possible.

"Still working on your little relationship column?" Even from thousands of miles away, the judgment seeps through her tone.

"Yes, Mom, I'm still working on my award-winning relationship column."

My mother's disdain for the dating articles I write is maybe the one thing we have in common. I was placed on the beat when I first started at my job, mostly because I was the only one on staff who was actually in a stable relationship at the time. And even though I've now been with the same publication for eight years and it's seen me through more than one breakup, I'm still stuck writing about love, when what I really want to be writing about is books and movies and television series, basically anything pop-culture related. I've always found solace in stories, and the only relationships I really care about (aside from my own) are the ones I ship on my screen.

Not that my mom would find that kind of writing any more worthwhile; she's never hid her contempt for my fandom obsessions.

"Well, I won't keep you from your very important job that surely benefits millions, I just wanted to let you know I'm going to be traveling for the next month at least and my cell service will be spotty." I don't know if she means to come across as condescending, but she sure has no problem putting down both me and my job every time we speak. Which luckily isn't too often.

"Setting up another girls' school?" I try to cut the attitude from my tone because, you know, setting up a school for underprivileged children is not actually a bad thing and doesn't deserve my sarcasm. Even if it means she's always put other children before her own. Despite the fact that I'm thankful for my good fortune, it still would've been nice to have had a mom at home.

"Yes. I don't suppose you would like to join me?"

"Some of us do have to work, Mom. You know, to pay our bills?" I take every opportunity to subtly remind her of her own immense privilege, mostly because I know it irks her.

My mother comes from money. And not like middle-class, invested-well money. Oil money. Big money. Money that, according to my mother, was earned by destroying the earth, and is therefore bad money. And I mean, she's not wrong. Once her parents passed and she inherited the trust, she made it her mission to spend as much of that money doing good works as physically possible. Which makes it really hard to be mad at her. Aside from my college fund and the money for my house, which I'm extremely grateful for, she refuses to send anything more my way, channeling it all into charities.

But it was never her money I cared about. The only time I ever dared to ask her to pay for something, it was for someone else. I admire my mother's mission and I can see all the good she does. But as her daughter, I wish I had gotten just a tiny sliver of the attention she gives to the kids she helps all over the world. I was basically raised by nannies, having never met my father and having no other family alive.

"Lana? Did I lose you?"

As if she ever had me. Or wanted me. I almost laugh. "I'm still here, but I gotta go. Good luck with the school." I don't wait for her to respond, knowing there's no *I love you* or *Take care, honey* coming my way. I let the silence of the car settle me as I head toward work.

Luckily, the office of *Always Take Fountain*—the hipster-chic web magazine I write for, name derived from the famous Bette Davis quote—is only a ten-minute drive from my house. I basically scored the Holy Grail of LA commute times and I've never been more thankful for it.

Unfortunately, ten minutes today is ten minutes too long. Ten minutes is just enough time for me to replay the traumatic events from the night before on a loop in my brain. And it's not enough time to figure out how I'm going to spin the whole breakup situation to the small, tight-knit group of colleagues I'm about to face. Colleagues who are expecting me to come in with a big-ass rock on my finger, not a big-ass hangover.

And I love my team of writer friends. Seriously, they are some of the best coworkers anyone could ask for. But, aside from Natasha, my editor/boss/CEO/mentor, they're all single and tend to live vicariously through my relationship milestones.

"Careful what you wish for, bitches," I mutter as I pull into a parking spot.

I push through the door to the wide-open loft space and find it suspiciously quiet. No one sits at the long white table in the center of the room or at any of the small desks scattered around the perimeter. The only people I see are our tech manager, Ian, and a couple of the behind-the-scenes folks, tucked into their corner on the far side of the room. My Birkenstocks slap loudly across the polished concrete floors, the exposed-brick walls and metal ductwork doing nothing to absorb the sound.

The door to the conference room is closed, which is unusual, and I start to get a sinking feeling in my stomach. I drop my purse on an empty desk and take a couple of steadying breaths. Marching slowly across the room like I'm on my way to the gallows, I tentatively push open the emerald-green door.

"Surprise!" a chorus cries out just before I'm wrapped in hugs, multiple pairs of arms encircling me.

"Congratulations, wifey!" James's booming voice reaches

out over all the others, loud enough to act as a gut punch on top of the shit sundae of the last twenty-four hours.

Could this day get any worse?

One of my best work friends, Tessa, grabs my hands, squeezing way harder than necessary. I do my best not to cry. Or throw up. Not sure which would be better (or worse) at this point.

Tessa's fingers are probing my most-definitely-bare left hand, as if by poking and prodding she might uncover a hidden diamond. When she finally accepts there's no shining ring to be found, she loosens her grip and meets my eyes. "Oh, honey. What happened?"

I don't know if it's her words or my overall appearance or the fact that I'm still standing in the doorway completely frozen, but a hush falls over the room.

"We broke up," I finally manage to choke out. And combined with the cryptic DM from Seth and the surprise phone call from my mother, it doesn't even feel like the worst of my problems right now. But it is the easiest one to say out loud. "He broke up with me. He dumped me."

"On your engagement night?" Corey shrieks, her voice so shrill I wince.

The room explodes with various cries of outrage and disbelief, every euphemism for male genitalia rocketing around the room so fast my already wobbly head spins.

Finally, a firm set of hands lands on my shoulders, shooing Tessa aside. Natasha's pale but bronzed, wrinkle-free face hovers inches away from mine. She has to squat to lower herself to my eye level. "Lana. Ignore everyone else in this room and tell me what happened."

And because I am nothing if not a dutiful employee, I open my mouth and spill everything, from the restaurant to the martinis to the blinding hangover. I leave out the DM from Seth and the second wave of drunk therapy it inspired, as well as the call just now with my mom—there's a limit to the amount of pity I'm willing to subject myself to. When I finish up with my word vomit—thankfully avoiding any real vomit—Natasha guides me to a chair and pushes me down.

Everyone else has already found a seat by this point, and somehow they manage to stay quiet until Natasha takes her spot at the head of the table. She remains standing, towering over all of us.

"What a fucking dick," Corey mumbles from my left.

Tessa, on my right, reaches over and squeezes my hand. "He doesn't deserve you."

I give them a small smile before turning my attention to Natasha. I've completely derailed this meeting with my lack of an engagement, and despite the concerned look she throws me, I know she's anxious to reveal her big surprise.

"Well," Natasha starts, her sharp blond bob swinging. "I know this is not how we expected this meeting to start, but we do need to get on with things. Let's get through pitches before I give you all the big news." Her voice is strident and commanding, and anyone who didn't know her would find her urge to move on callous. But Natasha has known me since I started here as an intern my junior year of college, which means she has seen me through two previous breakups, and she knows what I need most in this situation is to get on with work as usual.

I manage a slight nod and then I zone out. There's no

way my brain can process pitches and new ideas from the team right now, so I sink down in my seat and let the presence of my work family have a calming effect on me.

Tessa kicks it off with her most recent list of reviews. She started around the same time I did and holds my dream position: writing about books and entertainment. If it were anyone else, I'd hate her and be plotting her demise, but Tessa is basically the nicest person I know. She's unassumingly gorgeous, with bright-red hair and freckled white skin and these amazing emerald-green eyes.

After Tessa and me, Rob has been with *Always Take Fountain* the longest. He's our sportswriter, in his midthirties, Korean American, and as shy and stoic as he is hot. He and Tessa are my OTP, though I'd never tell either of them that because they might spontaneously combust from a combination of mortification and secret desire.

The first time Corey walked into the *ATF* office five years ago, I assumed she had been hired to make me feel bad about myself. She's a stunning white woman, tall and blond with legs like Naomi Smalls. She's also witty and smart and will absolutely cut a bitch. Despite our being near opposites, with her love for fashion and trendy social life, she quickly became one of my work besties.

James, sitting across the table from me and shooting me lots of winks and smiles, is the big brother of the crew. Literally and figuratively. He's got these luminescent golden-brown eyes and dark brown skin. He's six foot five and built like a linebacker, but despite looking like he could play pro sports, he's our resident foodie and restaurant critic. I originally started hanging out with him so he'd take me out to all the hot spots either for free or on the company's dime, but it didn't take long for us to build a genuine friendship.

I look at each of them as they go around the table, pitching their stories and giving updates on current projects. I don't process their words, just find comfort in their smiles as I take small sips from the cup of water someone thoughtfully placed in front of me. Ever so slowly, my stomach begins to settle.

If only I could say the same for my heart.

Natasha's voice cuts into my internal dialogue, saving me from myself. "Lana, normally I'd give you a day or two to pull yourself together and give me a new pitch, but . . ." She gives me a look that's not entirely sympathetic and finally takes a seat, letting her unspoken expectations complete her sentence. "You know your dating articles bring in the traffic we need. What can we expect from our resident relationship guide?"

"Wow, too soon, Natasha." Corey pats my arm.

"Would you rather talk just the two of us?" Natasha crosses her arms and leans on the clear Plexiglas table, her stare pinning me down and telling me in no uncertain terms that heartbreak or not, it's time to get back to work.

I shake my head. Having my friends surrounding me is the only thing keeping me together at this point. "No. I'm okay. Not exactly brimming with dating and relationship pitches right now, but I'm okay." And it's not true, obviously, not even close. But I will hold it together for the sake of work, and to save some tiny sliver of face in front of these people whom I love and respect.

And maybe, work-wise, this can actually be a good thing. I've wanted out of the dating game—writing about it, anyway—for months, even years, now. I want to write about things I'm passionate about, and I'm not all that passionate about relationships. But dating articles always bring in clicks, which *ATF* needs more and more of these days, and I'm incapable of saying no to Natasha. Perhaps the silver lining of being dumped by my would-be fiancé is finally getting the kinds of assignments I actually want to write.

"She'll come up with something fantastic. She always does." It's probably the closest Tessa has ever come to standing up to Natasha, and the gesture from my timid, people-pleasing friend soothes my battered and bruised heart.

"Do you have anything you'd like me to explore?" I can tell by the look on Natasha's face that she knows exactly what she wants me to write. Already ten steps ahead, she's just waiting for me to ask for it.

"I do, actually." She sits up even straighter, smoothing the already wrinkle-free front of her chic gray blazer. "Are you sure you don't want to meet with me alone?"

"I'm sure." The words come out much more confident than I feel. Because I know that look in Natasha's eyes. She's got a plan. A plan I'm probably not going to like.

"I want you to write about being single."

"Okay?" Other than laying out my heartbreak for the entire city of Los Angeles and the internet at large to see, that doesn't sound so terrible. Definitely not the exact assignment I'd choose for myself, but writing about being single does bring me one small step away from the relationship beat. Maybe it's a necessary first step.

"And about staying single." She levels me with a piercing look. "Which means you would need to stay so."

"Can she make you do that?" Corey mutters next to me.

"I'm not sure I get what you're going for." I keep my words even and level, doing my best not to show how much my insides are roiling. Not just at the thought of exposing myself—figuratively speaking—to our readers and the world, but also at the thought of being alone for any considerable length of time.

"You've developed a rapport with our readers, and I think a more introspective project could be a real breakout hit for the site, not to mention how good it could be for you personally." Natasha leans forward, blocking everyone else out of this conversation. "You know I care about you, Lana, and not just as an employee. I have watched you jump from mediocre boyfriend to mediocre boyfriend without ever taking a pause to ask yourself why someone as fabulous as you settles for mediocrity."

"That's true," Corey chimes in, killing the illusion that this is a private conversation.

"Thanks?" I cross my arms over my chest and sink back in my chair. It's really tempting to brush off Natasha's words, and I might, if they weren't an echo of May's earlier declaration. But just because I like being in relationships doesn't mean there's anything wrong with me. I just enjoy the comfort and security of having a steady boyfriend. I like having a support system and a place to go for every holiday. Is that such a bad thing?

"Sometimes it's better to have no boyfriend than a shitty boyfriend," James throws in as if he's able to see inside my head.

"You've all had shitty boyfriends," I mumble in weak protest.

"Yeah, we just don't keep them around as long as you do." Corey pairs her biting words with a sweet smile.

I duck my head, keeping my arms pressed tightly over my chest, as if that will somehow push back the tears. I know these are my friends and they love me, but it doesn't make it any easier to hear that basically everyone in my life thinks I'm a complete relationship disaster.

There are a few seconds of silence until Natasha finally breaks it. "As your boss, I think it would be fascinating to read about your experiences as you go from a serial monogamist to someone who's going to explore being single. You could reach a whole new audience. Think of all the things you can do and try . . . and write about." She taps her pen on her notebook. "And as your mentor, and your friend, I think this is something you should do. Take this opportunity to get to know yourself before you saddle up for another long-term relationship."

"Because if you can't love yourself, how the hell you gonna love somebody else?" Corey raises both hands as if she were on an episode of *Drag Race*. "Can I get an amen?"

No one responds, but she does bring a hint of a smile to my face.

There's another bout of silence, but this time it feels thoughtful and not constricting.

I mean, Natasha isn't exactly wrong. I've basically been

in a series of relationships since Seth Carson asked me to be his girlfriend when we were fourteen. Since then, I've never gone more than a couple of weeks between breaking up with one guy and dating someone new, usually attaching myself to whoever showed interest first.

Still, the idea of being single for an extended period of time feels daunting. Vaguely terrifying. What would I even do with myself?

"All kinds of things," Natasha responds, so I guess I said that last part out loud. "You could take a class."

"Or volunteer," Tessa suggests.

"Or have a one-night stand." This comes from Corey, but the rest of the group quickly nods their agreement.

"So what, once I check off all those boxes—not committing to that one-night stand, by the way—I'll magically be ready to be in a relationship again?" I guess I *could* volunteer or take a class. Though I'm definitely not here for sleeping with some rando for the sake of a column.

"Something like that." Natasha closes her notebook, signaling she's just about done with this meeting. "And maybe somewhere along the way, you'll figure out why you gravitate toward these kinds of relationships in the first place."

"Ooooh, therapy! Definitely put therapy on the list." Corey nudges me sharply with her elbow.

Natasha clears her throat, ending that line of conversation, thank Loki. "So. Now that we've covered pitches and assignments, it's time for the big news."

We all straighten up in our seats. Natasha has been hinting at this announcement for the past couple of weeks, but none of us have any real idea what it could be. I pray she hasn't decided to retire and leave us in the hands of someone else, because I don't know if I can handle another breakup right now.

Natasha clasps her hands tightly together, resting them on her closed tablet, a hint of a smile tugging on her bold red lips. "*ATF* has been acquired." She pauses as if she's expecting an immediate reaction, but the room stays completely silent. "The *Los Angeles Chronicle* bought the site, and we will now be operating under their umbrella."

I scan my friends' faces for some kind of indication of whether this is good or bad news, but we all wear matching confused expressions.

Finally, Corey comes out with it. "So, are we getting fired? What does that even mean?"

Natasha settles back in her seat. "No, no one's getting fired . . . at least not yet. For now, it doesn't mean many changes." She hesitates for half a second. "But in the long run, it does mean there may be opportunities for some of you to write for the *Chronicle*."

My heart jumps at this hint of possible good news. Natasha very pointedly doesn't look at me, as she's well aware of my desire to someday shift to writing for a paper like the *Chronicle*. "It also means that, for the next couple months at least, we've been asked to play host to a potential *Chronicle* employee."

James makes a face. "Are we going to become the new *Chronicle* training grounds or something?"

The skin around Natasha's lips tightens and I can see she's also not exactly thrilled at the prospect of mentoring writers just so they can go work at another outlet. But when she speaks, her voice is measured and even. "I don't believe so. In this instance it just happened to work out. We're looking to expand our staff and they wanted to try out a news guy to see if he could transition to more of a lifestyle brand."

"And when will said guy be joining us?" Corey asks the question innocently, but I know she perked up hearing there will be some fresh meat in the office.

Natasha checks her Cartier watch. "Hopefully any minute—"

"Hi, everyone, god, I am so sorry for being late on my first day. I feel like an absolute ass, but truly the traffic here is no freaking joke."

Everyone but me spins in their chair, attention swiveling to the doorway.

But I can't move.

Because I know that voice.

My finally-calmed-down stomach suddenly starts bouncing like it's in some nineties mosh pit. Voices swirl around me, but I'm in a foggy haze of a nightmare and I can't make out any actual words.

When I work up the courage to turn around, something like terror floods my veins; somehow I know my absolute worst fears are about to materialize.

Because there he is. Right in the doorway. Of the conference room of *my* office. A halo of golden light from the hallway surrounds him like he's freaking Captain America.

As if in slow motion, I push myself out of my chair. If only this were a scene in a movie, my hair flowing behind me as I gracefully turn. No longer dressed in leggings and an old shirt without a stitch of makeup on my face, I'm glamorous and gorgeous and completely poised and backed by a wind machine—as one should be when confronted with their ex for the first time in years.

Seth Carson.

The one who got away. Twice.

The movie in my head abruptly cuts to black as the real me stands, stumbles, and falls to my knees. "What the fuck are you doing here?" I manage to choke out before a trash can lands in front of my face. Just in time, as seconds later, I'm heaving up the entire contents of my stomach.

3

Is there anything worse than running into your ex when you least expect it?

—Lana Parker, "How to Rebound from a Broken Heart"

I COME BACK TO MYSELF SLOWLY, HAZILY, LIKE AN OLD-school radio tuning through static. A cool hand is rubbing slow and soothing circles on my back. There's a cloud of voices around me but I can't tell who's actually speaking. As I give a final heave, the clarity arrives.

"You're okay, you're okay." Tessa's comforting whispers sync up with her hand, which is tracing loops over my back.

I breathe in a steadying gulp of air, sitting back on my heels. "I'm okay."

Tessa, it appears, is the only one brave enough to be in the general vicinity of me right now. Everyone else has retreated to the far side of the room. I'm assuming that "everyone" also includes my vomit-inducing ex, but I'm too scared to turn my head and see.

Once it's clear I'm done flinging the contents of my stomach into the trash can, Natasha marches over, taking my elbow in her hand and practically yanking me to my feet. "Everyone, go do something productive," she commands. No one needs to be told twice.

My colleagues—my so-called friends—scurry for the door, along with the man responsible for my nausea.

Natasha pins him with a pointed look. "Seth. Meet me in my office in five minutes."

I refuse to glance at him, keeping my eyes glued to the floor.

Natasha continues guiding-slash-manhandling me down the hall and into the office's restroom, where luckily, a tray of amenities waits for occasions not unlike this one, though I'm guessing this is a unique set of circumstances.

I swish mouthwash around four separate times before I finally feel like the stench and the dry mouth have abated. After splashing cold water on my face, I run a makeup-remover wipe over my clammy skin, just in case. Tossing the wipe in the trash, my eyes catch on the bud vase sitting on the white marble. It holds a single sunflower, and my hand automatically travels to my ribs, pressing against the thin skin like I'm stanching a bleed.

Seth always brought me sunflowers.

I'll never forget the proud smile on his face the night of our first "date." He showed up at my front door with a single bright-yellow bloom, making sure I knew he grew it himself. We stuck it in a water glass because I didn't know where to find a vase and my mom was out of town. Not once in four years together did he ever gift me any other kind of flower.

For a long time, even well after we broke up, whenever I spotted a sunflower, it brought a wistful smile to my face. The sight of the bright-yellow petals stirred only happy memories of my high school sweetheart. The first boy I ever loved.

But now it feels like a cosmic joke. After an unfortunate run-in at our class reunion two years ago, now every time I see one of the godforsaken buds, my stomach sours. I'm tempted to yank the offending flower from its vase and rip the petals out one by one, but I think I've humiliated myself enough for one day.

I fix my messy bun as best I can and appraise my sorry self in the mirror, attempting to recover some small sliver of professionalism, all the while trying to puzzle out how this can actually be happening.

Seth Carson is here. In Los Angeles. At *Always Take Fountain*. My workplace. My home away from home.

When I walked out of that hotel ballroom two years ago, I thought I'd never see him in person again. I sure as hell never expected him to show up here. I'd thought it was well established that the West Coast was my turf. *Is* my turf.

Natasha leans against the doorjamb, and our eyes meet in the reflection of the mirror.

"Did you know?" I hold my breath as I wait for her to answer, unable to believe she knew about our history and brought Seth here anyway.

"I don't even know what I could possibly know." She sighs

at the confusion on my face. "Clearly this is not the first time you've met Seth Carson."

I shake my head, relieved to find the motion doesn't stir up any more nausea. "We dated, all through high school. He was my . . ." I want to fill in the blank with some sort of teen-angst throwaway, but even as much as I hate him, that would be unfair, and untrue.

"He was my everything," I finally say after a painful silence.

Natasha hands me a tissue, drawing my attention to the tears streaming down my face. "And it didn't work out."

I dab at my eyes before succumbing and scrubbing at them, not caring if they turn out as rough and raw as my heart currently feels. "No, it didn't work out."

"I take it that was his decision and not yours?"

I nod, blowing my nose loudly, as if the sound might end this conversation.

"And let me guess, you've been in a series of serious relationships ever since? With men who were never quite right?" Natasha looks at me as if she's piecing together the last decade of my life in one breath. She's way too on the nose for my liking.

But I can't deny the truth. "Yup."

She crosses her arms over her chest, leaning casually against the sink after checking for wet spots. "And how did Seth respond to the breakup? I imagine with all the traveling he's done for work it hasn't been easy for him to hold down something serious and long-term. Life on the road isn't exactly conducive to commitment and stability."

I huff out a sarcastic laugh. "From what I've heard, it seems like he goes through women like I go through books. Has a girl in every port, as the classics say."

"So serial monogamy isn't his thing?"

I swipe under my eyelids. "Quite the opposite, if the rumors are true." It took a while before anyone told me the gossip about Seth, and once I heard, I immediately wished I hadn't. Not that I could fault him for moving on—I certainly had—but the thought of his being with anyone else always stung. Might *still* sting on a low day.

Natasha hesitates for a second, but it's not like her to hold back and be tactful, and not even my tears will change that. They haven't before. "You're a smart, successful woman, Lana. It's been twelve years since you were together . . ." The *Why the hell aren't you over him yet?* is implied.

I could very well spill the entire dramatic saga right now, but I don't think I have the energy to make it through. "Yes, I know. I was okay for a bit, but we had an . . . encounter . . . at our ten-year reunion. It didn't end well."

I resolve to say no more, giving her just enough to justify my bitterness.

"You kids are going to be the death of me one day." Natasha sighs. "Can you sit in the same room with him at least?"

I pull myself up to my full height, taking a final swipe at my frizzy hair and red-rimmed eyes. "Of course I can." Despite my appearance, I am a professional.

"Good. Then meet me in my office. I need to make a quick call." She cocks her head at the door with a scheming glint in her eye, and I know I've been dismissed.

I take as long as I possibly can to walk the twenty feet from the bathroom to Natasha's office. Her door is wide open and Seth is sitting in one of the sapphire-blue velvet armchairs in front of her desk. I study him from behind, but there's not much I can discern from the back of his head.

I creep into the room slowly, as if Seth might not notice me as long as I don't make any sudden movements. My eyes stay firmly attached to the side wall opposite him.

The silence is suffocating.

"Parker."

It sends a short-lived thrill through me when he caves and breaks the silence first. Short-lived because the sound of my last name on his lips shouldn't still affect me.

"Seth."

"It's going to be very hard to work together if you won't even look at me."

I let out a humorless laugh. "Oh, we won't be working together."

He sighs, and I can practically see him rolling his eyes. "I get that this isn't ideal. Trust me, this was not in my original plans. But I'm here now, and I'm not going anywhere."

"Natasha isn't going to keep you on if I ask her not to." I try to infuse the words with more confidence than I feel. I like to think Natasha puts her employees first, but at the end of the day, this is a business, and if the order to train Seth came from the higher-ups—the brand-new higher-ups—I doubt there's any getting around it. Not that I plan to tell him that.

"Yeah, well, that's not really up to Natasha."

I swivel my head, finally turning to look at him. And

forcing myself not to react when I see he is staring right at me, his bright-blue eyes cocky and triumphant like he's still the teenage boy who always got exactly what he desired. I want to look him over from head to toe, sneer at the uniform of sneakers, baggy jeans, and a T-shirt he's been sporting since high school. But now that we've made eye contact, I know I can't be the first one to break it.

I used to be able to read those eyes like the hundreds of books cluttering my shelves, but now I don't know what emotions they're hiding. I try to drop a shroud over my own, closing him off from any hint of what's spinning through my brain. Though I'm sure the disdain is clear on my face.

Just as my unblinking eyes start to dry out, Natasha strides into the office, closing the door firmly behind her. I can practically hear the collective groan from the rest of the group, who I know were hovering just outside, hoping to eavesdrop.

Natasha sits in her enormous white leather chair, lacing her fingers together and placing them on top of her Lucite desk.

I sit up straight, my eyes flickering away from Seth and landing on her. I see him mirror my movements out of the corner of my eye. Suck-up.

Natasha looks back and forth between us, not saying a word as she completes some kind of internal assessment. Finally, she clears her throat and turns her attention toward Seth. "Lana tells me the two of you have known each other a long time."

"Yes, ma'am." Seth puts on his best charm-the-grown-ups voice.

Her lips pucker just a tad—Natasha hates being called *ma'am*—but she doesn't correct him. "All right then. Let's just get to it, shall we?" She doesn't wait for a response, and she has a familiar tone in her voice, one that means no one is going to like what happens next. "Seth, you've been foisted off on me as some kind of test run before you move on to the *Chronicle*, correct?"

He nods, staying silent and not repeating his *ma'am* mistake. He always was perceptive.

"Lana, you've been waiting for your chance to break away from the dating and relationships beat, correct?"

"Yes." I clench my hands together in my lap, not wanting either of them to see how tightly I've crossed my fingers, waiting for some smidgen of hope. Any hint that a golden opportunity is about to come my way.

"And *I* need to prove that this site can continue to bring in clicks, and, most important, ad dollars, under this new ownership." She leans forward and there's a glint of something just short of devious in her eyes. "So here's what we're going to do: a little friendly competition."

I shoot Seth a look for the first time since our staring contest was interrupted. He glances my way, a question in his eyes, but I don't pretend we can still wordlessly communicate, turning my attention back to Natasha.

"What kind of competition?" I don't bother attempting any enthusiasm.

A wide smile spreads across her face, and honestly I'm impressed her cheeks are that mobile given the Botox she got last week. "A dating competition."

"Absolutely not," Seth says, almost immediately.

"Oh hell no," I say.

This time I glare at him, because he should be so lucky.

"Relax. You're not going to date each other."

A slight sigh of relief escapes me, but I know enough to remain tense.

Seth raises his hand slightly, as if he needs permission to ask a question. Which, technically, as the newbie, he does.

Natasha ignores him. "Lana, you're a serial monogamist. Seth, you're a serial dater."

Seth sputters in indignation. "Excuse me? You just met me five minutes ago, how do you know anything about my dating life?"

She shoots him a dagger-sharp glare. "Am I wrong?"

His mouth opens and closes a few times, but Seth was never a good liar. "Well . . . no."

"Okay, good. Think about the potential here. You're two exes, high school sweethearts, and after your tragic breakup—"

"I wouldn't exactly call it tragic," I mutter.

"—after your tragic breakup, you each manifested your heartbreak in different ways."

"I was definitely not heartbroken," Seth insists.

Natasha barrels on as if she doesn't even hear us. "And now, twelve years later, you're thrust back together and finally ready to deal with your issues. Lana, you need to learn to live life on your own. Seth, you need to find a real relationship and settle down."

"I don't need to do that," we both say at the same time.

She looks back and forth between us a few times. “Well, you’re going to. Seth, you’re known and respected for your work in news, but the *Chronicle* has a news team. You need to try your hand at more lifestyle pieces; this layover here at *ATF* is your chance to prove you’ve got what it takes. You’re both professionals, you know a good story when you see it.” The dollar signs are practically cha-chinging in Natasha’s eyes. “Think of how big this could be. For both of you.”

“Let’s say I were to agree to this—and I’m not saying that I will—what are we talking here? An actual competition? What would that even mean? Terms? Rules? Prize?” Seth leans forward a little in his seat.

Natasha nods, jotting down Seth’s questions like she herself still needs to figure out the answers.

“None of that matters because I’m not doing this, no matter what the prize is.” I cross my arms over my chest and sink back in my chair.

“Even if it’s your own column in the *Chronicle*?” Natasha steeples her fingers together, resting her chin on her hands.

In the same breath, my boss and mentor is offering me my dream and using it against me.

She takes my stunned silence as a cue to continue. “I still need to work out the details, but here’s what I’m thinking: you will each come up with a list of ten tasks for the other to complete. Lana, your tasks for Seth should push him to be ready for a long-term relationship.”

Okay, not going to lie, the thought of coming up with ways to torture Seth does sound appealing.

“Seth, your list for Lana should have tasks that push her to explore being single and living life on her own terms.”

He shoots me a gleeful smile and my stomach turns.

"You'll each complete one task per week and write one corresponding article, which we'll post on Fridays. Winner gets their own column at the *Chronicle*, to do with what they wish."

"Who chooses the winner?" Seth asks with just a tad too much enthusiasm in his voice, like he's actually considering going along with this.

Natasha cocks her head to the side. "We'll nail down the logistics later, but let's let the readers determine a winner. They're our audience, aren't they?"

This time I'm the one delivering the gleeful smile. Our readers already know—and, if I may say so, love—me, which means I have the home-court advantage.

"Any questions?" Natasha doesn't leave space for us to ask any, not that my brain function could come up with one at this point. The events of the past twenty-four hours have left me in a weird fugue state where everything is made up and the points don't matter.

"Good. Since it's end of week and we've all had an *eventful* day"—Natasha pauses, sparing a gentle glance for me—"I'll be nice and give you until Tuesday morning to get your lists in my inbox."

Tuesday morning. That means I have three days to figure out how to best torture Seth and find a way to pay him back for marching into my territory, uninvited and unwanted.

Natasha, clearly done with the pair of us, waves her hand, shooing us out of the office.

I brush by Seth on my way out the door. "I'm going to make you regret the day you ever met me."

He snorts. "Who's to say I don't already?"

My mouth drops open and I make a very undignified sound of indignation.

Seth pushes right past me, heading straight for the main office door and out to the parking lot.

I, too, would love to make a break for it, but the moment Natasha's door closes behind me, I'm swarmed by a mini mob of frenzied coworkers.

Corey grabs my arm, giving it an urgent shake. "What the hell just happened?"

4

The best thing you can do in any heartbreak situation is lean on your friends.

—Lana Parker, "Top Ten Ways to Survive a Broken Heart"

I DON'T BOTHER TO PUT UP A FIGHT AS THE GANG STEERS me over to the long white coworking table in the middle of the office. Corey pushes me into a chair before hopping up on the table next to me. The others find actual seats, watching me with expressions ranging from curious to downright salacious.

Corey opens her mouth, but Tessa shoots her a look and she quickly closes it.

"Lana, are you okay?" Tessa asks quietly and calmly from my right-hand side.

I look at her, her bright-green eyes kind and open. And I burst out laughing. For the second time in this shitstorm of a day, uncontrollable giggles overtake me. I have to push back my chair because I'm doubling over with laughter.

"Am I okay?" I repeat when I finally get my laughs—which are on the verge of morphing into sobs—under control. "Let's see. First, my boyfriend of four years dumps me when I was expecting a proposal. Then I get the drunkest I've been since a misguided tailgate party freshman year of college. And this morning my hungover ass gets the full-on hit-and-run of learning that my other ex-boyfriend is now my new coworker." I hold up both hands, just in case any of them thought that was the end of it. "And NOW—and please hear that in the all caps it is meant to be in—my boss, who I thought actually cared about me, decides to pit me against said ex in some kind of masochistic *How to Lose a Guy in 10 Days* dating fucktastic challenge extravaganza."

Complete and utter silence echoes throughout the room.

"So, not okay then?" James pairs his sarcastic question with a cheeky smile.

I let my head fall to the table, the thunk reverberating from my skull through the rest of my worn-out body.

"Okay. Let's take this one step at a time." Tessa's voice remains calm and measured, which almost makes me feel worse. "I think we can go ahead and cross off last night's proposal-turned-breakup fiasco, yes?"

"Yes," I mutter into the cool white surface of the table. "Literally the least of my problems."

"Okay. So now on to ex-boyfriend number two."

"Wait, Seth Carson is your ex?" Rob doesn't even try to hide the awe in his voice.

I sit up and glare at him. "Why are you saying his name like he's LeBron James?"

He holds up his hands defensively. "I mean, he's no King James, but the guy is an amazing journalist."

"Yeah, well, he's also a huge butthead and we hate him."

James rolls his eyes. "Why do we hate him?"

Corey looks up from her phone, and she better not be live-tweeting this whole situation. "It doesn't matter. Lana says we hate him, so we hate him."

Rob shakes his head. "That's ridiculous."

"You know I love you, Lana, but you gotta give me more than he's a butthead." James crosses his beefy arms, leaning on the table and giving me a pointed look.

I press my lips together, weighing my options. I can either tell them the whole ugly truth, risking losing some of my closest friends to the enemy camp, or I can give them the SparkNotes version. I let out a long, dramatic sigh and decide to land somewhere in the middle. "Seth and I were close friends as kids, and we started dating when we were fourteen. We were more than just high school sweethearts; we were best friends. His home was essentially my home."

Tessa reaches over and squeezes my hand, maybe the only one who can understand the true depths of what that means to me since I've actually shared my mama drama with her.

"We broke up when I went away to college, and it crushed me. Eventually I was able to get over it and we were on okay terms. Stayed connected-ish over the years, mostly on social media. But we had a run-in at our recent high school reunion and it didn't end well." That's putting it mildly, but I'm pretty sure if I spill the whole story, I'll lose whatever tiny bit of dignity I might have left. "He crushed me, again. But it was even worse the second time around."

Another silence falls over the table.

James claps his hands. "Okay, fair enough. So we hate him. Now, what is this fucktastic challenge extravaganza you speak of?"

I groan, resting my elbows on the table and letting my hands do the hard work of propping up my head. "Natasha is pitting us against each other in a dating competition."

"I thought those only existed in rom-coms," Rob says.

"Can she do that?" Corey chirps.

I shrug, still unable to wrap my head around it, but also too mentally exhausted to examine it much further. "Who knows, but she's doing it. We each have to come up with ten tasks for the other one to complete, then the readers are going to choose a winner and that person gets their own column at the *Chronicle*."

James lets out a low whistle. "I guess that answers the question of whether or not the whole thing will be worth it."

"Yeah." I let his words run through my mind a couple of times. I've wanted a pop culture column of my own since high school, and only in my wildest dreams would that column exist in a paper like the *Chronicle*. And now I have the chance to gain just that. All I have to do is take down my ex-boyfriend with a set of tasks designed to humiliate him, and hopefully, make him cry.

Okay, that might be a little extreme, but at the very least, I want to make him hate his life for the next ten weeks.

"You have a scary look in your eyes." Corey scoots away from me.

I push back my own chair and stand. "I need to go somewhere I can think."

Tessa gently grabs my forearm. "Are you going to be okay? Do you want someone to come with you?"

I shake my head. "I appreciate the offer, but I'm good. Or at least, I will be once I win this competition and kick that motherfucker's ass."

"That's the spirit!" James cheers.

Blowing kisses over my shoulder, I head for the front door. "Thank you guys for everything, you're the best!"

Corey calls after me, "Make him rue the day you were born, bitch!"

An evil grin spreads across my face. Oh, I will.

#LANAVSSETH

This is the very beginning of the #LanavsSeth channel.

@James joined #LanavsSeth along with **@Corey**, **@Tessa**, **@Rob**, and **@Lana**

JAMES: Let's get down to business . . .

TESSA: To defeat the Huns!

COREY: To defeat Seth Carson!

LANA: OMG why is this even a Slack channel?

COREY: Because you need to come up with ways to torture your ex and who better to help you with that than us?

LANA: Okay fine. I could use some help. What makes a guy ready for a relationship and also what would make a bona fide player cry?

ROB: Deleting Tinder.

JAMES: Erasing all his booty-call numbers.

LANA: Could I get away with making that one task? To extend the opportunities for torture?

COREY: Totally.

LANA: Okay, what else?

TESSA: He should have to get a pet.

And keep it alive for the duration of the competition.

COREY: What about getting real furniture and more than one set of sheets?

JAMES: Make him go on a date with the same woman more than once.

COREY: And no sex!

ROB: Wow, that's harsh, guys.

TESSA: What do you think he's going to put on your list, **@Lana**?

LANA: I can't even think about it.

JAMES: I hope he makes you make out with a stranger.

COREY: Or go on a blind date.

TESSA: Or volunteer.

COREY: Yawn.

I'm still pushing for that one-night stand!

LANA: Don't even put that into the universe.

@Seth joined #LanavsSeth

SETH: Hey, guys. I see we're brainstorming list suggestions.

ROB: Welcome.

COREY: Traitor.

@Seth, don't even think about scrolling up.

JAMES: Dude. Now he's obviously going to scroll up.

SETH: Sorry, guys, all's fair in workplace competitions and sticking it to your ex.

LANA: Fuck me. I'm outta here.

COREY: Well, now that we have you here, **@Seth**, maybe you could tell us a little about yourself? Hobbies? Interests? How you came to be a fuckboy and why you moved to LA?

ROB: Jeez, **@Corey**.

COREY: What? Inquiring minds.

And it's always good to know your enemy.

SETH: That lovely misnomer aside, my hobbies are reading and writing. My interests are politics and people. I never would've described myself as a "fuckboy," I just never had time to date seriously.

COREY: Why'd you move to LA?

SETH: Oh. The weather, obviously.

COREY: Uh-huh.

5

If you know ahead of time you'll be seeing an ex, it's simple: look hot AF.

—Lana Parker, "So Your Ex Is Still in Your Life"

COREY FLUFFS MY HAIR FOR THE MILLIONTH TIME, smoothing down my ever-present flyaways before stepping back to give me one final looking-over. "This whole thing is a disaster waiting to happen, but I'm kind of living for it."

"Your support is overwhelming." I tug on the hem of my short black skirt, hoping for a few more inches of coverage.

Corey swats my hand away. "You look amazing. If nothing else, just know the internet at large is going to see you as a total hottie."

"Well, that *is* the most important thing," I say sarcastically, fiddling with the gold book-shaped pendant hanging around my neck.

She swats my hand again. "Stop fidgeting. Be confident and bold, let them know you know you've got this."

"And if I definitely don't got this?"

She grins. "Fake it, baby."

Right. Fake the confidence. Somehow I don't think even Meryl Streep could put on a convincing enough performance in this situation, but I try to shake off the overwhelming sense of impending doom and steady my nerves.

Our attention swings to the creaking office door. Seth has finally decided to bless us with his presence, and he looks about as happy to be here as I do.

Corey drops her smile as she gives Seth the same once-over she just gave me. "Is that seriously what you're wearing?"

The faded-jeans-and-sports-T-shirt look worked for Seth in high school, but we're not teenagers anymore and on a grown-up Seth, it reads as sloppy, especially for the video we're about to film. Of course, a less-than-ideal wardrobe hasn't ever derailed his potential for . . . railing. His bad clothes are still outshone by his stupid perfect face.

Seth doesn't bother to address Corey's question, and he barely even greets either one of us. "Can we just get this over with?"

I roll my eyes. "Corey and I have been here for a half an hour already. We're the ones who've been waiting for you."

"Well, I'm here now."

"Then I guess we'll jump right to it. Wouldn't want to keep the great Seth Carson from his next big important story."

Corey's eyes flit between the two of us. "This is going to be a total shit show." She sounds way too excited by the prospect.

"I can't believe we're doing this," Seth mutters as we cross to the filming area.

We pose in front of the exposed-brick wall of the office, the large skylights overhead bathing us in a perfect golden glow. We leave a good six feet of space separating us.

"We wouldn't have to be doing this if someone had stayed on the other side of the country where he belongs." I toss my hair, trying to find some of that fake confidence Corey recommended.

"You don't own Los Angeles, Parker."

"I might as well, as you'll see once the readers start chiming in." I'm faking it till I make it, and it sort of works. Either my faux poise or my determination to not lose even more face in front of Seth pushes me to stand up straight, ready to nail this thing.

Natasha emailed us both on Saturday outlining the logistics for the dating fucktastic challenge extravaganza. We're each to complete one task and corresponding article per week. We'll be awarded points for the comments and clicks our pieces receive, but the majority of the competition will be determined by a reader vote, which will happen at the end of the ten-week challenge. And then she directed us to both be in the office bright and early Monday morning to film an Instagram Live, introducing our followers and readers to the competition.

As if Mondays weren't already terrible enough.

Corey, our social media expert, adjusts her phone on its tripod. "I'm going to need you two to stand a little closer together, we're not exactly working with a huge frame here."

We each take half a step in, shooting daggers while we do.

Corey sighs, marching over and pushing the two of us together so our shoulders are brushing. "I realize we'll be lucky to escape this without bloodshed, but the faster we get this finished, the faster you guys can retreat to your separate corners."

I shift a little so the pointy part of my elbow connects with Seth's ribs.

"Really, Parker?" He gestures to Corey. "Did you see that?"

Corey grins from behind the tripod. "See what?" She fiddles with her phone for a second. "Okay, once I give you the signal, we're live. Emphasis on the *live*. Like people will be watching this as it's happening. Please, for the love of god, keep that in mind." She holds up some pieces of poster board with the finer details of the challenge written in big black letters. "I outlined a little bit of who should say what, but—please don't make me regret this—you should also feel free to ad-lib a little."

I glare at Seth before schooling my face into a pleasant smile. Like there's nowhere I'd rather be than standing next to my ex-boyfriend and introducing this pile of bullshit to the world.

Corey taps around some more and then gives us a big thumbs-up. She mouths *good luck* to me and oh Hela, this is really happening.

As soon as he gets the signal, Seth turns on his signature charm—the same charm that won him both class president and homecoming king. "Hey, everyone, happy Monday!

Thanks for joining us this morning. Most of you probably don't know me, but my name is Seth Carson. I used to write freelance, but I'm a recent transplant to LA and am thrilled to be joining the team at *Always Take Fountain*. I'm sure you all know my colleague here, Lana Parker."

It isn't until Seth nudges me with his elbow that I realize I'm meant to speak now. "Hi, everyone!" My voice comes out too high and too chipper, but I barrel on. "As Seth said, I'm Lana Parker, but you probably know me better as your resident dating and relationships expert."

Seth chuckles.

I shoot him a dirty look but keep on with my upbeat banter. "I've been writing the love advice column here at *ATF* for eight years, and while I love writing about being with your perfect partner, for the next ten weeks, I'm going to be trying something a little different. Seth, why don't you tell the viewers about our friendly competition?"

"I'd love to, Parker," he says, as smooth as a game show host. "But first, I think they need to know a little bit about our history, don't you?"

My mouth falls open for longer than a second before I remember we're live. I clamp my lips shut, speaking to him out of the side of my mouth. "What are you doing? That is not in the outline!"

Seth ignores my death glare, his gorgeous smile sparkling "Come on, Parker, it's important for our viewers to know about the past before they can fully appreciate the present."

I catch Corey's eye, flashing her an *Oh shit please help me* look, but she shakes her head, lips pursed tight; a shiver of fear darts through me, not just at the thought of our history being spilled live on the internet, but at the thought of having to relive it myself. I turn to Seth, a pleading look in my eye. "Seth, I'm sure the viewers don't really care about our very-much-in-the-past past."

He hesitates for only a second before turning his attention back to the camera, his cheesy, too-wide smile permanently in place. "Parker and I were high school sweethearts, folks. Isn't that just the cutest? We dated all four years and were even voted Most Likely to Grow Old Together."

"And that's the end of that!" My voice sounds frantic and shrill, and I don't even care because I just need this to be over. I continue on before Seth can reveal any other personal tidbits to a live audience of probably thousands. "So as I said, Seth and I are going to be engaging in a little bit of a *friendly* competition like professional adults, if Seth is even capable of that. One thing he definitely is capable of is jumping from one woman to the next, but for this competition, he'll have to quell his manwhore urges and prove he's ready for a serious, long-term relationship."

There's an awkward amount of silence and I chance a quick glance over at Seth, surprised to see something like hurt lingering in his eyes. But it disappears as quickly as it came, leaving only a fake smile and too-bright eyes.

"You're probably wondering about Lana's part of the challenge, and I'm thrilled to tell you your intrepid relationship guide is going to have to put her serial monogamy aside and enjoy the single life. As her ex-boyfriend, I can promise you, there is nothing Lana hates more than being alone!" He punches me lightly on the shoulder, like we're still best friends.

I grit my teeth and try to force my face into a smile. "I have no doubt I'll be able to crush this competition. I'm single and ready to mingle!" I can't help but cringe at my own cliché declaration.

Seth covers his heart with one hand. "While I'm finally ready to settle down and make some lucky woman very happy."

I snort. Loudly. "Hopefully Seth has learned the definition of *serious* and *settle down* sometime over the past twelve years!"

Corey waves a wild hand at us, holding up one of her poster boards, pointing at the information written on the card.

I open my mouth to expand on the finer details of the competition, but Seth beats me to it.

"Maybe the most exciting thing about this challenge is that you, the readers, will help select a winner!" He winks at the camera.

I roll my eyes and push myself forward so I'm blocking him from view. "That's right! Your clicks and comments will be converted into points, and at the end of the ten-week period, there'll be a final vote where you get to decide who has done the best job with their mission." I toss my hair over my shoulder. "I'm confident you'll see how committed I am to finding myself and award me the final prize!"

Seth nudges me out of the way. "And I'm confident Lana couldn't find herself if she had a personal GPS."

"Well, take it from me, folks, Seth doesn't know the first thing about making a woman happy." I spread my arms wide, almost smacking him in the face.

"That's not what you said at the reunion." He raises his eyebrows and smirks.

I keep on my scary-cheerful presenter voice to hide the trembling. "We're definitely not going there in front of a live audience, Seth. Thanks so much for joining us, and keep an eye on the site for our first series of challenges, coming soon!"

Corey stabs at her phone a couple of times and an absolute, suffocating silence fills the office. She finally breaks it. "Ummm, shit."

I take it that means the stream has ended.

Ohmigod. The stream. That was all streamed. Live. To who knows how many viewers. My entire body heats with the red flames of embarrassment.

I feel Seth behind me and my skin crawls. I cannot believe he was about to air our dirty laundry in front of Thor knows how many followers.

"Parker." He's dropped the phony presenter voice, and the single word from his lips is low and rumbly. Like he's also just realizing what we put out on the internet for the world to see.

I spin around, venom in my eyes and my voice. "Seriously, Seth? Fuck off."

For a second, a flicker of shame lights his eyes. But then they harden against me. "We're supposed to exchange task lists tomorrow, and I, for one, would like to be professional about this."

I scoff, crossing my arms over my chest. "Why start now?" I gesture back to the area where we filmed. "That was a fucking disaster."

He smirks, mimicking my pose. "I bet it brought in the viewers."

"Am I supposed to be excited about thousands of people watching you make me look like an idiot?" I clench my fists. I've never wanted to punch someone before, but I can clearly visualize how good it would feel for my fist to connect with his pretty little face.

His shoulders fall just a tad. "I wasn't trying to make you look like an idiot."

"If that were true, you wouldn't even be here, Seth." I pull myself up to my full height because I will not allow this man to crumble me. Again. "I'll meet you tomorrow to exchange lists, but after that, I don't want to talk to you. You may not be taking this seriously, but I am. This is *my* career on the line. I don't care what you have to work out with Natasha; work from home, come in only when I'm not here. I don't care. *ATF* is *my* turf and I refuse to see you if I don't have to." My chest tightens, likely due to the steady stream of rage flowing through me.

Seth's voice softens and his hand drifts up like he's tempted to reach for me. "Lana, I wasn't trying to hurt you . . ."

I ignore his protest, pushing past him and out the door, determined not to look back.

MY ANGER AND frustration toward Seth simmer in my blood from the moment I leave the office until I wake up the very next day. I still have trouble believing my self-assured but sweet first love has morphed into this complete jackass—willing to infiltrate my territory and embarrass me in front of thousands—but here we are. Whatever. All I have to do is make it through one more conversation with him and I can put him firmly back in the past. Where he belongs.

As I get ready for our meetup, I dress in one of my favorite outfits, wanting to feel comfortable yet cute. Pulling on a long chiffon pleated skirt in a mint green, I top it with a vintage Wonder Woman shirt, an image of Diana in her power pose in black and white. Tying the shirt in a knot just under my ribs, I hope some of her strength will trickle through to me. I slip on flat gold sandals and dangly gold earrings, grab all my work stuff, and head out.

I arrive at Constellation Coffee two hours before my designated meeting time with Seth. To say I'm anxious about this exchange is an understatement. Not only do I have to see Seth face-to-face after the disaster that was yesterday, but we foolishly agreed to do this outside the office. At least at *ATF* there's a chance someone else would be hanging about if we needed interference. Especially once I see what kind of torture he's come up with for me. Torture I'm sure has only gotten worse over the past twenty-four hours. Thank Loki I get to deliver some torture in return.

After ordering an iced hazelnut latte, I find a table in the back of the shop and hunker down. I wanted to arrive early to calm my nerves, but now that I'm here with no other assignments to work on, all I've done is give myself plenty of time to psych myself out. I use the time to write reviews of the last two books I read for my personal blog, which is my happy place, but even writing about books doesn't help take my mind off what's coming. I'd really rather just get it over with at this point and put myself out of my misery.

So it's actually something of a relief when Seth pushes through the front door of the café only an hour later. He orders and his eyes find mine as soon as he turns to look for a table.

If I was hoping for my anger to cancel out his hotness, well . . . I'm shit out of luck. It's been hard to give him a full once-over since every time I look at him lately, my eyes are squinted in a glare. But since today is the last time I plan on seeing him, I allow myself a complete perusal.

Today he's in jeans and a gray T-shirt, just tight enough to show off both his biceps and his sculpted forearms. When we were teenagers, his dark hair was long and floppy, hanging in his eyes à la Leonardo DiCaprio in *Titanic* (a.k.a. peak hotness). Now it's cropped shorter, showing off his strong jaw, which is covered in a layer of stubble he never would've been able to grow in high school. It doesn't look like he's combed said hair or shaved said stubble, but this only adds to his appeal, which, given how long I spent getting ready for today, should make me hate him. And it totally does.

He gives me a brief nod of acknowledgment. "Parker." He dumps his stuff on an empty chair before grabbing his coffee.

I sit up straight. And maybe stick my chest out a little, but I can neither confirm nor deny. "How do you want to do this?" I don't even let him take a sip of coffee before cutting right to the chase.

This doesn't stop him from taking a long swig before he answers me. "Should we go through the lists item by item?"

I was going to suggest that myself, just in case I need to make last-minute adjustments depending on what he came up with for me. But now that he's suggested it, I can't allow it. Narrowing my eyes, I shake my head. "Nope. I'm not going to let you sneak any changes in. You hand me your list and I'll hand you mine."

His lips turn down, but he shrugs. "Fair enough." Reaching into his messenger bag, he pulls out a lined piece of notebook paper, and I have a sudden flashback to junior year, when he used to write me notes every day during study hall. Most of them were just pithy witticisms about what he'd observed that day in class, but sometimes they were more serious, detailing things he wanted out of life. Where he saw us down the road. What he hoped we'd achieve, both together and as individuals. He was a beautiful writer, even then.

He clears his throat, shaking me out of my reverie. And fuck that reverie. That Seth no longer exists, and even if he did, that's all in the past. This whole dumb experiment is about finding myself, not about romanticizing my high school relationship.

I flip open my silver Avengers notebook and rip out the list I made for him. "Ready?"

"Do we need a countdown or something?"

I glare at him, tossing his list across the table and snatching mine from his hand.

There are a couple minutes of silence as we each take in what the other has written. My eyes scan the page quickly, looking for any grenades, before they travel back to the top of the paper and I read it through more carefully. I take more time than I need because it's easy to see I've been way harsher on Seth than he has been on me. Most of the items on this list are similar to what I would've done for my original assignment, before this became some ridiculous competition. And there's one particular item I expected to see, thanks to my lovely coworkers and our Slack conversation, but it's conspicuously missing.

"Any questions?" Seth finally breaks the silence, his tone and expression equally unreadable.

"You left off the one-night stand?" I know I should take this gift and run with it, but I can't help but wonder if he left it off on purpose. And if he did, for what reason. It certainly wasn't to be nice.

He studies his own paper, keeping his eyes busy and away from mine. "Yeah, well, there are limits, I guess. I don't want to push you to do something like that if you're not ready or don't want to." He almost immediately ruins the considerate sentiment. "Besides, I'm planning on winning even without humiliating you."

My eyes narrow. "So, what, you think I'm incapable of doing it?"

"I know you're more than capable." His eyes finally meet mine and they are lightning, his lips curling up in a smirk.

My cheeks heat and my lips part, just the slightest bit. We sit for an uncomfortable minute, the flush spreading down my neck and to my chest, as my very stupid and unhelpful brain plays a montage of all the doing it Seth and I used to, well, do.

I clear my throat and pick up my pen, striking through *Get a guy's number* and writing in *Have a one-night stand*. I regret it almost immediately, but I refuse to let that show on my face. I throw down my pen quite triumphantly considering the colossal mistake I just made. "Do *you* have any questions?"

"Nope." He crosses his arms and leans on the table, bringing him close enough into my bubble that I get a whiff of him. He still smells like sunshine and salt.

The scent threatens to bring up even more powerful memories, so I sit back in my chair to create as much distance between us as possible. I narrow my eyes at him. "I really want to win this, you know."

"So do I." He raises his eyebrows in a challenge.

"I've been in LA for longer than you've been a writer."

He shrugs. "Doesn't mean I want it any less."

"Why do you?"

"Why do I what?"

"Why do you want to work for the *Chronicle*? Why here? I'm sure you could have gotten a job anywhere. Why trample on my home turf?" The words come out sharp, laced with all the anger I felt yesterday and this morning. Anger that was slipping over the last few minutes of this conversation. I latch on to it.

Something that looks like sadness flashes through the blue of his eyes for half a second before they harden to steel. "It was always the dream, right? Living and writing in LA?"

Yeah, it was. *Our* dream. One he gave up any right to

when he took all our fantastical, young-and-in-love plans and Hulk-smashed them to smithereens.

My breath hitches in my chest. "That was a long time ago."

"I suppose." He pushes his chair back with an obnoxiously loud scrape. "I'll text you if I have any questions."

"Guess that means I have to unblock your number."

He pauses, his hands on his thighs as he's about to stand. "You really blocked my number, Parker?"

I meet his gaze dead-on. "Can you blame me?"

He doesn't flinch under my glare. Shaking his head slowly, he rises from his seat. "Whatever. Think you can manage to be professional for the next ten weeks?"

I bite down on my lip to hold back my retort—*Think your mom can manage to be professional for the next ten weeks?* Instead, I nod, coolly, calmly, totally unfazed. "Good luck, Seth. You're going to need it."

He rolls his eyes, spinning on his heel and marching out the front door without a backward glance.

And I'm glad he doesn't turn around, because I most definitely can't seem to tear myself away from checking out the rear view.

Lana's List for Seth

1. *Get actual furniture and household items (i.e., linens and towels)*
2. *Update wardrobe*
3. *Set up a dating profile on a relationship-seeking app/website*
4. *Go to therapy*

5. Delete Tinder and all booty-call numbers from phone
6. Get and care for a pet
7. Go on at least three dates with the same person
8. Keep a plant alive for the duration of the competition
9. No sex for the entire ten weeks
10. Find someone to be happy with long-term

Seth's List for Lana

1. Go on a blind date
2. Go to therapy
3. Take a class on something that's new to you
4. Play tourist in LA for a day
5. Kiss a stranger
6. Go speed dating
7. Volunteer
8. ~~Get a guy's number~~ Have a one-night stand
9. Take a vacation by yourself
10. Learn to be okay with being alone

6

Best friends pretty much always have your best interests at heart, even if it doesn't always feel like it.

—Lana Parker, "What Do I Do When My BFF Hates My Partner?"

MAY EXAMINES THE LINED PIECE OF PAPER WITH A SMIRK on her face.

"You know how much I hate that face." I rub both of my temples, resting my elbows on the wooden table at one of our favorite bar/cafés, Bon Vivant, where I've gathered my entire support system to help me make sense of my life.

"Look, I know Seth and I haven't met, but after reading this list, I like him already." She slides the paper back to me and takes a sip of her white wine.

"According to the best-friend code, you're obligated to hate him." I scan the list again even though I already have it memorized. "Although truth be told, he could've done me dirtier."

"I'm sure he's done you plenty dirty before." Corey's eyebrows dance up and down.

"Excuse you, we were children." I toss one of my french fries across the table at her. Though she's not wrong.

May picks up the discarded fry and eats it in one bite. "Enough about Seth and his dirty, dirty ways. We really need to talk about this list, *and* that video."

Tessa removes said list from my hands before I can crumple it into a ball, shooting me a sympathetic smile.

Dipping a fry in ketchup and swirling it around for way longer than needed, I avoid looking at any of them. "I don't really know what there is to say about the list. I don't think it'll be that hard to accomplish most of the tasks." Emphasis on the *most*.

"Sure. Volunteering, taking a class, playing tourist in LA, those are all things you might've done anyway." Corey crosses her arms, leaning on the table.

"Yeah," May chimes in. "Were your life not centered around someone else and their wants and needs."

I sit back in my seat, crossing my own arms over my chest. "I don't think I did that."

She purses her lips, not saying anything. Tessa and Corey flash me similar *not buying it* looks.

"Okay, fine. Maybe I did that sometimes, but it's not like my life fully revolved around Evan's."

"Not just his, LP. Mine and your colleagues'. Natasha's too." May gestures around as Tessa and Corey nod. "It's not an inherently bad thing, you know. You just don't usually like to do things on your own, and so you sometimes let your own wants and needs take a backseat."

"You say it like it's a bad thing." I swirl another fry in

ketchup, no intention of eating it, just needing something to do with my hands.

"Okay, fine. Sometimes I think it's a bad thing." May chugs the remainder of her wine.

"Let's try something." Tessa reaches over and pats my hand. "An easy question. If you could do anything, job-wise, what would you do? No caveats, just whatever you wanted, sky's the limit."

"I'd write about books. And probably TV shows and movies too. Have my own column where I could talk about the things I'm passionate about." I don't even need time to think about it because I've been thinking about it for the past eight years.

"Or maybe your own website where you could write about whatever you wanted?" Corey gives me a pointed look, her eyebrows practically touching her hairline.

I stick my tongue out at her. "You all know why I don't promote my blog. It's my personal space to write about whatever I want." I hear the echo as the words trail out of my mouth.

May leans forward. "You know between my PR skills and your social media presence we could easily make your blog a legitimate hit."

"No one wants to read my fandom ramblings."

Corey shrugs, refilling her wineglass from the communal bottle. "I read your fandom ramblings and they're so good they almost make me care about superheroes and droids."

"That doesn't mean it could ever be something that

makes me enough money to pay the bills." And yes, I'm super lucky to not have nearly as many bills as the average millennial Angeleno. But even still, living in LA doesn't come cheap.

"How do you know if you don't try?"

I sit with the question for a minute.

May takes advantage of my silence. "Maybe instead of devoting time to a man, you can devote your time to building something for yourself."

I bristle a little, not fully ready to hear my friends' advice. "Well, maybe I could have, but now I'm going to be spending all my time accomplishing these tasks for some stupid competition. I won't have any free time to do anything."

Corey rolls her eyes. "You still have plenty of time. If it's something you want, you'll make time."

"Well, if and when I win this whole thing, I'm gonna get my own column anyway, so why should I spend the energy reinventing the wheel?" I try to hide the whine in my voice with a long sip of the wine in my glass.

May leans over and refills it for me. "Whatever, LP. If you don't want to do it, don't do it. Find something else. Learn to crochet or train for a marathon."

We all make a face at the idea of me running.

"Whatever you decide, maybe you should use this opportunity to do something for yourself. Not for a guy or *ATF* or Natasha or us. Something that's just for you." Tessa's sweet smile is maybe the only thing that could wear me down.

"Fine. I'll think about it." I finish off my wine, setting the empty glass down not exactly gently. "Let's talk about someone else's problems. May, any news on the promotion?"

She holds back her smile. "No official word yet, but I'm pretty sure I've got it in the bag. Now, stop trying to change the subject."

"Shush, you are brilliant and beautiful and perfect. And you all are the best friends a girl could have." I purposefully make the words sound over-the-top, but I spot no lies among them.

"Don't think you can distract us with compliments." Corey pushes her wine aside, signaling she means business. "As the only witness to the live shitacular from yesterday, I need to know only one thing." She pauses dramatically. "What the hell happened at your reunion?"

I exchange a heavy glance with May, the only person I told about the experience.

Tessa catches the pained look on my face. "You don't have to tell us if you don't want to."

Shaking my head, I steel myself to relive that night. "No, it's fine. It was going to come up sooner or later." I take in a deep breath. "Basically, I may have drunk too much and confessed my still-kind-of-there feelings for Seth."

"And by that she means she propositioned him," May interjects.

I glare at her. "Okay, yes, so I propositioned him and he turned me down. And not in a nice, *I recognize you were once the love of my life* kind of way. In a brutal, stab-me-in-the-heart way. It went beyond just embarrassment. It was cruel."

There's silence for a full minute.

"Wait, wasn't your reunion two years ago?" Corey asks.

I nod, already knowing where this is going.

"Weren't you with Evan then?" She's trying not to sound super judgmental, but it doesn't work.

"In my defense, Seth didn't know I was dating someone. And Evan wasn't there."

May leans across the table and pats my hand. "Not the defense you think it is, sweetie."

"Okay, fine. It was a dick move on my part. But he was a complete asshole about it and I haven't seen him since. And now, thank Thor, I don't ever have to see him again."

THE NEXT DAY, Natasha calls me into her office as soon as I step through the door. It's been two days since the disaster video, my first article is due in a week, and I haven't even figured out which task I want to do first. The only bright spot is I haven't seen Seth since we exchanged lists, and I'm intending to keep it that way. A quick glance around the open space reassures me he's not there, but I duck into the safety of Natasha's office with my head down, just in case.

"Sit down," she commands, pushing the door closed behind me.

I sink into one of the soft chairs, the apology already on my lips. "I know how unprofessional that whole live video was and I'm so sorry, Natasha. You know I never do anything like that, I don't know what came over me."

She sinks into her chair and levels her stare at me. "You think I called you in here to ream you out?"

"Yes?"

An almost-smile cracks her face. "Lana, that video has brought in more likes and views and new followers than anything we've posted in the past five years."

Well, shit. On the surface that seems like a good thing, but it doesn't help the nausea stirring at the thought of people actually watching our implosion. "Great," I manage to choke out.

She raises one perfect eyebrow. "I take it that means you haven't watched the playback? Or read the comments?"

"Never read the comments." It's always been my policy, but even more so when I know I embarrassed the hell out of myself.

"The comments made it pretty clear that the readers want to see more of you and Seth together. Whatever happened years ago, your chemistry is still off the charts."

I laugh hollowly. "Well, too bad for the readers. We already exchanged lists. Now we're just working on our tasks and articles. Separately."

"Or, you work on your assignments together."

My brow furrows, scrunching up in confusion. "The whole point of my list is that I do things on my own. I'm supposed to be focusing on learning to love myself. Can't really do that when I'm hanging out with my ex." Whom I hate.

"The whole point of your list is to bring in clicks, Lana. It would be stupid not to take advantage of this viral video and bring in new readers. If they want to see the two of you together, then that's what we're going to give them."

My heart thuds out an accelerated beat. She can't actually be asking me to do this. "So you want me to, what, just hang out with Seth twice a week for the next ten weeks?"

"Some tasks you'll still have to complete on your own—therapy, for example, and the one-night stand, of course." She throws me a piercing look. "But anytime you can do it together, you will. Think about what this kind of attention could do for you. The *Chronicle* will surely take notice."

Yeah, but at what cost? I told Seth I never wanted to see him again, and I meant it. "I don't think I can do this, Natasha."

"You can. And you will. I already talked to Seth. He knows you'll be reaching out to set up a schedule." She gestures toward the door, dismissing me.

"Seriously? I don't get any say in this?" Natasha has never been the soft and fluffy kind of boss, but she's also never dismissed my concerns out of hand like this.

"I'm beholden to a bigger boss now, Lana. This is my final decision." A trace of sympathy flashes in her small smile, but it's gone a heartbeat later.

I push out of my chair, too stunned to storm out of her office.

Seth: Assuming you've unblocked me and this message goes through, what tasks do you want to tackle first?

Lana: You're unblocked. For now. I don't care which, as long as it's fast. Which of yours can we do quickly?

Seth: Easy. Furniture. I need some. I'd like to sit on something other than a milk crate.

Lana: Wow. Milk crate, huh? Very grown-up.

Seth: In my defense, I've been living out of a suitcase for the past six years, and before that I was living with my parents. I'm kinda starting from scratch here.

Lana: Stellar defense.

Lana: I'm free tomorrow. I'll pick you up at 10.

Seth: And for your first task?

Lana: I was hoping you'd forgotten.

Seth: Not a chance.

Lana: Ugh. I guess I'll get the blind date over with. I'm sure Corey or James has someone they could set me up with.

Seth: I'll be taking care of the date portion.

Lana: I don't want to date you.

Seth: Yeah, obviously. Same.

Seth: But don't worry. I have the perfect guy in mind.

Lana: Mansplainer?

Lana: Gym devotee?

Lana: Misogynist?

Seth: The whole point of the date is to go in blind.

Lana: Oh fuck, all three?

Seth: Do you think, at least for the duration of the time we're being forced to spend together, we can put the combat on hold?

Lana: Scared?

Seth: No.

Seth: I just don't want to spend the next ten weeks fighting with you. Can we call a truce?

Lana: Fine. Truce for now.

Lana: But I reserve the right to revoke said truce at any time.

Seth: Good night, Parker.

Lana: Good night, Seth.

7

If you want to know if you're compatible with someone, take a trip to IKEA.

—Lana Parker, "How to Know When You've Found the One"

HAVING A CLEAR PLAN FOR OUR TASKS DOES LITTLE TO soothe the frustration radiating through me. As soon as we say good night, I drop my phone and head directly into my home office. I stand in the center of the room, the original hardwood floors covered by a soft sky-blue rug. Almost the entire space is lined with wall-to-wall bookshelves, and they're filled to the brim. I have a really hard time letting go of my books, and since I read anywhere from fifteen to twenty a month, those shelves are packed. Not just with books, but also with candles and mugs and goodies collected from my multiple bookish subscription boxes.

On the one wall not encompassed by shelves, I have a long white desk, neatly cluttered with supplies and piles of notebooks. Floating shelves hang above it, my collection of superhero Funko Pop!s on proud display. Framed *Playbills* fill in any of the open wall space, and a rolling cart of my TBR books lives next to my desk.

Just to the left of where I'm standing is a cushy gray armchair and a small birch side table, a tall gold reading lamp perched overhead. I sink into the chair with a sigh. Closing my eyes, I attempt to clear my mind.

The readers want to see more of you and Seth together.

Not the defense you think it is, sweetie.

Lana, I wasn't trying to hurt you . . .

Ugh. What has become of my life? I push out of the chair and head over to my desk. Next to my laptop is a pile of books I put aside to review. Opening up my computer, I log on to my blog site and click *New Post*.

I started this blog about four years ago, right before I began dating Evan. I'd just had my heart broken—again—and the last thing I wanted to be writing about was finding love. I bought a domain and figured out how to post, and it felt good, purposeful. Even though my blog has never been fancy or intended for public consumption, it's always been mine. I blog about new Marvel movies and the books I've read, all the things that annoy me about my fandoms and all the things I love about them. It's where I published my five-thousand-word treatise on why the end of *Game of Thrones* was a detriment to society. And where I espoused my love for the purehearted goodness of *Schitt's Creek* and *Ted Lasso*. I've taken solace in pop culture since I was young, and this blog has become the place where I get to show my appreciation.

And yeah, maybe no one reads it except my few closest friends. But that's okay. The point was never to make it my job. Now, though, writing about these passions will be my job, once I win this stupid competition. And I *will* win this competition.

I KEEP UP my positive thinking as I make the short drive to pick up Seth the following morning.

Seth's place is not what I was expecting. Mostly because it's a house, not some run-down apartment. Not that I think he'd gravitate toward a run-down apartment, but the LA housing market is a bitch and he did just get here. And he doesn't even know for certain if he's staying yet.

So the cute little bungalow, in need of some love but located in a primo spot in Highland Park, catches me off guard. I park my Prius behind a different Prius and make my way to the front door, stepping carefully through the weeds littering the yard.

Seth opens the door before I can even knock, a snarky grin plastered on his face. "Hey." He gestures for me to step inside, sweeping his arms wide like he's welcoming me to a Renaissance castle.

The inside doesn't seem to be in much better shape than the outside, though at least everything looks clean. And empty. Seth wasn't exaggerating about the milk crate, which sits in the center of the living room, in front of the small TV residing on its own crate. There's a card table and a single folding chair in the dining area. I'm scared to even look in the bedroom.

"So when you said 'starting from scratch,' you meant actual literal scratch." I begin making a mental list of everything he's going to need, then pull out my phone to start taking notes because I'm never going to remember a list this long.

He runs a hand through his hair. It's a classic Seth move, and it leaves his hair sticking up all stupid cute—not that I notice. "Actual literal scratch."

"Please tell me you're not sleeping on an air mattress." I hesitantly head down the hallway, equal parts worried and intrigued as to what I might find.

There's one bathroom, still outfitted in the original tile, which is old enough to be back in style. At least he has a shower curtain up and a towel hanging over the bar affixed to the wall. I peek my head into the first room I come across, but there's not a single thing to be found inside. The next room I come to is his bedroom. There's a mattress and even a box spring, though both rest in the middle of the room, sitting on the hardwood floor, without a bed frame or nightstand in sight. A table lamp sits plugged in in the corner, on top of a stack of books.

"Not bad, considering I just moved in, right?" He creeps up behind me and I almost jump out of my skin.

"At least it's clean." I stride farther into the room to avoid having to turn and look at him, unwilling to give him even the smallest amount of affirmation. "Did you buy this place?"

"Renting. For now. I made a deal with the owner that I'd do some work on it while I'm here, try to get it in presentable shape. In exchange he's going to give me first dibs before it goes on the market."

"You're planning on staying then. In LA, I mean." The thought makes my stomach spin. I pivot so I can see him in my peripheral vision.

He leans against the doorjamb, hands shoved in his pockets. "I've been living out of a suitcase for what feels like a decade. It's time. I want somewhere I can call home."

Home. The word pierces me right in the chest. I'm sure for him it's just a simple phrase. A place to sleep at night, make coffee in the morning. Seth has always had a home, a place to go to where he's loved and accepted no matter what.

For me, it's a feeling that I've always been searching for. And Seth is the only person who ever truly made me feel like I was home.

I clear my throat, turning my attention back to the windows, which look original and in need of a fresh coat of paint. "We should probably head out. Lots to buy today."

He takes a tentative step inside the room. "Yeah. So about that. I'm obviously up for buying some essential pieces, but I'm not really looking to spend a ton of money. This place isn't technically mine, and I don't officially have a job until I win this competition."

I push past him out of the room, ignoring his cocky—and asinine—claim. "Luckily we're fifteen minutes away from one of the country's biggest IKEAs. I'm sure we'll find what you need and stay on budget."

"IKEA?" He says the word as if I suggested we pick out a couch from Satan's Furniture Emporium deep in the bowels of hell. Which I guess is fair.

"Oh man, I should've made that part of your list. Build an IKEA dresser with one of your dates."

"I think I would've forfeited on sight."

"Is it too late to edit our lists?"

"Yes." He grabs his keys and wallet from the kitchen counter and gestures for me to lead the way. "Okay if you drive? I'm still not used to the traffic, and the freeways here are no joke."

"Wait, did the great Seth Carson just admit there's something he can't do?" I was already planning on driving anyway. Seth was never a big driver; he only got his license in high school so he could commandeer his mom's van for our make-out sessions, and given his nomadic lifestyle of recent years, I assumed he was still hesitant about getting behind the wheel. But that doesn't mean I'm going to give up the chance to poke at his ego.

"It's not that I can't, I just haven't had a lot of practice." He puffs up his chest. "I'm secure enough to admit when I need help."

I lead him to my car and unlock the doors, both of us climbing in and buckling up. "The only way to learn is to just go for it, but I'm going to let you take care of that when my life isn't in your hands."

"Gee, thanks."

"Watch and learn."

I'm what many would probably deem an aggressive driver, but I learned quickly that Los Angeles's freeways (and streets, for that matter) are as cutthroat as its signature industry. What would be aggression anywhere else is practically passive here; it's cut off or be cut off, drive not the speed limit lest ye be passed on all sides and honked at from here to oblivion.

The exhale of relief Seth lets out once we're safely parked at the Burbank IKEA is well earned.

I pull out my phone as we ride the escalator up to the top level. "Okay. So bare minimum you need a couch, a bed frame, and a dining room table and chairs. How are you doing on linens and towels?"

"Fine, I guess?" He shrugs, his eyes widening as we crest the peak of the escalator and the showroom spreads out in front of us.

"Do you have more than one set?" I grab a free measuring tape, weaving through the crowds congregated at the beginning of the labyrinth.

"Do I need more than one set?" His voice sounds far behind me and I can practically see him trying to politely maneuver his way through the sea of people without stepping on anyone's toes. Amateur.

I don't slow down, following the path of arrows on the polished concrete. "You obviously need more than one set. However, I find Target the superior option for affordable linens and towels."

Seth finally catches up to me, fear in his voice as he falls into step beside me. "Do we have to go there too?"

I shoot him a pitying gaze. "Not today." Someone pushes past me, knocking me into Seth. His arm jets out to steady me, grasping my waist and keeping me upright. His fingers squeeze into the curve of my hip, like muscle memory kicks in. He releases me after just a few seconds too many.

My breath quickens in my chest and I don't think it has anything to do with the marathon-like pace I've been setting.

"So what's first?"

"First?" It's like the removal of his hand from my body has removed my brain from my skull right along with it.

A knowing smirk teases his lips. "What are we shopping for first?"

"Oh. Right." I look around the wide-open-yet-crammed-full-of-people space. "Couches," I blurt since they're the first item I see. I barrel through the crowd to the displays, moving from one couch to the next as I test them all for comfort and durability.

Seth stops in front of the cheapest one, plops down on it for half a second, then jumps back up. "This one will do."

"Seriously? You can't just buy the first one you try."

"Why not?"

"It's like a car or a house or a significant other. You don't marry the first person you date." I want to shove the words right back in my mouth the second they break free. They hang heavy in the air as an alternate future looms before us, the two of us shopping for furniture under totally different circumstances. If anything, years of people-watching at IKEA have taught me that kind of trip typically ends in either a screaming match or the silent treatment.

That wouldn't be us though, a very mean voice in the back of my brain insists. We'd be the couple zipping through the aisles, Seth pushing me as I rode a cart like a skateboard. The pair sharing an ice-cream cone, actually looking forward to an evening of putting together the mind-bending puzzle they call furniture, because it would mean spending time together.

"Would that have been so terrible?" Seth's voice is so soft I barely hear it, his question revealing a similar could-have-been scene played out in his own mind.

"Yes." My one-word response is stark. And a lie.

He exhales sharply, like he's been punched in the stomach.

I busy myself with my phone, letting Natasha's marching orders distract me from dumb things like feelings. "Sit and pose, try to look pretty. We need something to post on Instagram."

Any hint of emotion drops from Seth's face, replaced with his signature cocky charm as he perches on the arm of the sofa. "I always look pretty, Parker."

He flashes a charismatic grin and I snap the photo before we continue on.

SETH ONLY GRIMACES a little when he's given his final total at checkout, sliding his card through the reader and taking his receipt. The grimace gets a little deeper when he pays to have everything delivered to his house.

"You had to drive a Prius," he grumbles at me as we make our way to the food court.

"I'm saving the planet, jerk." I order us each a vanilla cone, hand over my two dollars, and lead him to the only open table. Of course, it's the tiniest one possible and our knees brush together once we're both in our seats. I scoot my chair back, putting some space between us and taking a moment to remind myself that the little zings from his touch don't magically heal the damage he's done.

We sit in our awkward, hostile-lite silence for a minute, both of us focusing on our cones and avoiding looking at each other.

"So how do you like working for *ATF*?" Seth extends his long legs, one on either side of my chair, encroaching on my space in a way he knows irritates me. Even though they don't touch me, I can feel his legs surrounding me.

I ignore the overwhelming urge to play footsie and focus on how much of the truth I want to share. Is he asking just to be polite and make conversation, or is he trying to get insider info? Does he want to compare publication stats so I can be intimidated by the great Seth Carson? I mean, I know how lucky I am to have a stable writing job with steady pay and benefits, but it also doesn't feel anywhere near as important as what Seth has done with his own career. Not that I ever had a nose for "serious" journalism, but I certainly never pictured myself as LA's millennial Carrie Bradshaw.

If Seth notices my reticence—and I'm sure he does—he just sits silently while I puzzle it all out, his attention focused on his ice cream, his tongue swirling through the sweet cream like I'm not supposed to notice.

And I'm so distracted by the sight, by the way his tongue swipes at the cool vanilla, that I start speaking without a filter. "I like *ATF* a lot. The crew is great, they're some of my closest friends. And Natasha is a really good boss. She genuinely cares about us, not just as employees, but as people."

"Do I hear a *but* in there somewhere?"

I shrug, swiping a lick of my own cone. "It's not what I would choose to be writing."

His feet hook around the legs of my chair. "Yeah, to be

frank I didn't expect to find your name listed under dating and relationships."

"Because I'm so bad at them?" The heat in my voice is enough to melt the ice cream.

"Because it's a waste of your talents. And it's not your passion." He meets my gaze head-on, his mouth devouring a bite of his cone.

I nudge his feet away from my chair and ignore the fire in my belly as I remember what else that mouth can do. "How would you know anything about my passions? Believe it or not, people do change over the course of twelve years."

He's quiet for a minute. "Fair enough." He doesn't point out that it was the very chance to write about my passions, a column dedicated to that piece of my heart, that convinced me to agree to this whole competition in the first place.

It irks me, the way he still seems to know me. The way I don't feel like I know him.

His tongue swipes another lick of ice cream. "Are you free this Saturday?"

For a second, it sounds so much like he's asking me out on a date that I freeze up.

"Brian wanted to confirm your blind date."

Oh right. The blind date. That Seth is setting me up on. I feign nonchalance. "He's giving up his Saturday night for a blind date? What's wrong with him?" I bite off a chunk of my cone with a satisfying crunch.

Seth doesn't answer my inquiry, just continues to tap away on his phone, not paying me any attention.

"Fine. Yes, I'm available Saturday." I finish eating my cone, wadding up the wrapper and stopping just short of throwing it at him.

He still isn't looking at me, his eyes now seemingly glued to his screen. "Great. He'll meet you at Little Dom's at eight."

I wrinkle my nose at the restaurant choice. Not that there's anything wrong with Little Dom's; the food is great. It's just a known haunt for lots of celebs and you usually don't go there unless you have a business meeting or are trying to catch a glimpse of Jon Hamm. Though I certainly can't fault anyone for wanting to try to scope out Jon Hamm.

"Is that okay?" Seth breaks me out of my daydream involving me in a Christina Hendricks–worthy corset and Jon Hamm undoing the laces.

"What? Yes. Fine. Little Dom's at eight." I stand and toss my wrapper in the trash, trusting Seth will follow me. There's no way he could find his way back to the car on his own.

The ride to his house is mostly silent and uncomfortable. We seem to find ourselves in these brief moments of blast-from-the-past banter, only to minutes later be jolted back to the memory of the last awful time we saw each other, or to our present circumstances, pitting us against each other. It's a mind fuck, and after almost a full day of it, I feel like I have emotional whiplash. So when I pull up in front of his house twenty minutes later, I don't bother to park or turn off the car.

"So you're coming over this weekend to help me put all this shit together, right?"

I scoff. "Dude. I wouldn't even help my best friend put IKEA furniture together." Not that May would ever shop at IKEA.

He pauses for a second, one hand on the door, the other on the armrest in the middle of the car, which all of a sudden feels very close. "Sometimes I forget we're not friends anymore." His words are quiet, heavy and pained.

My breath catches in my chest, my instincts screaming at me to reach out for that hand sitting so close to mine. I close my eyes and shake the vision out of my head. "We haven't been friends in a long time, Seth."

I avoid looking at him, and after another silence, I hear him climb out of the car, shutting the door firmly behind him.

This time I don't watch him walk away.

8

You couldn't pay me a million dollars to go on a blind date.

—Lana Parker, in conversation with friends, two years ago

I DON'T REALLY KNOW WHY I SHOW UP TO THE OFFICE the Friday after IKEA. I don't have anything to write about yet, seeing as how I won't have completed my first task until I go on my blind date tomorrow night. But that doesn't stop me from strolling in the door, coffee in hand, bright and early at ten a.m. My eyes quickly scan the room, but I don't spot a head of dark hair and broad shoulders.

Which is totally a good thing.

I drop my stuff at the long white communal worktable in the center of the open space, going through my perfunctory setup, even though I have literally nothing to work on.

Luckily, Corey saunters over, hopping up on the table next to my computer, her tiny ass still nearly managing to knock over my coffee.

"Sooooooo," she drawls, leaning back on both hands.

I make a grab for my coffee, saving the precious lifeblood before she spills the entire thing. "So what?"

She rolls her eyes. "How was your first date with Seth?"

"It was not a date."

Tessa exits the office kitchen, dunking a tea bag in a mug proclaiming we should Write Drunk Edit Drunker. "Oooh, are we talking about the IKEA date?" She slides into the chair across from me. The fact that they are here in the office on a Friday speaks more to their want of gossip than to the need to get work done, and they both settle in.

I push my laptop away from me. "Guys. It was not a date. And how did you even know we went to IKEA?"

"The *ATF* Insta Stories. You posted like five times." Corey doesn't even have to say the *duh* out loud; it's implied.

"I only posted because Natasha demanded it, and if you actually watched, then you know it was merely furniture shopping." And a little erotic ice-cream eating, but they don't need to know that. "The whole thing was just a reminder of all the reasons we broke up. I wouldn't even be talking to him if I didn't have to."

"Yeah, it's bullshit she's making you do this whole thing, but don't act like hanging out with Seth Carson, mega hottie, is a total sacrifice."

My hackles spring to action hearing that descriptor come from Corey, who is at least ten times hotter than I am. "Kindly remember that 'mega hottie' is also my ex-boyfriend."

"Is that argument supposed to help your case?" She grins at me, kicking her legs back and forth.

Tessa clears her throat. "Anyway. Are you all ready for your blind date tomorrow night?"

I prop my elbows on the table and cradle my head in my hands. "If by 'ready' you mean 'totally dreading it,' then sure. Absolutely ready."

"Come on, what's the worst that could happen?" Corey chides.

"I could end up dead and dismembered, my body locked in his trunk?"

"I think it might be time to lay off the true-crime docs." Tessa smiles at me over the rim of her mug, knowing full well she's the one who got me hooked on them.

"Also, Seth knows this guy. It's not like he's some stranger you met on Craigslist." Corey grabs one of my pens and starts drumming it on her thigh.

"Do people still do that?" I take the pen from her, placing it on the other side of the table and out of her reach.

"Only people with a death wish." Corey hops off the table and heads back to her workstation, calling over her shoulder, "Have fun on your date, wear something slutty!"

I turn to Tessa. "Aren't we not supposed to say the word *slutty* anymore?"

Tessa shrugs with a smile. "She means it as a compliment."

I lace my fingers together around my coffee mug, tracing the outline of Captain Marvel's super suit with my thumb. "Have you ever been on a blind date?"

"Oh god no." Her eyes widen and she takes another quick sip of tea. "Though I'm sure it's great. Yours is going to be great."

I blow out an exasperated sigh. "What have I gotten myself into?"

She pushes out of her chair, coming around to give me a side hug. "Just think about how awesome it's going to be when you're writing your own column. You've been waiting for this for a long time. Grit your teeth, buckle down, and get it done. It'll be worth it in the end."

"Assuming my blind date doesn't kill me."

"Assuming that." She blows me a kiss, heading back to her desk. "Text me if you need an emergency bailout!"

I SHOW UP to Little Dom's at eight fifteen on Saturday night, not knowing much about blind dates, but for sure knowing I don't want to get there first. All Seth provided me with was my date's name, Brian, and luckily that's enough for the hostess to point me in the right direction.

At first glance, Brian is just a half step below my type. He has fair hair and light eyes, a little too frat boy for my tastes, but he's dressed nicely, and he stands up to greet me when I approach the table, so I figure he can't be all bad.

"Brian?" I hold out my hand as he rises from the booth. "I'm Lana."

He holds back for just a second before launching himself at me in a full-body hug.

"Nice to meet you." He pats my head, which is currently shoved almost directly into his armpit. "You look great."

"Thanks, you too." I extricate myself out of the danger zone, which smells more like Axe than BO, though I'm not sure that's better. We slide into seats on opposite sides of the booth and I immediately peruse the menu so I have somewhere to direct my attention. This already feels weird, and that hug didn't help. What are we even supposed to talk about? I literally know nothing about this man aside from his name. I guess I could ask him things about himself, but where do I even begin? And why am I so bad at this?

Our server, who already has impeccable timing, shows up just as the silence becomes awkward. We order drinks and our food, and suddenly the security blanket of a menu is whisked away and our server abandons me, and we're left all alone.

Brian flashes what looks like a very forced smile. "So, Seth says you're a writer too?"

I nod, glomming on to this most basic of conversation topics. "I am. I've been on staff at *Always Take Fountain* since I graduated from college."

"And you write the dating section?" He picks up his fork and begins to lightly drum it against the table, like he somehow knows it's my biggest pet peeve.

I lace my fingers together tightly, keeping them locked in on my side of the table so I don't yank the fork out of his hand. "Yup."

"That's cute."

"Cute?" I gratefully accept the glass of wine the server delivers and take a sip, steeling myself for his response.

Chugging half of his beer in one go, he slams down his drink and wipes his sleeve across his mouth. "Yeah, a dating column. It's cute. Very *Sex and the City*."

And suddenly his bad manners are the least offensive thing about this date so far. Because yeah, I may have similar thoughts about my job, but I'm the only one allowed to talk shit about it. Brian-who-I-just-met-five-seconds-ago certainly is not.

I grit my teeth. "And what do you do, Brian?"

"Oh, I'm a writer too. But I write important stuff. News, politics, you know."

"Yes, I have heard of news and politics, seeing as I have a journalism degree."

He grins at me. "I have a master's."

I flick my wrist, checking the time on my nonexistent watch. "Well, would you look at the time? I gotta go." I grab my purse and prepare to slip from the booth.

He chuckles and mutters, "That was even easier than I thought."

I stop my butt midslide. "Excuse me? Did you just call me easy?"

Brian freezes, clearly caught. "Um, no? I mean, yes. Yes I did. You're so easy."

I narrow my eyes, giving him my best Natasha impersonation. "How is me leaving ten minutes into the date easy, Brian?"

His skin pales, and instantly I know. "Um . . ."

"Did Seth put you up to this?" I demand.

"Maybe?" His voice rises absurdly high.

"That motherfucker." I sit back in my seat, swallowing down the rest of my wine. "Of course he finds the worst guy possible and sets me up for failure," I grumble, sort of under my breath but not really.

"Hey." Brian sits up indignantly. "I am not the worst

guy possible." He waves his hands around. "That was all for show."

"What was all for show?"

"The intrusive hug and the condescension."

"And the beer chugging?"

"Yes, that too." His cheeks flush and it's a little endearing. "Look, I owed Seth a favor, and he asked me to come meet you and just be an asshole the whole time. He said to keep up the act for as long as it took to get you to bail and not finish the date."

"You know, this is why everyone hates straight dudes." I raise my hand, signaling to the server to bring me another glass of wine.

Brian sighs. "I'm sorry. Dinner is on me."

"Yeah, no kidding." I study him for a second, and he flashes me a sheepish grin.

"I can go, if you'd rather be alone."

"That depends. Are you actually an asshole?"

He smiles wider and a dimple pops in his left cheek. "I try not to be."

I sigh, not willing to admit he's got me somewhat charmed. "Are you actually a news writer?"

He shakes his head. "No, I do write and edit, but for a website. We cover pretty much everything entertainment, movies, TV shows, comics, the works."

"Really?" I perk up just a tad. "I'm kind of a pop culture nerd."

Brian's eyes spark at the mention of pop culture, and from there our conversation evolves easily, starting with our favorite TV shows and movies, leading into some spirited discussions about the direction of the MCU and where we each feel it needs to go. He scores a lot of points with me by not making the basic white-man criticism of too much pandering with all the new women-led projects. He doesn't complain once about Captain Marvel, which basically makes him a unicorn among man-nerds. After our initial hiccup, the conversation flows effortlessly through dinner and dessert and even an after-dinner drink.

"So how did you first get into all of it? Books, movies, TV? Were your parents in the business?" Brian spins his wineglass around on the table.

It's a fair question, especially when you live in LA. It's not his fault he doesn't know how much the simple inquiry stings.

I take another sip of wine. "No, my parents didn't get me into it. The opposite actually."

He raises his eyebrows. "Oh?"

I shrug like this whole line of conversation is no big deal. "Yeah. I was alone a lot as a kid. My dad was never in the picture and my mom was always traveling for work. I sort of turned to movies and books and TV to find a family?" I chuckle, even though nothing about it is funny. "That sounds really pathetic, doesn't it?"

Brian reaches across the table and gives my hand a quick squeeze. "It's not pathetic at all. I think a lot of us turn to the characters we see on the screen and the page to find some kind of acceptance."

A smile spreads across my face and I'm surprised to find it's actually genuine. "I never really thought of it like that."

He swigs the last of his drink. "That's what's so great about art, the profound impact it can have on its audience."

My smile fades just a tad. Even though I haven't necessarily articulated it that way before, Brian's summed up the main reason I want to be writing about my favorite entertainment enterprises. Because they do mean something to me, and they mean something to a lot of readers and viewers out there, much more than some stupid listicle featuring the ten best breakup songs.

Brian gives me a soft smile while I digest his words. "Should we head out?"

I nod, not quite able to return his grin.

After he pays the check, he walks me to my car and leaves me with a kiss on the cheek and a promise to text and set up a second date, to which I wholeheartedly agree. I was so worried about this blind date, and despite a disastrous start, it turned out better than I could've ever expected.

It isn't until I'm home, face scrubbed clean and brushing my teeth, that a niggling little worry starts to poke at the edge of my brain. It makes sense that Seth would send one of his friends in to try to get me to back out of the task. But why would he chance sending someone like Brian, someone I could legitimately have a connection with? The question rolls around in my mind until I'm curled up in bed watching the latest episode of *Ted Lasso*.

And it hits me after a particularly poignant pep talk onscreen. I'm such an idiot. I'm a first-class moron. Of course Seth wouldn't set me up with someone awful. My whole aim here is to stay single, and what better way to challenge that, to make me forfeit the competition, than to present me with a guy I could totally see myself in a relationship with?

Sneaky bastard. I can't believe he would sink so low, play so dirty, right on my very first task.

And I can't believe I not only fell for it but also had no qualms about accepting a second date with Brian. Competition aside, I'm supposed to be finding myself and shit, not jumping into another relationship I'm not actually ready for.

But it's far easier to blame Seth for this mishap than to recognize my own patterns, so I go to bed vowing to get back at him tomorrow. He thinks he knows me, thinks I'm just going to roll over and give up, let him have this win.

Well, that motherfucker has another think coming.

9

As that one guy said that one time, all's fair in love and war.

—Lana Parker, "How to Win Back Your Partner"

THE MORNING AFTER MY SLIGHTLY-TOO-SUCCESSFUL blind date, I make two pit stops before driving over to Seth's house. Armed with a set of sheets from Target and a *Fittonia* plant personally recommended by one of my favorite small plant shops, I knock on his door, plastering a sweet smile on my face as it swings open.

A smile that quickly freezes when it takes in a shirtless Seth, greeting me in nothing but a pair of baby-blue basketball shorts. Seth was an athlete all through school and always in great shape, but he still had a teenage lankiness to him. Now he has man muscles instead of boy muscles. Holy Hemsworth, I can actually see the outlines of his abs. Fuck me if he doesn't have that perfect V, pointing directly where I know I shouldn't be looking. And I probably shouldn't be thinking the phrase *fuck me* anywhere near this whole situation.

With a self-satisfied smirk when he catches me gawking, he crosses his arms over his chest, further emphasizing the bulges of his biceps and shoulders. “I didn’t expect to see you here this morning. To what do I owe the pleasure?”

I clear my throat and force myself to meet his eyes. Eyes that are all twinkly with his misguided assumption that he’s pulled one over on me. He thought he could one-up me on my very first task, but last night he declared war. Even if he doesn’t know it.

“Well, my date with Brian went so well last night, I wanted to come over and say thank you.” I hand him the potted plant and a bag containing the sheet set, along with a sickly-sweet smile. “A combination housewarming and thank-you present. I thought I’d get ahead on the houseplant task and the woman at the shop said these are easy to care for.” I make sure I open my eyes just a tad wider than usual, turning up the innocent act as much as I dare without going overboard.

I actually asked the woman at WildFlora for the most sensitive of plants, one that would require a ton of work and attention but didn’t have a big reputation for being difficult. Hence the *Fittonia*, which most people have never heard of. Those who have know that this dramatic bitch faints when she doesn’t get enough water. She’s high-maintenance and sensitive, and therefore the perfect plant for Seth and his challenge.

Seth takes my offerings out of my hands with a skeptical look on his face. “Should I be scared?”

I roll my eyes. "It's just sheets and a plant. I really do want to thank you. I never thought I'd find someone I clicked with so easily, especially not so soon after the breakup."

He tries hard to hide the glee, but he forgets how well I know him. "I'm so glad you guys hit it off. Brian is great."

Seth's stupid confidence strikes a new spark of rage within me, but I push down my ire, feigning newly coupled-up bliss. "He is, isn't he?" I throw in a sigh of longing, just to really drive it home.

He goes for it, and his grin widens as he realizes he's got this competition in the bag. Too bad he doesn't know that I know that he knows. "So are you going to see him again?"

I bite my lip like I'm holding back a grin of my own. "Yup. I can't wait!" I pull my car keys from my cross-body purse and give him a cheeky little wave. "Well, I'm off to work on my article. Have a great rest of your day, and enjoy your plant!"

His eyes narrow just a tad and I really hope I didn't take it too far. That chipper voice coming out of my mouth was definitely several octaves higher than usual.

But too late if I did. I bound down his front steps and slide into the front seat of my car.

#LANAVSSETH

Friday, 8:03 A.M.

JAMES: Today. is. the. day.

COREY: Yay!!! I can't wait to read your article, **@Lana**!

TESSA: I'm sure it's amazing, **@Lana**!

ROB: I'm sure both articles will be amazing.
COREY: Traitor.
ROB: Hey, clicks are clicks and that's good for all of us.

10:14 A.M.

COREY: They're up!!! So good, **@Lana**! "Joe" sounds perfect!
TESSA: Such a great piece, **@Lana**!
ROB: Isn't your whole goal to not start a new relationship?
LANA: Thanks, Captain Obvious. And thanks, friends! Appreciate your support!

1:42 P.M.

JAMES: Damn, these pieces are doing numbers. **@Ian**, can you give us some stats?
ROB: You know **@Ian** never checks the Slack, he's too busy with site maintenance.
COREY: Yeah, he has real work to do, unlike the rest of us.
SETH: I see my article is generating lots of comments.
LANA: I'm sure that photo of you posing in an IKEA bed has nothing to do with it 🙄
SETH: You took that photo.
LANA: Only because you threatened to tell Natasha if I didn't.
SETH: Not my fault the readers find me appealing.
LANA: Barf.
SETH: Good one.
LANA: I'm sure your appeal will fade as soon as they get to know you.

SETH: They already know you and yet I don't see them commenting on your piece . . .
JAMES: Wow, you two. Get a room. Or a DM thread.
COREY: Ha! Have you seen all the comments shipping them? 😄 If only the readers could see this!
LANA: We can see that, you know. Also, gross.
SETH: Yeah. Barf.
LANA: Good one.

5:36 P.M.

SETH: I'm up to 200 comments. How many do you have, **@Lana**?
LANA: Shut up.
SETH: Oh, you haven't checked? Let me check for you. It's seventeen. So few, I had to spell out the number. Just a little journalism humor for you.
LANA: Fuck off.

10

Is my new Ektorp sofa the key to all my romance woes?
Now that I own a dining table AND four chairs
(hold your applause until the end, please),
will I finally find the woman of my dreams?

—Seth Carson, "Some Assembly Required"

I STAB ANGRILY AT MY PHONE SCREEN, CLOSING THE *ATF* site. It's been two days since our first articles went live and Seth's piece still has the majority of the comments. Seth is also still continuing to gloat about his lead in the work Slack, which used to be my favorite time-waster. Now, like the rest of my life, my work happy place has been commandeered by my stupid ex. Shoving my phone back in my purse, I cross my legs tightly, my foot swinging in impatience. Not only is Seth an arrogant bastard, he's also late.

Okay, only a minute late. But still.

I spot him a second later, striding toward where I sit on the edge of the fountain in the middle of the Americana outdoor shopping center. I'm here against my will today for Seth's makeover challenge. I argued he could've managed the task with some online shopping, and, most important, without me, but in Natasha's words, it's all in the name of "content." Seth gives me a small smile when he sees me, but I pretend not to notice him.

My anger and frustration falter in my chest as I take him in. He's wearing a navy-blue T-shirt and jeans, topped with a black baseball hat. Aviator sunglasses cover his eyes, and I wonder if he's hiding from his emotions as much as I am.

Because there's no denying the swoop in my stomach at the sight of him. The way my chest tightens when I stand and he gives me a perfunctory side hug. The way the salty, sunshine scent of him immediately sends me back to the days when I thought our life together was going to be happy and perfect and beautiful.

Just as there's no denying that I still can't forgive him. For twelve years ago, for two years ago, for coming to LA, for this whole ridiculous competition.

Neither of us says anything for a moment; we just stand there in stilted silence.

Seth shoves his hands in his back pockets and clears his throat. "This place is cool."

I nod, gesturing with a limp hand to the mostly fancy shops around us. "I come here a lot."

"Cool," he says again.

I tilt my head in the direction of the H&M just across the way, wanting to get this over with as soon as humanly possible. "I figured we could probably get everything we need there."

"Lead the way." He's adopted his professional voice, the

one he always used with teachers and parents. It's smooth, with just a hint of charm, and also completely lacking Seth's usual warmth.

We head into the store and up the escalator to the men's section. I wait for him to take this chance to gloat about his article's success in person. Every time I catch a glimpse of him from the corner of my eye, he's got a smirky smile on his lips, but he stays quiet. He knows he doesn't have to mention he's kicking my ass. He knows it's something I can't stop thinking about and how much I hate losing. Especially to him.

"Do you have any ideas about what you want to look for?" I half-heartedly finger a blue checked button-down shirt.

He shrugs, removing his sunglasses and hanging them from the collar of his faded T-shirt. "I never thought my style was all that bad, to be honest."

I give him a once-over. "It's not. You've got the whole *Avenger trying to disguise himself as a civilian* look down pat."

He cracks an almost genuine smile. "You always did love the Avengers."

"Even Chris Evans can't deny the power of a good suit." I find a spinning rack of collared shirts and riffle through, picking out a few in shades of blue, colors that will make his eyes pop.

Seth takes the chosen shirts from me. "I guess I leave my fate in your hands then."

And with that, he dutifully follows me around the store as I pull different pieces for him to try on. Once we both have our arms loaded with garments, we make our way to the fitting room. Surprisingly, there doesn't seem to be a huge crowd and Seth is able to snag one of the bigger rooms.

"Are you going in with him?" the attendant asks.

"Oh hell no." I shove the pieces I've been carrying into Seth's arms and shoo him into the dressing room, flashing the attendant an apologetic smile. Finding a spot near the door, I lean against the wall and brace myself. I'm not an idiot, and I'm not blind. No matter how weird and uncomfortable things are between us right now, seeing Seth looking better than usual is going to have an effect on me.

I only ever saw him in a suit a couple of times, but the boy cleaned up well. The man, I'm sure, is going to look like he's fresh off the pages of *GQ*. My fingers subconsciously drift to the sunflower tattoo inked on my right rib cage as I'm both blessed and cursed with a vivid memory of prom night our senior year.

Seth arrived to pick me up dressed in a fitted black suit, about as basic as a prom-night look can get. Only he paired it with a mustard-yellow tie. It made about zero sense, in terms of style or otherwise, until he unearthed the plastic container holding my corsage. Somehow he'd convinced the florist to make me a sunflower corsage, even though the bloom itself was bigger than the palm of my hand. We both fell into a cascade of giggles as he slipped the elastic band over my wrist, the huge flower obscuring almost my entire forearm.

A throat clearing pulls me out of my haze of memories.

Luckily, Seth's taking wardrobe baby steps, coming out in fitted jeans and one of the button-down shirts I picked, sleeves rolled up to perfectly display those damned forearms.

"What do you think?" He tugs a little on the collar of the shirt.

I clear my own throat so the words don't come out mangled. "Looks good. Casual but professional."

"Great." He nods succinctly before heading back into the dressing room.

Next, he comes out in another button-down, this time tucked into gray slacks. My mouth goes a little dry, so I merely give him a thumbs-up and send him back to try on the next. And I'm glad I've had a bit of mental prep time, because when he comes out for the third time, I almost fall over. Thank Odin for the wall holding me up.

The suit is navy blue, paired with a white shirt covered in minuscule gray dots. It fits him like it's been custom made, and I've never seen him look so good.

I hold up my phone to snap a photo. "Natasha wanted me to post on our Stories," I say as an apology. I turn my attention to the camera to distract myself from the vision in front of me, though all it does is force me to focus on him even more. I capture a few photos and then swipe over to Instagram and the *ATF* account.

The attendant gives Seth an appreciative once-over. "Fit is just about perfect, but you need to see it with a tie." He riffles through the stray garments littering the fitting room counter.

I can't look at him any longer, afraid I might spontaneously combust, so I pretend to be engrossed in my phone. I share one of the photos of Seth to *ATF*'s Instagram Stories while the attendant helps him with a tie. Reactions to Seth in a suit pour in almost immediately. Most of them are versions of flames and heart eyes, but many are much more graphic than that. All of them make my stomach turn.

"Much better," the attendant finally says.

Taking in a long deep breath, I raise my eyes, praying I'll be unaffected. I've already seen him in the outfit, there's nothing adding a tie can do to make the searing attraction I clearly still feel for Seth any stronger.

Except the tie the attendant has fitted him with is yellow. Mustard yellow. Sunflower yellow.

"Just imagine a different color." The attendant misinterprets the pained look on my face.

But Seth knows. His eyes meet mine and they are blazing yet soft, and I know he remembers every single detail I was just picturing not five minutes before. He gives me a small smile, and it's both sad and sweet and the most genuine emotion I've seen from him since he arrived in LA.

"Looks great," I finally manage to choke out.

Seth takes that as his cue and heads back into the dressing room. When he reemerges, he's in his original clothes, arms laden with items to purchase. I stand off to the side as he checks out and pays. A flash of yellow catches my eye as the cashier is bagging up all his new clothes.

He bought the tie.

My heart implodes.

Without excusing myself, I rush to the front of the store, pushing my way outside, finding a shady spot away from all the foot traffic of the midday shoppers. A stupid piece of shiny fabric should not be the thing that sends me over the edge. But it just might be. He bought the tie. He bought it, knowing full well what it means and what it represents. One little glimpse of sunflower yellow brings back all the memories I've been trying so hard to forget—trying so hard to bury under our banter and verbal sparring. I wrap my arms around my midsection, as if I can somehow hold myself together.

I shut my eyes tightly, forcing myself to focus on more painful memories of Seth. The horrible reunion night rushes in, burned in my brain, and I sink into the emotions. The shame and the humiliation. The rejection and the hurt. And the anger. The pure, unfiltered anger.

Anger is easy. Anger doesn't leave any room for what might have been. Anger doesn't allow for confusion and what-ifs.

"Parker? Are you okay?" He places a single hand on my shoulder.

I spin around to face him. "No, I'm not fucking okay!" A few people stop or turn to look at us, and I remember we are in public and lower my voice. "I'm not okay, Seth. Why the fuck did you buy that tie? More important, what are you even doing here, honestly? Do you really think you can just waltz into my life and insert yourself where you don't belong? After everything you did!"

His eyes harden, shifting from concern to ire in the span of a few seconds. "What *I* did? Are you kidding me? What about what *you* did?" He takes a step closer into my space. "You are not the victim here, Parker."

I take my own step closer, shortening the distance between us until just a few inches remain. "Neither are you, Seth."

He lowers his head, his mouth a breath away from my ear. "I'm allowed to be angry too."

"Well then, if you're so angry, why are you here?" My heart pounds so loudly I'm afraid he'll hear it. There's so much heat between us—the furious feelings and the tension and the proximity—my skin tingles from head to toe.

He pulls away just enough so he can look in my eyes. "I don't know, Parker. I just couldn't be anywhere else."

After another glance full of emotions I can't parse, he gives me a helpless shrug, turns, and walks away.

11

They say the clothes make the man, but to be totally honest, I've always thought that line was kind of bullshit. Swapping out an old T-shirt in favor of a spiffy button-down doesn't change who I am underneath, does it?

—Seth Carson, "Head to Toe, Let Your Whole Body Talk"

I HAD ORIGINALLY PLANNED ON SAVING THERAPY FOR much later in this whole competition process, because honestly, I know I'm going to need it once I've been alone for a few weeks. But after May's nudge to do something for myself and seeing how torn up I got from just one shopping session with Seth, well, the need for therapy has been expedited. I'm no stranger to the process, so I schedule an appointment with my favorite former therapist, Dr. Lawson. She's kind but tough and already has the backstory on my mom, so hopefully I won't need to repeat that mess.

So of course her first question after the standard "how are you" is "How are things with your mother?"

I sink back into the plush navy-blue love seat in the center of her office. "Um, fine, I guess. Nothing much has really changed there, I don't think."

"When was the last time you spoke with her?" Dr. Lawson pulls her eyes from her notepad and studies me while I fidget.

"A couple weeks ago. She was traveling but she could be home by now." The throw pillow in the corner is calling my name, begging for me to pick it up and hug it to my chest, but I don't want it to seem like I'm hiding anything, so I clasp my fingers together to keep from reaching for it. "But that's not really why I'm here."

Dr. Lawson picks up her pen. "Oh? What can I help you with today?"

I let out a long breath. "Well. I just got out of a relationship. A long-term one. I thought we were going to get engaged, and instead he ended it." How has it only been a couple of weeks since Evan and I broke up? It feels like forever given how little it matters at this point. If our breakup hadn't spurred this whole competition, he probably wouldn't even be a blip on the radar, which only further reinforces how completely wrong we were together.

Dr. Lawson's pen scratches across the paper, but she doesn't say anything, so I keep talking.

"And then my best friend, May, pointed out that I have trouble with being single, that I tend to jump from relationship to relationship. And when I told Natasha—my boss—she basically said the same thing and challenged me to stay single, for myself and for work. She wants me to try a bunch of new things and write about it for the website."

Dr. Lawson's eyebrows raise, just the slightest bit.

I take a sip of water before I continue. "And then my high school ex-boyfriend showed up. He has an interim position at our site and when it came out that he never has serious relationships, Natasha turned it into this whole competition thing. My tasks are supposed to help me branch out and explore being single, and his are to prep him for a relationship. The winner gets their own column."

"Wow." Her pen glides across the paper for a solid minute. "That was a lot."

"Hence my being here." I need someone to tell me how to feel about all of this, because I sure as hell have no idea.

"What kinds of tasks are on your list?"

"Mostly easy stuff like 'take a new class' and 'volunteer.'" My cheeks heat as I think about the other, not-so-easy things, but I'm not ready to share those checklist items just yet.

"And how do you feel about your boss demanding this of you?" It's amazing how she asks such a judgmental question in such a totally nonjudgmental manner. I need some lessons on how to do that.

"I mean, she didn't exactly demand. She presented it as an opportunity for me to move from writing about relationship stuff to getting a column where I can write what I want." The pillow is practically calling my name now. It's perfectly shield sized.

"And do you agree with May and Natasha?"

"About what?"

"Do you think you're a serial monogamist, that you have trouble being alone?"

Fuck it. I grab the pillow. Squeezing the throw tightly to

my chest, I take my time before answering. "I think all evidence of the last sixteen years would point to that being true. I've had one steady boyfriend after the other, ever since I was fourteen." I do some quick math. "More than half my life."

"Would you say you feel more comfortable when you are in a long-term relationship?"

"I guess that's a fair statement."

"And why do you think that is?"

"I was hoping you could tell me that." I give her a cheeky grin, which she doesn't return.

"You know me better than that, Lana." She puts her notebook down on the side table next to her chair. "Why do you think you gravitate toward serious relationships? What's the appeal of a commitment over dating casually or being single?"

I blow out a long breath. "I guess given the erratic comings and goings of my mother throughout my life, I'm probably looking for something steady and permanent, since those things were missing from my childhood."

Dr. Lawson raises her eyebrows and tilts her head. "That sounds very reasonable."

A harsh laugh puffs out of my chest. "That was a little too easy."

"Why does it have to be hard?"

Well. She's got me there.

"What's so scary about being alone, Lana?" She sits back in her chair and folds her hands in her lap.

"I don't know. It's been so long since I've been alone, I haven't really had a chance to think about it." And I realize the deeper truth of that. The last time I was "alone," I was thirteen. So much in my life has changed since then, obviously, but I still have that ever-present desire for companionship. For a place or a person to call home.

"Do you want to accomplish the things on the list? Are they things you're interested in? Feel comfortable with?"

"I think *want* might be a strong word, but I could see how some of them could be good for me." I place the pillow back in its corner. "I actually already checked one off. I went on a blind date."

"And how did it go?"

I laugh before chugging another long sip of water. "A little too well. I really liked him and we made plans to meet up again."

She doesn't say anything. She does that sometimes when she wants to push me to the conclusion on my own.

"Which, yes, I realize is a pretty strong indication that the whole serial-monogamist thing is totally true."

"Okay. That's good that you made that connection." She picks up her notebook and pen again and jots down a few more notes. "How do you feel about completing the rest of the tasks?"

"Okay, I guess." I shrug. "I'm pretty sure Seth—that's the high school boyfriend—tried to sabotage me by setting me up with someone he knew I would like. It makes me feel more determined to prove to him that I can actually do this."

"What would you say you want more, the chance to write this column or the opportunity to beat Seth?"

I wrangle my face into a smile, even though the question alone makes me uneasy. "Can't it be both?"

"Is it important for you to impress Seth?"

"Our relationship ended a long time ago. His opinion doesn't matter much anymore." That almost sounded convincing.

"And you don't feel you have any lingering feelings for him?"

"Well, I mean, the guy was my first love. But I wouldn't exactly say we left things on good terms. Any lingering feelings are of the annoyed and angry variety." And the physical-attraction variety, but that's an insignificant detail.

Dr. Lawson takes note of that, and I know it's not going to be the last I hear from her about Seth. "You're determined to complete the challenge and stay single?" She's studying me with a gaze that's way too knowing.

I nod. "I am." I decide to be fully honest, because what's the point of therapy if you hide things from your therapist? "But I'm definitely freaked out by the idea of being on my own."

"What's the worst that could happen if you stay single?"

"I could miss out on a fabulous relationship with the love of my life?"

"With Seth?"

I shake my head and avoid her stare and conveniently forget that tidbit about not hiding things from your therapist. "Not him. Obviously. But maybe someone else, like my blind date or even someone I run into on the street tomorrow."

"If a relationship comes along when you're not truly ready for it, is it actually the best relationship for you?"

"That's a little too philosophical for me, Doc."

"I want you to think about that." She checks her watch. "And I want you to think about why you need a long-term partner. I'm not going to lie, Lana, this whole work assignment feels like it's bordering on inappropriate, but at the same time, I think some elements of it could be good for you. I'd like for you to think about this like less of a work project and more of a life project."

"I hope you have a lot of availability in the coming months," I joke, even though I'm totally serious. Something tells me I'm going to need it.

#LANAVSSETH

ROB: For those of you keeping track, current standings are as follows:
Seth: 63 Lana: 41

JAMES: Closer than I expected.

LANA: Wow. Rude.

COREY: I still don't understand how these totals are being calculated.

ROB: It's not hard. I created a system.

COREY: Whatever. Just glad to see my girl is within striking distance!

TESSA: **@Lana**, your second article is so good 😊 I love how vulnerable you were, I think that's really going to resonate with readers.

LANA: Thank you, friend! I hope so. Everyone should be in therapy.

COREY: Word.

There's even more shipping this time around 😄

LANA: Thanks for pointing that out. Again.

SETH: I know it's not a competition, but I do already have double the number of comments on post #2.

Oh wait. It is definitely a competition.

LANA: The only reason you do numbers is because you include a photo with every column and people in LA are swayed by good looks.

SETH: So you think I'm good-looking?

You don't need to answer that. I know you think I'm good-looking.

LANA: I hate you.

SETH: Don't hate me because I'm beautiful.

JAMES: Guys. Again. Get a room. Or a DM.

12

Sometimes it would feel really nice to be able to punch your ex right in the face.

—Lana Parker, "What Not to Do After a Breakup"

"I CAN'T BELIEVE I LET YOU TALK ME INTO THIS." MAY drags her feet through the parking lot as we make our way to the front door of the boxing studio, located in a nondescript strip mall somewhere in the Valley.

"I bribed you into it." I hold the door for her, knowing if I don't usher her into the building before me, she might make a break for it.

"One round of drinks is not nearly equal to the pain of a kickboxing class."

We cross through a small lobby and into the large gym area. In the back stands a boxing ring that looks straight out of *Rocky*. It's surrounded by several punching bags, all hanging from metal chains bolted into the ceiling. I'm immediately intimidated, until May nudges me over to the side and into a small classroom-looking space. One wall is fully covered in mirrors, the floor is a cheap-looking laminate, and only a few other people mill about the room, which smells in that way all gyms do, musty and sweaty. Gross.

We find a spot in the back of the room, away from the small crowd of fellow students, tossing our bags along the mirrored wall.

"Should we stretch or something?" I half-heartedly pull one arm across my chest like we did in high school PE, which is essentially the last time I worked out. I'm trying to push myself out of my comfort zone, but I might have pushed a little too far.

May shrugs, using this chance to blatantly check herself out in the mirror from every possible angle. "At least my ass looks good in these pants."

"Your ass looks good in all pants."

"Duh. And all without ever having to kickbox."

I shake out my arms and sigh. "Look. It's one hour. One hour and then I can check this task off my list."

"How did you convince Natasha to let you do this one on your own? I thought you and Seth were supposed to be doing all these assignments together."

I purse my lips, leaning to one side and stretching my torso. "I didn't tell her. Or him."

May pauses her self-perusal. "I'm sorry, do my ears deceive me? Did you, Lana Parker, blatantly ignore a directive from your boss?"

I spin around so I don't have to face her, forgetting there's a mirror behind me until she catches my eye in the reflection. "The spirit behind this assignment is that I should be doing things on my own. So, I'm doing this one on my own."

May cocks a finger gun at the me in the mirror. "Sort of."

"Still counts." I break eye contact and pause for a moment. "Besides, I needed a little breather from Seth."

May bends over to touch her toes, seemingly to stretch, but mostly to give the few attendants an even better view of her butt. "I take it you will be picturing his face when aiming all the kicks and punches this evening?"

My first thought is that I could never hurt such a pretty face, but I'm smart enough not to say that out loud. "Yup."

"Hmmm." She straightens and levels a piercing look at me. "So there definitely hasn't been even a hint of feelings resurfacing for one Mr. Seth Carson?"

I delay answering by taking a long sip from my water bottle. It's pointless to lie to her, though that doesn't mean I'm not tempted to try.

"Oh shit, you're totally in love with him again, aren't you?" May's voice isn't exactly subtle or quiet, and the other members of the class turn to look at us.

I shush her, my eyes narrowing. "I'm not in love with him, but I can't help it if being around him brings up old feelings. Hence his not being here."

"Love feelings?" Her voice takes on a wheedling tone and she clasps her hands together like a Disney princess.

"No. More like nostalgia feelings. And anger and hurt and humiliation feelings." Though I have to admit, if only to myself, it's the former that I find more disturbing.

"All right, let's get started." A gruff rumble from the front of the room saves me from having to introspect even further.

I gesture helplessly to May, like I'd be happy to continue this conversation were it not for scary-looking instructor man.

And he's most definitely scary. He's at least six foot four and as wide as a house. He's got a black bandana wrapped around his forehead, and his pale face is accented by sunburned cheeks and a stubbly black and gray beard.

When he tells us to come forward, we scurry up to the front of the room.

The instructor introduces himself as Duke, and that's where the pleasantries end. We start with a "warm-up" that has me panting for breath after just a few minutes. At one point Duke looks at me in the mirror and mutters something that looks like "Pathetic."

So yeah, we're off to a good start.

After the warm-up, Duke has us wrap our hands in some kind of tape. One of the other women in the class takes pity on May and me and helps us before Duke can see that we're unable to complete even this simplest of tasks.

Once everyone's taped up, Duke demonstrates a few moves for the group. A jab. An uppercut. Some other moves that I'm sure have technical names I can't remember. And then he just starts yelling out different combinations and we try our best to keep up. He tells everyone to partner up, and May and I cling to each other like we're on the *Titanic* and it's going down.

But Duke has other plans. He points to May. "You. Over there." He directs her to a guy standing by himself, who's not exactly cute, but also not *not* cute. Duke gives me a sadistic grin. "You're with me."

I let out an actual whimper.

May saunters over to her new partner, and I'm not sure if her slow walk can be attributed to her wanting to show off her assets, or if she just can't make her legs move any faster.

I swallow audibly as Duke bears down on me. "It's my first time."

He grunts. "Yeah. I could tell." He slips what look like padded oven mitts onto his hands. "Let's start with jabs." He holds up his pads in front of his face.

"You want me to hit you?"

He nods. "Don't even pretend like you could hurt me."

Well, that's rude. I throw a jab with my right hand. My fist connects with the pad, but it barely moves. That definitely just hurt me more than it hurt him.

"Pitiful."

I try again, putting a little more muscle into it this time. It barely moves again.

"What are you doing here?" Duke asks as I throw another half-hearted punch, this time with my left hand.

"I'm here for a work assignment." It takes me a minute to get the words out because even with my wimpy excuse for punches, I'm still winded.

"Bullshit."

This time I go for a combo, right left right.

"Why are you here?"

I pause for a second, blowing a loose strand of hair out of my face.

"Do not stop. And answer my question."

"I'm here because I'm forcing myself to branch out and try new things." I hit him with three quick jabs, all with my right hand.

His mouth moves a fraction of an inch, possibly in some sort of sign of approval. "Why?"

"Why do I need to try new things?" I throw an uppercut into my next combo and don't wait for him to answer. "Because I was stuck in a pattern. A pattern that was bad for me."

"Dating the wrong people?" He starts to shuffle on his feet a little, forcing me to move with him if I want my punches to connect.

"Am I that obvious?"

He shrugs, and when my next punch lands, he gives me a bit of resistance, which I take as a good sign, even though my arms already feel like spaghetti without his pushing back.

"I have been known to focus more on being in a relationship rather than who I'm in the relationship with."

"Who left, your mom or your dad?"

I risk pausing again, letting my hands fall to my knees while I catch my breath.

Duke gives me all of ten seconds before he nudges me back into formation.

I wait for him to repeat his question, but he just lets me punch his padded hands.

"I never knew my dad. My mom was there, but not really. Being maternal isn't exactly her thing." I'm thankful that the boxing is leaving me winded, covering how I have to force the words out. Even though I've mostly come to terms with my relationship with my parents, it still sucks.

"So you had two shitty parents?" he asks, as if he's inquiring about the weather.

"Yup." And all of a sudden, something that I've accepted

for over a decade makes me angry. Impossibly angry. Which is convenient, since I currently face a large man permitting me to punch him.

"Does that make you mad?"

"Of course it does." Jab, jab, uppercut.

"What else makes you mad?"

"People who don't understand that they're not wanted."

He raises an eyebrow and dances around a bit, forcing me to follow. "Is this person hurting you in some way?"

"How do you know it's one specific person?"

He pauses long enough to give me a look.

I punch him again. "Fine. No, he's not hurting me. Not physically anyway."

"Then why are you letting him affect you?"

I don't answer for a second, focusing on aiming my punches at the center of his gloves, picturing Seth's face right there on the vinyl.

"Why are you holding on to your anger?" Duke swipes his pad, aiming for my head.

I instinctively duck and come up swinging, connecting with his pad with a forceful jab. "I . . . I don't know."

He cracks a smile for the first time, distracting me so he can take another swing. "Tell me all the things you want to say to him."

I just barely manage to get out of the way of his pad, stumbling back a few steps in the process. "What?"

"You heard me. Pretend I'm him. Role-play, or whatever the shrinks like to call it."

My eyes narrow as I think about all the things I want to

say to Seth. All the things I've been holding in for the past twelve years. Things that I shouldn't—couldn't—say to his face. I throw a punch. "I hate you for making me fall in love with you." I hit Duke's pads again, channeling the anger into my fists. "I can't believe you let your pride get in the way of our plans." A one-two combo flies at him. "That's for breaking my heart. Twice." Duke's face blurs, replaced by a more familiar one with bright-blue eyes. "That's for coming to LA and for infiltrating my happy place and for trying to steal my job." I pause for just long enough to catch my breath so I can punch with the full strength of both my body and my heart. "That's for taking away the only home I've ever known. And that's for humiliating me. And leaving me. And rejecting me. And breaking me." My hands fall to my knees as I struggle to force air into my lungs.

Duke gives me a not-so-gentle thwap on the back. "Feel better?"

I nod, my neck the only muscle not limp as a noodle. I let myself really think about the question. "Yeah. Actually, I do."

"Good. Don't hold on to that shit. It only hurts you, not him." Another thwap and he trots away, calling over his shoulder, "I'll see you next week."

I collapse on the wood floor, reaching for my water bottle. The anger—along with a gallon of sweat—has trickled out of me. My body feels depleted, but my mind is racing.

Duke might be giving Dr. Lawson a run for her money.

Shifting my feet under me, I attempt to stand and promptly fold back into the floor.

May stumbles over to me but is smart enough to stay standing. "I hate you."

I hold out my hand and she hoists me up with far more grunts and groans than should be allowed. "Would it help ease your pain if I told you I think I just had a major breakthrough?"

She slings a sweaty arm around me and we trudge out to the parking lot. "Breakthroughs can't buy me drinks."

13

Journaling is always a good idea; write down your true feelings and don't hold back.

—Lana Parker, "New Hobbies to Try When You Find Yourself Suddenly Single"

I CLIMB OUT OF MY CAR AT THE *ALWAYS TAKE FOUNTAIN* office two days after kickboxing, a latte in one hand and a croissant in the other. My body still aches, and even the simple act of opening the office doors sends a wave of dull pain through my biceps. Our third set of articles is due soon, and I need this one to be good. I have to close the gap between Seth and me if I'm going to have any chance of winning this competition. Normally I'd head to one of my favorite coffee shops when I'm on deadline, but I'm hoping the added pressure of being in the office will help me churn out my best work.

Only subconsciously, I might also be hoping to run into Seth. Not because I'm dying to see him, obviously, but because I'm mildly curious to know how he's doing with his task for this week. And maybe test out that whole letting-go-of-the-anger deal.

I'm the only one there aside from Ian, our web tech manager, which is probably for the best since I won't have any of my colleagues to distract me from writing. I hole up at one of my favorite tables, open my laptop, and get to work.

Writing about the kickboxing class itself is surprisingly easy. Duke is a character in his own right, and whether I want to admit it or not, the experience was therapeutic to say the least. Where I stall out is the ending. I want to win this competition. And to do that, I need the readers to be on my side. Which means my writing needs to be compelling, and in order to be so, it needs to be honest. But I don't know how much I want to reveal about Seth and me and our previous relationship. Yes, everyone knows we dated thanks to our viral Instagram shitstorm, but I haven't exactly filled the world in on the finer details of our breakup. Or our meltdown at the reunion. Yet for me, the most important part of the kickboxing experience was being able to physically express my anger toward Seth, and a little bit toward myself, and how that helped me let go of it.

And I'm as surprised as anyone to find out I really did let go of it. It's been two days since the literal blowout, and while I certainly wouldn't classify my feelings for Seth as suddenly warm and fuzzy, the rage has faded. Hopefully it stays that way the next time I see him in person.

I settle on a middle ground for my article, detailing how kickboxing allowed me to work out some long-held-in anger, painting my vulnerability all over the page. But I decide to leave Seth's name out of it. For the readers, my anger was directed at some unknown person instead of my competitor. I'll save the major reveals for later, if at all, but I'm finally offering something of myself in my writing, and hopefully it will resonate and bring in the engagement I desperately need if I want to catch up.

"You missed a comma right there." A finger points over my shoulder, nearly touching the screen of my laptop.

I jump back. I was so deep in my zone I didn't even notice anyone else come in. "This is my first draft, asswipe."

"Nice to see your insults haven't changed since sophomore year." Seth leans against the edge of my desk, making himself perfectly comfortable in my space.

"Nice to see you're still a condescending jerk about grammar." I scoot my laptop and my chair a few inches away from him.

"Working on your column?"

"Obviously." I angle my screen so he can't see it.

"When do I get to read it?" He crosses his arms over his chest and gives me what I'm sure he thinks is a charming grin.

"When it goes live on the site." I click *Save* and shut my computer before he can do something truly obnoxious and juvenile like grab it out of my hands. It's what high school Seth would've done, although back then the gesture would've been teasing but gentle. And he would've fixed all my grammar mistakes without giving me shit for it.

"I gave my draft to Natasha two days ago."

"Well, good for you."

"And I've already got a jump on one of my long-term tasks." He pulls out his phone and opens something on the screen. "Meet Harry." He shoves his phone into my sight line.

"You got a fish." I try to not be charmed by the bright-blue fish, swimming happily in a tank outfitted with a neon-green castle and bright-pink and orange rocks, but I don't manage very well. "You know, when I tasked you with getting a pet, I meant a cat or a dog or even a bunny. Something that requires care and nurturing."

He grabs the phone from my hand. "Fish require care. I have to feed him and clean his tank."

"You know that wasn't the point."

"I guess you should've been more specific then." A cheeky smirk slides across his face. "Besides, I'm learning a lot about myself by having a pet fish, which is the whole purpose of the assignment, right?"

I sigh, rubbing my temples, hoping to dispel my sudden headache. "I'll have you know I'm learning a lot about myself too, but unlike you, I'm taking it seriously."

"Oh? I'd love to hear the details."

"No." Like I'm going to divulge my therapy-worthy secrets. He can read about them on the internet like everyone else.

"Ouch." Seth stands, stretching his arms over his head, which of course causes his blue button-down shirt—one of the ones we bought together—to rise, revealing a tiny peek of that cut-from-marble stomach. "Well, I'm off to work on my dating profile, you know, for one of those real-relationship-finder sites . . ." He lets the words dangle, though I don't know how he wants me to fill in the blank.

But my curiosity is piqued. "Oh?"

"Yeah. I've been working on it for a few days and I just can't seem to get it right." He makes a weird sort of half grimace, half winky face.

"How come?"

Seth has the nerve to look sheepish. And the nerve to look adorable while doing so. "I don't know what to say about myself to make a woman like me."

It would be sweet if it weren't utter bullshit.

"Since when do you have a problem with confidence?"

"Since I got my heart broken, of course." He gives me an endearing smile, but there's a bit of sadness behind his eyes, like maybe he really did experience heartbreak at some point.

I roll my eyes, tempted to tell him karma is a bitch. If he didn't want his heart broken, he shouldn't have broken mine. But I've let go of that. And what better way to test myself than to help Seth with this task. "Lead the way."

Seth's brow furrows. "What do you mean?"

I sigh and push out of my chair. "If anyone can make you sound appealing, it's me."

His lips part just the slightest bit, giving away his genuine surprise. "You want to help me write my dating profile?"

"Of course not." I gesture for him to start walking. "But I will anyway."

His eyes narrow suspiciously. "Are you going to make me sound like some kind of asshole?"

Crossing my arms over my chest, I glare at him. "One:

you wouldn't need my help with that. Two: I don't feel the need to try to sabotage my competition, which is more than I can say for you."

"What did I do?" He sounds like we're fourteen again and his mom is yelling at him for pestering his older sister.

I raise my eyebrows. "Brian."

A triumphant grin tugs on the corner of his mouth. "Oh yeah. That was fun."

I sit back down. "Never mind. Offer retracted."

He taps his foot against mine. "You really want to help me, Parker?"

"Again, no I don't." I force a small smile, determined to prove to myself that I can do this, that I learned something and am growing as a person and blah blah blah. "But I will."

"Did you have some sort of magical personality transplant or something? I thought you hated me, Parker."

"I don't hate you." I shrug and spin my chair just slightly away from him. "But I can't promise this goodwill will last forever."

He opens his mouth like he has more to say on the topic but seems to think better of it, pushing off my desk and gesturing for me to follow.

Seth has set up shop at one of the cubicle desks stationed around the perimeter of the open space, right under the large windows. None of us have specific desk assignments, since we're in and out so frequently, but he's picked one of the better spots. In addition to his laptop, he also has an old-school Mead spiral notebook, which he quickly shuts and shoves to the side. He drags over an extra chair, gesturing for me to sit in the one in front of his computer.

"All right. Let's see what you've got so far." I pull the laptop closer to me. "'Seth, age thirty, writer.' Wow. I can see you put a lot of time and effort into this."

"I told you I was stuck." He pulls his chair close enough to me that he can dig his elbow into my ribs. Of course he hits my one ticklish spot like Hawkeye hits a target.

I attempt to duck out of the way but end up getting nudged again, leading me to giggle like a contestant on *The Bachelor.*

"You still have the same laugh."

"You're still a huge butthead."

"Good one."

"Do you want my help or not?"

He folds his hands in his lap, flashing me a contrite smile.

I roll my eyes again and turn away from him. "Okay. What do you think is the number one thing women are looking for in a man?"

"Money?"

I start to rise because no demonstration of personal growth is worth having to listen to my ex make misogynistic jokes.

He grabs my arm, laughing at his own misstep. "I'm kidding. Good god, you know I'm kidding. Because that's the number one thing women are looking for."

"Immaturity?"

"A sense of humor." He grins, his eyes twinkling like he's genuinely enjoying this.

"You're incorrigible." And fuck if I'm not also somewhat enjoying this. It's like that whole letting-go-of-my-anger thing actually worked, though somehow this feels even more dangerous.

"But I'm right, right?"

"Yes. Sense of humor is the number one thing women are looking for, and so despite my moral qualms with lying on your dating profile, we'll put that first."

"'Silly and snarky sense of humor'? You always did love alliteration."

"You always did love making me do your work for you."

"Hey! That's not fair. I wrote your chemistry final paper for you." He tries to give me another nudge, but I successfully duck this one.

"Only because I wrote your essay on the French Revolution."

"That was only so you'd have an excuse to watch your *Les Mis* VHS on repeat."

"'I may have trouble admitting when I'm wrong, but what man doesn't?'" I narrate out loud as I type the words onto his dating profile.

"Rude."

"You know what? Why don't you walk down to the coffee shop at the end of the block and get me a hazelnut latte, and while you're gone and not being a distraction, I will write something that is truthful and not totally unflattering."

"Not totally unflattering . . . can't wait to see the kinds of dates that brings me." But he doesn't argue, pushing back his chair and striding out of the office without a backward glance.

Once he's left the building, I turn my full attention to the dating profile. And my fingers hover over the keys; I'm unsure of what to write. Letting go of my anger is one thing, but helping him win this competition is another. I could use this moment as payback—he pretty much admitted he set me up with Brian to mess with me—but my thirst for revenge seems to have been slaked. I decide to stop thinking and just write.

My name is Seth and I'm a thirty-year-old writer who just moved to Los Angeles. I know right off the bat that makes me a total cliché, but I already have a very successful career and I relocated because I am looking to settle down in one place, and with one woman. The people who know me best would probably tell you I have a great sense of humor, am always willing to try something new, and am loyal to the people closest to me. My ex-girlfriends would probably tell you that I'm a good cook but suck at doing dishes, I'll always let you control the playlist during road trips, and I pride myself on doing a good job of taking care of you. Not like in a sugar-daddy way, but in a make-you-soup-when-you're-sick way. I don't know if I believe in "the one," but if she's out there, I would love to find her.

I reread the words I've written, satisfied I've crafted a profile that will appeal to the average Los Angeles woman. I read it again and catch all the truths about Seth, all the little things I know about him that most others don't. And it starts to do funny things to my insides. They get all warm and squishy. Because what I wrote isn't even a stretch. Seth *is* funny and loyal and adventurous, and he truly does the best job of taking care of people.

A cup of coffee appears before me just as a sheen of tears springs up in my eyes. I grab my latte with a quick muttered thanks and farewell, and bolt from the desk before I do something foolish.

I run—almost literally—into Tessa as I'm barreling my way out the front door of our building.

"Hey!" Her hands grasp on to my forearms, steadying us both while somehow managing to not spill my coffee in the process.

I keep my head down to hide the tears I know are still shining in my eyes. "Hi. I was just leaving."

"No worries. How is everything going with your latest article?" She keeps her hands lightly gripping mine, like she knows I need the extra support.

"Fine, I guess." I shuffle my feet, anxious to be in my car, music and AC blasting.

Her voice softens. "And how are you feeling about, you know . . . ?"

"I'm pretty sure I'm already over Evan. He and I really weren't compatible, so it was a good thing in the long run." I look everywhere but at her.

"And how are you feeling about Seth?" Tessa finally drops her hands.

I miss their warmth and steadiness almost immediately. "There's nothing to feel. All of that is in the past."

She gives me a soft smile. "Okay. Well, I'm here. When you're ready."

"Thanks." I force myself to return her smile before I stride to my car.

My phone buzzes with a text before I can even close my door.

Seth: Hope everything is okay.

Seth: Thanks for the profile. It's perfect.

I shove my key in the ignition. Because it's not perfect. It's just honest.

Me: Just because I don't hate you doesn't mean we're friends.

I regret the text almost the second it's sent. But it's out there, and despite several attempts, I don't know what else to say to soften the blow.

I scoff to myself, luckily in the privacy of my car. Why do I need to soften the blow? I might be able to forgive Seth for his many past transgressions, but that doesn't mean we're now BFFs. I have plenty of BFFs already. I don't need another one.

R2-D2 chirps, pulling me out of my inner debate.

Seth: I know.

I wait for another text to come through, but nothing else appears. No typing bubbles hover in my messages. And as unsatisfactory as his two-word response might seem, I appreciate it. There's no demand for friendship. No declaration of an attempt to wear me down. Just an acknowledgment.

It's exactly what I needed.

I spend the first few minutes of my drive replaying everything from my previous session with Dr. Lawson. She wanted me to think about why I was really so willing to put myself through this challenge, to complete the tasks Seth set for me. Of course I want to win—I want the new column position—but I think I also want to push myself, to see what I can be without a partner constantly standing by my side.

I know if I head straight home right now, I'm likely to spiral, caught up in either the what-has-beens or the what-could-bes, and neither would have a good outcome. So instead I drive to one of my happy places, a tiny vintage movie theater in Los Feliz.

After scoring a sweet parking space, I buy a ticket for the latest Marvel release, treat myself to some popcorn, and settle into a slightly sticky seat. I've already seen the movie—on opening night, of course—but these films provide a comfort I'm desperately seeking, and for the next two and a half hours, all I have to worry about is defeating the bad guys and saving the day, with the reassurance it will all be okay in the end.

It's a balm to my soul.

When I finally do arrive back at home, it's evening and the sky is blanketed in pinks and oranges. It's magic hour in LA, so I take my laptop out to my tiny backyard and open up my blog. And I write. I write about letting go of the past, and finding solace in places that might seem strange, and how I used to lose myself in the pages of books and images on-screen. How I used to lose myself in other people. And how I don't want to do that moving forward.

I save the blog post as a draft before shutting my computer. Normally I don't hesitate to publish posts, but this one feels too personal, too raw, even if the only people who read my site are my closest friends. For a brief second, I consider sending it to Seth. Of all the people in my life right now, he's really the only one who would truly understand my feelings. He knows where my solaces came from and why.

But I dismiss the thought as easily as it came. Seeing Seth in the office today, falling back into our old banter patterns, it might have been fun, but it can't happen again. It'd be too easy to continue that slide, fall back into not just patterns but feelings. And too much has happened between us; I can't let myself go there, even in my head.

Seth Carson is my past. And this assignment, this project, this competition, is all about looking toward the future.

14

It's not always easy, putting all your personal stuff out there on the internet for the whole world to see.

—Seth Carson, "Profile Me, Baby"

#LANAVSSETH

ROB: For those of you keeping score, current standings are Seth: 91 Lana: 79

COREY: Closing the gap, bitches!

TESSA: Another stellar piece this week, **@Lana**!

COREY: Totally! You almost made me want to try kickboxing! Almost.

ROB: Seth's comments are still outpacing Lana's this week, but Lana's have shown an uptick.

COREY: Whose side are you on?

ROB: I am on no one's side because there shouldn't be sides because we're grown-ups.

LANA: Some more than others.

SETH: I appreciate your support, **@Rob**.

@Lana, sorry about the ass whooping, I promise I'm not trying to totally decimate you.

LANA: Fuck off.

SETH: You were saying some of us are more adult than others?

LANA: I hate you.

JAMES: Get. a. room.

Seth: Did you also receive a cryptic email from Natasha?

Lana: "Be at the below address tomorrow at 10:00 am"? Yes. Yes I did.

Seth: Should we be scared?

Lana: Probably.

Lana: Also, if you're still feeling iffy about driving in LA, you should take a Lyft. The address she sent is right in the middle of Hollywood and traffic and parking will be a bitch.

Seth: Will do.

Seth: And thanks.

Lana: Any hits on your dating profile yet?

Seth: Um, yes?

Seth: Is that something you wanna hear about?

Lana: . . .

Lana: I don't know what I want anymore.

Lana: See you tomorrow.

I REREAD THE short text conversation between me and Seth during my Lyft ride to our mystery destination. I don't know what Natasha has planned for us, but I'm certain I'm not going to like it. And I'm even more certain I'm not going to like spending the day with Seth.

He was much easier to deal with when I only felt overwhelming wrath at the mere sight of his stupid pretty face. Now that I've become the bigger person and all that bullshit, I can't seem to get a handle on where we stand.

I don't even know where I want us to stand. Other than several feet apart. Definitely not close enough that the salty sunshine scent of him brings back memories of hour-long make-out sessions and cuddling during movie nights.

"Here we are," my Lyft driver says, and I realize I must have been staring into space for an awkward amount of time.

"Thanks," I mutter, hopping out of her Prius without really paying attention to where I'm landing.

But one look at what's parked along the curb a few feet away from me and my stomach sinks.

My phone chirps with a text at exactly ten o'clock.

Natasha: Surprise! I'm sending you and Seth on your tourist-in-LA day!

Me: You mean the tourist day I was supposed to enjoy ALONE?

Natasha: Minor detail. Take lots of pics, post some Stories, and enjoy the ride!

I shove my phone in the back pocket of my jeans, glad I dressed for comfort instead of style today. "I do *not* get paid enough for this shit."

Seth climbs out of the backseat of his own Lyft a minute later, also dressed for comfort in fitted jeans and a white T-shirt. Of course, his simple ensemble doesn't do anything to take away from his hotness, which is just rude.

He joins me on the sidewalk, his eyes locked on the monstrosity in front of us. "Please tell me this isn't what we're doing today."

"It is. Natasha just texted me. It's my 'be a tourist in LA' assignment." I gesture helplessly to the double-decker bus, painted a blinding neon orange with the words *See the Sights* emblazoned on the side, along with neon palm trees, a bright sun, and blue waves painted with actual glitter.

For a second, we just stand in pained silence. At least this time, we're not the ones causing the pain.

Seth shoves his hand through his hair. "Okay. Well, we have two ways to go about this. We either pout the entire time like teenagers—"

"I like that option, let's do that." I cross my arms over my chest and stick out my lower lip.

"Or," he barrels on as if I never spoke, "we make the best of it and actually try to have some fun."

"I know I should choose option B, but I'm still very much an advocate for A." I sneak a peek at him out of the corner of my eye, trying not to smile when I catch him rolling his eyes with a grin. I make him wait all of ten seconds just to make a point. "Okay, fine. We'll try to make the best of it." I march over to the guy standing at the bus's entrance, clipboard in hand. "Is there booze on this ride?"

"No, ma'am, but we make several stops throughout the city and you can hop on and off at any stop."

Wow. A bus ride, no booze, and a *ma'am* all in one.

Seth steps up next to me, giving the guy our names in exchange for two hot-pink wristbands. He gestures for me to board first.

"Top or bottom?" I practically dare him to go for the obvious joke.

"I think making the best of it means we head to the top level, Parker." He raises one eyebrow as he deftly avoids my sex pun setup.

I ignore him, carefully climbing up the winding staircase and heading for a seat all the way in the back. Of course the entire upper deck is packed and there's only one bench seat available. I slide in first, pressing up against the wall.

Seth folds himself in next to me, and despite my best efforts, it's impossible for us to keep even a sliver of space between us. His jeaned thigh presses against my jeaned thigh, and heat that is surely coming from the sun beats down on us.

Seth pulls a baseball hat from his back pocket and slips it over his dark hair, which seems to have grown even just in the short time he's been in town. "Remember how we always used to sit in the back of the bus on class trips?"

A smile tugs on my lips despite my best attempts to stifle it. "You held my hand for the first time in the backseat of a bus."

A soft chuckle escapes him. "I don't think I've ever been more nervous in my life."

"I doubt that." I nudge him with my elbow because suddenly, sitting here pressed up against him, it would be so very easy to reach down and pick up his hand.

"Parker. Come on. I'd been in love with you since I was six. It took me eight years to work up the courage to hold your hand." He gives me a nudge back, and the movement causes our hands to brush each other. His fingers twitch and I wonder if he's fighting the same instinct I am.

Then he abruptly pulls his hand away and turns his attention to the front of the bus, where our tour guide is welcoming us. So maybe not.

"We'll be exploring some of the most famous sights in Los Angeles today, with multiple stops at several different landmarks. Buses run every half an hour, so feel free to hop off, do some exploring, and join us again whenever you're ready." The bus lurches away from the curb and our guide continues talking, narrating the history of Grauman's Chinese Theatre and the Walk of Fame as we putter our way down Hollywood Boulevard.

As we head toward the Sunset Strip, an awkward silence descends. It's not actually quiet, since we're surrounded by chattering tourists and the honking horns of LA traffic and the drone of the tour guide, but in our little five-foot-by-three-foot bubble, the silence is thick.

"I got really drunk there one night." The words fall out of me as we pass by one of the Strip's dive bars. I don't know what makes me overshare, other than needing to break the quiet tension somehow. "They have margaritas that are literally the size of your head."

Seth's eyes twinkle with laughter. "Drunk Parker is a sight to behold."

"Um, excuse me, I think I was only ever drunk once in your presence."

"Once was enough." He clears his throat. "And it was twice, actually."

Just when I thought we were making progress.

"If today is going to hold any possibility of fun, it might be better not to mention that whole situation." I direct the words at the bars and clubs we're currently driving by, half hoping he won't hear them.

"You're probably right about that."

I whip my head around to face him. "I'm sorry, did you just say I'm right?"

That familiar smirk tugs on the corner of his lips. "Just this once, this one time, on this one occasion, you might be right."

"What's that you said? Lana is always right? Weird, I totally agree! Look at us agreeing and getting along!"

He laughs, for real, causing his shoulders to move even farther into my space.

I can't seem to make myself shift away.

We fill the next half hour with innocuous conversation. Seth asks questions about my experiences at some of the places we pass. I fill him in with stories about the city and May and our coworkers.

"I see why you love working at *ATF*," he says after I tell him about one of our epic nights at the Abbey.

"The people are great." It's a simple statement of truth, one that also gives me pause for a second.

"But . . . ?" Seth knows me too well and can likely see the wheels turning in my head.

"But I'm beginning to wonder if I stay for the people and not for the work." If I'm being totally honest, I'm not just beginning to wonder. I've been wondering that for longer than I'd like to admit.

He's quiet for a second, his eyes studying my profile as I determinedly keep my gaze focused straight ahead. "You deserve to write what you want to write, Parker. And your dating columns are great, but they're also a waste of your talent."

"You've read my columns?" I turn my head just slightly, allowing me to catch the expression on his face changing.

His cheeks flush, the crimson spreading to his ears, a sure sign he's said more than he intended. "I read a few. When I knew I was going to be stuck at *ATF* for a bit. Not before that or anything."

"Hmmm." I let my knee press into his. "I've read everything you've ever published."

"You have?" His fingers dance closer to the seam of space separating our thighs.

"Of course I have." I turn to face him fully. "It's brilliant. You've always been brilliant."

His eyes meet mine and my breath halts in my chest. "Parker . . ."

"Our next stop is the Grove shopping center, along with the Original Farmers Market. This is the place to hop off if you're in need of a snack!"

"Well, I for one am starved!" I stand up too quickly and have to reach for Seth's shoulder to steady myself as the bus comes to a quick stop. His hand snakes around my waist, keeping me upright. He doesn't release it when he stands—after the bus has ceased moving—and suddenly I'm tucked into his side and all I want is to bury my face in his chest and breathe in every inch of him.

Then he steps away, into the crowded aisle.

But his hand reaches back. And I take it.

Our fingers automatically intertwine and he squeezes gently, and I wish I could see his face, but instead I follow his broad back as he leads us down the winding stairs and out to the sidewalk.

There's a moment's hesitation when we hit the ground. Seth lets his hand drop and I have to shove my hands in my pockets so I don't try to grab it back.

He adjusts his hat. "Where to?"

"You ready for a drink?"

"Fuck yes."

"I know the perfect spot."

We spend the next couple of hours exploring the Original Farmers Market, which butts up to the Grove, an outdoor shopping mall of sorts. The Grove itself is not one of my particular haunts, but I love coming to the farmers market, which is full of dozens of stalls serving everything from pizza to donuts to the best Brazilian barbecue I've ever had. Since it's adjacent to the CBS studios, it's also a good spot to low-key celeb-watch, which I most definitely partake in whenever I can. Even though I've had plenty of sightings by now, seeing the rich and famous out in the wild still gives me a little thrill every time.

We eat a bit of everything and indulge in some local beers and wines, avoiding heavy topics and heavy looks and any hint of physical contact. I force Seth to buy one of those "I ♥ LA" shirts, telling him it's a rite of passage even though no one else I know has one. He humors me and even poses for a photo in it in front of the old-school trolley that circles the area.

The earlier tension has dissipated, due to either the alcohol or the extended time spent in each other's company, and I'm finally able to relax and actually enjoy being with Seth.

I wait until we both have a couple drinks in us before I attempt to dig in a little deeper. We're sitting at a high-top bar table in the very back of the farmers market, a beer in front of each of us. As soon as we sat down, Seth spun his hat around backward, leaving his eyes unguarded and looking so much like his high school self I almost choked on my drink.

"How are your parents doing?" If I were completely sober, I know it would hurt to even ask. Not because of the question itself, but because I hate not already knowing the answer. Seth's parents were the closest thing to a functioning family I ever had, and the loss of them in my life still hurts every time I think about it.

Seth pulls the cardboard coaster from under his beer and spins it a few times. "Good. Really good, actually. They both retired three years ago. Now they're just busy living their best lives." He visibly softens the moment he starts talking about his favorite people. Seth and his family were always close in a TV-sitcom kind of way, their connection and love completely genuine and not codependent or weird. "Lizzie got married a few years ago and just had her second kid, so they help her out with childcare a couple days a week."

I knew some of this from my occasional Instagram stalking, but I smile and nod as if this is all new information, all the while trying not to think about my life's alternate timeline. The one where I was invited to the retirement party and planned Lizzie's baby shower. The one where my ovaries squeezed every time I saw Seth holding one of his nieces. "I hope your parents manage to find some time for themselves too."

He tucks the coaster back under his drink. "They do. They take a couple of vacations every year. Sometimes it's just driving around and finding a new local spot, but at least once a year they leave the country and go explore somewhere remote."

"Does your mom still host holidays for the entire neighborhood?" Thinking about the holidays I spent with the Carsons, the holidays I could have spent with them, pierces through me. Their home was always overcrowded with both people and love.

"Of course. Seems like we have more and more people every year. Sometimes I wonder where we'll go when we outgrow the rec room." A soft smile pulls on his lips and he leans forward in his seat, the motion bringing us closer together. He clears his throat. "How are things with your mom?"

I'm tempted to blow off the question, but the alcohol has relaxed me enough that I don't mind sharing. And the truth of the matter is no one else in my life truly understands my relationship with my mother. On the surface, it's hard for others to fault a woman who set me up financially and devotes her life to helping others.

But Seth had a front-row seat to my childhood, and he knows. He gets it in a way no one else ever could.

"Mostly it's more of the same. The last time we talked she was heading out to open another school. She called to let me know she was leaving and made sure to throw in a few career jabs while she was at it."

Seth grimaces, hiding it with a swig of his beer. "I take it she doesn't make the time to read your work? If she did she would know how great of a writer you are."

"I thought you only read a couple of pieces." I arch a single eyebrow at him in surprise.

"I may have stumbled across one or two others over the years." Another flush colors his cheeks. "But anyway. I'm sorry things haven't gotten better between you two."

I shrug, turning my attention to the sticky tabletop. "At least we're not living in the same city anymore. No one knows her out here, and I don't have to hear all the endless praise, which is nice." It was tough as a kid, to hear my mother lauded for all her accomplishments when I constantly felt abandoned and neglected.

Our server comes around and we pay the check, needing

to head back to the bus so we can make our way to its final stop.

“My mom still asks about you, you know. Every few months.” Seth stands, stretching a little before turning to head back to the bus stop.

The words knock the wind right out of me.

Mrs. Carson—Linda—was always more of a mother to me than my own. The idea that she still asks about me after twelve years, still cares about my well-being when by any stretch I am fairly and rightfully just a figure from the past, means more to me than I could have expected.

“Parker?” Seth reapproaches the table, his hand outstretched.

And I take it, letting him help me off the stool.

Neither of us lets go this time, not until we’re forced to separate by a kid sprinting away from his mother, who throws a hasty apology over her shoulder as she darts by after him.

Seth gives me a sad sort of smile and we make our way back to the bus in silence.

15

You want your first kiss with a new partner
to be electric, but don't be surprised if it sometimes
takes some practice to work out the kinks.

—Lana Parker, "It's in His Kiss"

Lana: Thanks for hanging out with me yesterday. Never thought I'd say this, but your company actually made being a tourist in LA somewhat close to enjoyable.

Seth: Of course. I had fun ☺

Seth: Kind of felt like old times.

Lana: Yeah, except we didn't need Lizzie to buy us beer!

Seth: Lol.

Lana: What's your task for this week so I can figure out my schedule?

Seth: Oh, I have therapy this week so you get a break, I guess.

Lana: Oh. Cool. Well, therapy is great, so have fun?

Lana: Good luck?

Lana: What's the proper therapy send-off?

Seth: Lol. Not sure there is one, but thanks for the thought.

Seth: What are you planning for next week?

Lana: Sadly, it's time to kiss a stranger.

Seth: Oh. Not sure I want to be there for that one.

Lana: Yeah, I figured. I'll take May. She'll make me follow through.

Seth: Have fun?

Seth: Good luck?

Lana: Ha. Thanks.

Seth: I guess I'll see you when I see you?

Lana: That is how that works.

Seth: Good night, Parker.

Lana: Good night, Seth.

I DON'T SEE Seth in person for a few days after that, not that that prevents him from being a constant presence in my brain. I may or may not have shown up at the office every day this week, hoping to catch a glimpse of him. Which is why when I met with Dr. Lawson again she was finally able to force me to talk about Seth.

Okay, so I opened my mouth and blurted it all out the second I sat down on the sofa, but it felt like she metaphorically pushed me in that direction.

And while it felt good to word-vomit all my convoluted feelings out into the ether better known as her office,

I didn't exactly leave with a ton of clarity. Clearly, I don't *not* have feelings for Seth. And to expect otherwise would be silly. He was a huge part of my life and those kinds of relationships leave a lasting imprint, even long after they've ended.

The problem is I don't know how I feel about Seth in the here and now. He still makes me laugh. He's still kind and loyal. He still cares about his family and does a good job of taking care of those around him. He still embodies so many of the things I want in a partner.

And he's still absolutely drop-dead fucking gorgeous. And judging from the sparks ignited by a mere thirty seconds of hand-holding, I'm still very much into him. Physically speaking.

But that doesn't change the fact that I am not ready to be in a relationship. With anyone. And it most definitely doesn't change the fact that Seth broke my heart once already and then stomped on it again ten years later, just for good measure.

When I asked the doc what I should do about Seth, she gave me the standard I-can't-answer-that-for-you line, which, of course, did nothing to help me in the immediate sense. And now here I am, putting the finishing touches on my look for the evening, waiting for May to arrive so we can go hunting for a stranger. A stranger for me to kiss.

I really do need to work on my timing.

I adjust the neckline of my little black dress, pulling it down just a smidge, right as R2-D2 chirps, letting me know May is out front. I lock up my house and bound to the passenger door of her Mini Cooper.

She whistles as I slide in the front seat. "Damn, girl. You look hot."

I'm tempted to brush off her compliment, but instead I decide to accept it. "Thanks, you too, but no surprises there."

"Where to?"

I give May directions as we take off; I've thought long and hard about where my stranger-hunting safari will take place. We listen to Britney extra loud as she drives us through the city and to the Sunset Strip. As we get closer to our destination, May starts to give me the side-eye.

I direct her to a lot and fork over twenty dollars in cash to park. Climbing out of the car, I take my time to adjust my dress and use my reflection in the window to touch up my lip gloss.

May circles the car and watches me with her hands on her hips. "Lana, please tell me we are going to one of these swanky-ass hotel bars and not where I think we're going."

I link my arm through hers and guide her out of the parking lot. We don't have to go far before she can see where we're headed and she stops in her tracks, pulling me to a halt next to her.

"Lana." This time she crosses her arms over her chest, which does more to boost her va-va-voom appearance than the simple gesture ever could for me. "Explain. Now."

"We're going to a bar so I can find a stranger to kiss. Also so that I can buy your promised round of drinks for accompanying me to boxing."

"It's been over a week and my ass is still sore, so you'll be buying more than my first round. But I will not be distracted by the lure of free drinks."

I tug on her arm to pull her away from the middle of the sidewalk. "My task is to kiss a stranger. So we're going to a bar, which is likely full of strangers."

"We're going to a dive bar, LP. It is one of my favorite dive bars, but a dive bar nonetheless." She throws her arms up in dramatic frustration. "This place is filled with tourist bros. You are not going to find someone suitable—or sober—to kiss here and you know it."

"Excuse me, we come to this bar all the time. Are we not suitable? Besides, I'm not looking for Prince Charming here. Just a pair of lips." I loop my arm back through hers and pull her down the road a bit, till we reach Cabo Cantina.

Which is in fact a dive—a dive full of the kinds of guys I could never be attracted to. Which may or may not have been my intention.

It also hasn't escaped my notice that I brought us to the very bar I pointed out to Seth on our tour, like somehow having that measly shared experience with him created some sort of magnetic pull between me and the Cantina.

Once we're inside, May leads me directly to the bar. "I'm going to pretend you picked this spot so you don't become emotionally attached to your kissee and not because you're secretly hoping you won't find someone to kiss." She gives me one of those *I'm not mad, I'm disappointed* looks.

I know she's trying to help, but it cuts me like a knife. I'd rather be just about anything other than a disappointment.

"What'll it be, friends?" An extremely attractive bartender tosses two coasters our way and looks at us expectantly.

"Margaritas. Big ones. She's buying." May jabs her index finger into my shoulder. Hard.

"Ow."

"That is the least of what you deserve."

The bartender returns with two margaritas, each of which is served in a glass as big as a fishbowl.

"Talk about liquid courage." I have to use two hands to lift my glass, clinking it against May's before taking a long sip.

Before I forget, I pull out my phone and snap a selfie, posting it to the *Always Take Fountain* Instagram account with the caption "Out on the town to complete my next task 😉"

While I'm there, I scroll through some of our more recent posts, the majority of which feature Seth or me or the both of us. The pictures from our tourist day are some of the account's most liked ever, the comments full of followers telling us how cute we look together.

And they're not wrong. In each of the shots, we look happy and comfortable and content.

I swipe out of the app and tuck my phone back into my cross-body purse so I'm not tempted to spend the night Instagram-stalking myself. When I turn my attention back to May, she's already chatting up a trio of very good-looking men.

"This is my best friend in the world, Lana." She throws her arm around me once I join the conversation, apparently all her earlier anger erased by one giant margarita.

"You look really familiar," one of the hotties says, leaning in very close as he shakes my hand. "I'm Ben."

"Hi, Ben!" I let him press his cheek to mine in a sort of air kiss. Wow, he smells good. "I'm pretty sure I'd remember your gorgeous face."

He grins and gives me a little wink before gesturing to his companions. "This is my boyfriend Justin and our best friend Tom."

I wave to the others, all while slurping down a quarter of my drink in one go.

May and I chat with the guys for the duration of our first round of drinks, after which May switches to water since she's driving, and I have another margarita because I have a death wish. Our new friends are wonderful and, honestly, the perfect answer to my task at hand, but I still can't bring myself to ask one of them if they wouldn't mind kissing me simply for posterity.

We've been at the bar for maybe forty-five minutes when May nudges me in the ribs. Hard.

"What the fuck, lady?" I rub my side and drink more alcohol all at the same time. "Duke really rubbed off on you, and not in a good way."

"Shit fuck fuckety fuck. Do not turn around," she hisses under her breath.

In my inebriated state, nothing could get me to turn around faster than trying to catch a glimpse of whatever it is she doesn't want me to see. And with my spinning motion, I quite literally fall off my stool.

Ben catches my elbow before I hit the ground. "You okay?"

I straighten my dress with a flustered smile. "Good. Thanks."

May slips her arm through my elbow, attempting to steer me away from the bar.

I plant my feet and refuse to move. "What is the problem?"

"We need to leave." Her eyes dart back and forth through the crowded space.

"Why?" My buzz is buzzing, and while I don't know much, I know I haven't accomplished what I came here to do. "I still need to make out with someone!"

"Forget about that, LP. You're just going to have to trust me." She yanks on my arm again, but I don't budge.

Stomping my foot like Veruca Salt, I cross my arms over my chest, just sober enough to know that the move doesn't look as good on me as it did on May. "I got all dressed up for this bullshit and I'm not leaving without kissing someone!"

"Would anyone care to explain what's going on?" Justin's eyes dart between May and me like we've completely lost it. Which we have.

May ducks into the circle of guys and gives them the basic rundown of tonight's mission.

"So does anyone want to help me out and kiss me?" I bat my eyes at the guys, quite proud of both my patience and my commitment to this assignment.

"Hey, Parker."

Well, fuck.

I really should've trusted my best friend.

Because of course there's only one person who would raise eight million alarm bells and be more than enough cause for hightailing it out of here. I keep my back to him, instead watching the faces of May, Ben, Justin, and Tom as they watch the moment unfold. May looks worried but also a little self-satisfied, and the guys all wear matching gleeful expressions, like they know something good is about to go down. At my expense. Traitors.

Ben nudges my shoulder, spinning me around to face Seth.

Seth, who is not alone.

Seth, whose eyes meet mine and don't let go for a solid minute. And when they do, they travel down to the deep V of my dress.

A throat clears.

"Oh. Shit. Sorry." Seth puts his arm around the woman. "This is Jessica."

And oh my fucking god. This is his date. He's on a date. Maybe even a second or a third date. And he brought her here. To the bar. Where I'm supposed to be kissing a stranger.

What the actual fuck.

I plaster on a Joker-like smile. "So nice to meet you, Jessica. I'm Lana."

Her eyes widen a little at my name, but she just shakes my hand with a soft smile on her equally soft-looking lips.

"Wait! That's where I know you from." Ben smacks his forehead. "You're writing that article series," he says to me. "And you're her challenger," he says to Seth.

"And would you be the guy she's going to be kissing?" I never actually had a dad around to question the boys I dated, but Seth sounds exactly like what I always imagined.

"Dude, we're literally all gay." Justin says this like it should be obvious.

Seth's eyes cut to mine. "You were going to kiss a gay guy for your task?"

I shrug, reaching back for my margarita and taking a long swig, pretending I didn't hear a twinge of hope in his question. "You got a fish."

Ben's eyes, which have been darting back and forth between Seth and me like we're engaged in some kind of Ping-Pong match, widen to the point of ridiculousness. "I've been following your columns ever since that disaster of an Instagram Live video you guys did. I can't believe the two of you used to date!" He turns to Seth. "Wait, is she the one you wrote about in your first article, the one who broke your heart?"

"Um, no!" I protest with more than a tinge of a whine. "I most certainly am not." I gesture to Seth, urging him to clear the air before things get even more awkward and embarrassing and I lose my built-in backup kissers.

But Seth doesn't say anything. He doesn't confirm Ben's assertion, but he sure as fuck doesn't deny it either. Instead he just runs a hand through his hair, looking like he wishes he were anywhere but here.

Which is his own damn fault, because no one invited him here in the first place.

"Um, would anyone care to fill me in on what exactly is going on here?" Poor Jessica. She looks lost and confused, standing as close as possible to Seth, even though he dropped his arm from around her shoulders nearly the second introductions were done.

"Yeah." I thrust my chest out and try to look imperious, focusing on indignation so I don't have to think about Seth's words—or lack thereof. "What are you even doing here?"

The color still hasn't completely returned to his face, and a grimace seems permanently attached to his lips. "You pointed it out the other day on the bus. It looked like a fun place and we had a date planned for tonight, so here we are."

My eyes narrow, because that feels a little too convenient.

May leans into our little circle. "Wait. You brought your date to a bar that your *ex* pointed out to you?"

"May," I hiss under my breath, punching her at the same time for good measure.

Jessica's face falls. "Maybe I should go."

No one says anything for a minute. I wait for Seth to protest, to tell her to stay, or better yet, to agree to go with her, but he just keeps staring at me, like he's trying to impart some silent message only I can understand. Only, I don't understand.

"This is bullshit. I have a mission to accomplish." I turn back to the bar, gesturing for Ben and Justin to help me up. I clamber my way to standing on the bar in a manner so ungainly the Coyote Ugly team would weep.

"Parker, what are you doing?" Seth reaches for me, as if to help me down, but I ignore him.

Once I'm stable on the bar, I turn to the room at large. "Are there any straight guys out there willing to kiss me for like a minute or two?" I yell the words at the top of my lungs, and though there is no literal record scratch, there's most definitely a metaphorical one. The silence that follows is long enough to border on insulting, but to be fair, I think everyone is just as surprised and confused by my proposition as I feel.

"Jesus, Parker, you're going to hurt yourself, get off the bar." Seth's hand is still raised, waiting for me to accept his chivalry.

"No. I need to complete this task and there's no way I'm going to let you sabotage me." I push his hand away and narrow my eyes. "That's why you really came here, isn't it? You're trying to keep me from completing another task."

He flashes me what I'm sure he thinks is a charming smile. "If I say yes, will you get down?"

"No." I stick my tongue out at him and then turn my attention back to the rest of the crowd, most of whom seem to be watching this exchange with too much interest. "So yeah, any kissers out there?"

"Fuck yeah!" a male voice finally calls from somewhere in the depths of the bar.

A second later, he sweeps through the crowd like a white knight on a horse. And he's cute. Thank Thor. Though even if he weren't, I don't think I'd care at this point.

He holds out a hand to help me off the bar. "I'm—"

"Don't tell me!" I take his proffered hand and hop down with as much grace as I can muster. "Sorry, but for this to be as official as possible, you have to be a stranger."

He shrugs. "Whatever works."

And with that, he sweeps me into his embrace and lays one on me, much to the delight of the crush of people surrounding us. As kisses go, it's definitely not terrible. The stranger's lips are warm and soft and even though he tastes like beer, it's not overwhelming or gross or stale.

It also doesn't affect me nearly as much as Seth's squeezing my fingers.

It's over before I can take in anything else. He returns me to a standing position with a grin. "Not bad for a stranger. Though if you want to become *not* strangers, I'd love to get your number."

I'm about to politely decline when I feel an imposing presence hovering over my shoulder, pressing way closer to me than necessary.

Seth lowers his voice at least an octave. "She's not interested."

I whip my head around. "Excuse me? Who the hell asked you?"

"The task is over, Parker. You kissed a stranger, now he can move along."

"What if I don't want him to move along?" I do, obviously, want him to move along, but not if it means Seth gets away with this possessive alpha bullshit.

Seth leans down, his lips brushing my ear. "We both know you don't want him, Parker."

The contact and the words send a jolt through me, and my mouth goes dry. I want to shove him away and rip into him for pulling this macho act with me. But I can't seem to move.

Someone nudges me, and it shakes me out of my haze. When I look up, my stranger has disappeared. May and the guys are watching us with wide-open eyes. And Jessica looks crushed.

I take a step away from Seth. "Maybe you should worry about your own date and leave mine alone."

"Lana . . ." There's a hint of protest and more than a little sadness in the tenor of his voice. He looks like someone just canceled Rachel Maddow.

I let my fingers brush against his, just for the barest flash of a second. I watch his breath catch in his chest and feel mine do the same. "You should go."

He spins on his heel without another word. Jessica doesn't meet my eyes, silently following Seth out of the bar.

"Hey." May hands me a fresh margarita. "That is a him problem, not a you problem."

"What the hell was that?" I fold myself back into the group, and even though I just met these guys an hour ago, they comfort me like we're lifelong friends. "He was the one who assigned the task in the first place! It is not his place to go all overprotective big brother!"

The guys and May exchange looks. Looks that say *Who's going to tell her.* Looks that say everyone here gets it but me.

Ben places a warm hand on my shoulder. "Let's just say the vibes weren't exactly overprotective big brother, honey."

I take down a long gulp of margarita, afraid to even ask the obvious question.

"That was a jealous boyfriend if I've ever seen one." Justin pairs the stark words with a gorgeous grin.

My laugh is forced and fake. I go in for another sip of margarita, but the tequila is sour in my mouth. "That's definitely not it. We just barely got back to being friends."

They all give me an *Oh, sweetie* smile, even May.

And I get it. I'm sure it's easy for an outsider to misinterpret Seth's actions. But I know him better than anyone, and Seth Carson is not jealous. Jealousy implies feelings. And feelings are things we can't have for each other. Not anymore.

16

One, going to therapy is awesome and everyone should do it if they can. Two, therapy should be FREE because see point number one. Three, I've only been to a couple of sessions, but I already feel a sense of inner peace that three months of crying alone in bed did not bring to me. Weird.

—Seth Carson, "Check Your Mental Health Before You Wreck Your Mental Health"

WHEN I WAKE UP THE NEXT MORNING, MY FUGUE STATE isn't due to the alcohol. Not even a margarita the size of my head could mess with me the way Seth Carson does. The events from last night have been playing in my mind like I'm a Loki Variant trapped in some kind of nightmare loop reel, and each time I run it all through my brain, I come out with less clarity and more embarrassment.

On the one hand, I accomplished another task, and it was one of the ones I was dreading the most. Five down, five to go. On the other hand, that was so much mess Andy Cohen couldn't even begin to untangle the web of what-thefuckery. Was I really the one who broke Seth's heart? How is that even possible when I'm the one who got dumped? And why did he get so upset about my kissing someone when he's technically the one who made me do it?

My phone chimes with a text as I'm vacillating between pity for myself and pity for Jessica, who really got thrown into the deep end last night.

Seth: The way I see it, we only have one more task left that we have to do together.

Seth: So let's figure out a plan for this volunteering thing and get it over with.

Well then. I guess we're done mincing words and playing nice. If he wants to be done with me and move on, then who am I to argue. Wouldn't want to unknowingly break his heart again.

I don't have a plan for volunteering just yet, and I don't particularly like his tone, so I don't respond to his text. I toss my phone to the side before I finally pull my lazy ass out of bed and into a hot shower. Coiling my wet hair into a messy bun, I leave my face mostly bare before slipping into one of my favorite dresses: a navy-blue T-shirt silhouette with a white pattern that from far away looks like an abstract print but up close is really all the droids from *Star Wars*.

I have two articles I need to write, and given how things are shaking out with the competition, they need to be good. But I don't want to go into the office and risk running into Seth, so I shoot Tessa a text to see if she wants to meet up at

Alcove for a coffee/work/vent session. She promises to meet me there in an hour, so I grab my stuff and head out, knowing I need at least a little alone time to get some work done before I fill her in on everything that happened.

After I nab a primo parking spot, I order my coffee and pastry and snag a table on the expansive patio, taking just a few minutes to breathe in the fresh city air. Once my food and drink are delivered, I open my laptop and pull out my notes about the tourist day. I think this one has the potential to be a real knockout piece, but also, given how I spent the entire day with Seth, I know I have to be careful not to spark another round of shipping among the readers. He'll have to appear to some extent, but maybe instead I can focus on writing about moving on from the past and finding closure in unexpected places. Maybe tie something in about appreciating said past but not lingering on it, much like the tour did with old Hollywood landmarks.

Writing about kissing a stranger isn't going to be so easy. Even though Seth and I found something bordering on friendship on my tourist day, I can't help but wonder if we totally blew up our fragile peace last night at the bar.

But it's not like Seth has any right to be upset. He's the one who assigned me the task in the first place. He wasn't even supposed to be there. And while I was merely kissing a stranger and sending said stranger on his merry way, Seth was there with an actual date. Probably some perfect marriage-material girl who will help him find his long-term potential and finally heal from his heartbreak or whatever.

If I was worried about how long I'd be bitter about this

whole "woe is Seth" deal, something tells me the limit does not exist.

"Your face is doing that scrunched-up thing again. Like you're thinking about someone who really pissed you off." Tessa grins as she sinks into the seat across from me, hefting her bag onto an empty chair.

I open my mouth to deliver some kind of witty retort but find I don't have one.

Her eyes automatically soften. "Oh, honey. What happened?"

Not skimping on the details, I barf out everything that went down between Seth and me not only last night, but over the past couple weeks. The flirty banter, the supposed broken heart, the tentative truce, and the look on his face when he left the bar. I avoid her gaze until I finish spewing everything out, which turns out to be a good decision because the kindness and sympathy in her eyes make me want to cry.

Okay, so I may let a tear or two slide anyway.

She pushes back her chair and stands, coming around to wrap me in an awkward seated hug.

I hastily wipe under my eyes. "Thanks. I don't think I realized how much I needed that."

She sits back in her seat and looks me dead in the eye. "We have two options here. I can go get us a round of mimosas and we can talk about how much men suck and we hate them. Or I can go get us a round of lattes and we can try to actually work some of this out and hopefully get you some clarity."

"I don't know if actual clarity is possible without me talking to him, which I'd prefer not to do right now." And to be totally honest, I'm not sure what he could say at this point to make me feel any better.

She shakes her head. "I don't mean clarity about him, I mean clarity about you."

I flash her a cheeky grin. "It's going to take more than a mimosa or a latte to get that."

"Okay." She gives me a look and slowly reaches over to grab her laptop from her bag. "Quiet writing time works too."

"Fine, let's maybe hold off on work for just a minute." I shut my own laptop with a sigh. "Between you and boxing I wonder why I'm paying my therapist."

"Because professionals still know better than friends." She stands again, wallet in hand, to head inside and order more coffee. "Though you definitely need all the help you can get."

I sit back in my chair and close my eyes for a half second before my phone pings with another text. I should've turned off my notifications, but I open it anyway, too used to jumping at the sound.

Natasha: Seth reached out to me about the volunteering assignment. I took the liberty of setting you both up at a teen writers workshop next week. I'll email you the info.
Me: Sounds good.

I can't even be annoyed that Seth went somewhat behind my back and talked to Natasha about my own task. At least it takes the decision out of my hands, and soon, the teamwork portion of the challenge will be complete. From there it will be every person for themselves. The end of this competition can't come fast enough.

Tessa returns with two iced lattes in hand.

I take mine gratefully. "Thanks for this, and for listening, as always. I appreciate it."

She raises an eyebrow. "But . . . ?"

"But I think I'm done talking about this for today. We're almost through most of the assignments, and with any luck, I'll win and Seth won't even stay in LA. This angst will all go away when I don't have to see him anymore." Because that's definitely what I want here. To not have to see Seth anymore.

Tessa looks like she's close to calling bullshit, but she doesn't push me. "Whatever you want, hon."

"If you really want to help me, you can distract me with an update on the you-and-Rob of it all." I flash her a weak smile.

Her cheeks color at the mere mention of his name. "There's not much to tell there."

"You like him." I purposefully don't phrase it as a question.

She studies the top of her latte with great interest. "I do. But . . ."

I knock her foot with mine under the table, a small reminder that I'm here for her too.

"But I kind of made a promise to myself that I'm not going to moon about anymore. If he likes me, he knows where to find me." She meets my eyes and gives me a sheepish shrug.

"We're well into the twenty-first century, Tess, you could

totally make the first move." I wrap my hand around my coffee cup, wondering if I'm giving her actual good advice or just the advice I'd want to hear in this situation. Because if I were in her shoes, I'd totally make the first move. But Tessa isn't me. "If you're not comfortable with that though, you don't have to, obviously."

"It's not that. I mean, it is that a little, but it's more like I want him to want me enough to make the move himself, you know?"

I nod, even if I'm not sure I relate. "Well, if he doesn't, he's a moron."

She rolls her eyes and turns her attention to her laptop, gently ending the conversation.

I shift my focus to my own computer, and instead of talking out all my relationship drama, I write it out, pouring everything I've got into my next piece. I've got a competition to win.

#LANAVSSETH

ROB: Things are getting interesting around here. Current standings: Seth with 124 and Lana closing in with 116.

TESSA: Woohoo! Nice work, **@Lana**!

LANA: 😘

COREY: All right. You know I am firmly #TeamLana, but I gotta say, **@Seth**, your piece today is awesome. Therapy for the win!

SETH: Thanks, **@Corey**, that means a lot ☺

LANA: Yeah, thanks, **@Corey**.

COREY: Your article was great too!

JAMES: You couldn't pay me a million dollars to get on one of those tourist buses.

LANA: It actually wasn't as bad as I thought it would be.

SETH: I thought it was a lot of fun.

TESSA: I guess any activity can be fun with the right company ☺

LANA: I wouldn't go that far.

Though maybe you all would like to join me for a kickboxing class?

JAMES: Since when are you down with working out?

LANA: I'm down for anything that lets me imagine punching my ex in the face . . . purely for physical fitness purposes of course.

SETH: And here I thought we called a truce.

LANA: Calling a truce doesn't mean I wouldn't enjoy punching you.

SETH: You should probably bring up your anger issues at your next therapy appointment.

LANA: You should probably not be such a butthead.

JAMES: Do I have to say it every time?

GET. A. ROOM.

17

Whatever happened to meeting people face-to-face?
Remember those few months when
speed dating was all the rage? Good times.

—Lana Parker, "Are Dating Apps Our Only Hope?"

A FEELING OF DREAD POOLS IN MY STOMACH AS I PEEL the thin paper backing off the "Hello My Name Is" tag and stick it to my dress. And it has nothing to do with not wanting to leave any adhesive residue on my favorite sundress—royal blue and swingy, clinging in all the right places, with a tiny Captain America shield embroidered on the sleeve.

I slap a fake smile on my face as I turn and survey the half-full room. Apparently speed dating isn't really a thing anymore, which isn't all that surprising given the heteronormativity of it all. In order to find an event so I could complete my task, I had to travel to a church all the way in the Valley. Somehow, I ended up back in the Valley.

I find myself in a large, nondescript multipurpose room,

the carpet a drab gray, the walls a dingy cream that probably used to be white. There are small tables set up in a large circle in the center of the room, each with two folding chairs, a number, and a bud vase with one wilting flower. People mostly in the thirty-to-forty-five age box mill around the room, and it resembles a junior high dance, boys on one side and girls on the other.

I make a beeline for what looks to be the bar, only to find it's a self-serve drink station stocked only with water and lemonade. Which I guess makes sense since we're in a church. Even though I'm pretty sure Jesus had a thing for wine and would certainly not begrudge a girl some liquid courage before this whole evening gets under way.

The good news is that the horrible traffic I sat through got me here just a few minutes before the event is scheduled to start. By the time I help myself to some lemonade, our host for the evening is already directing us to our assigned seats.

"Welcome, everyone. Thank you so much for coming. I'm sure many of you are already familiar with how speed dating works." The woman, who appears to be in her mid-forties, shoots some knowing looks around the room, presumably at the repeat customers, although their very presence doesn't exactly make for a ringing endorsement of the event's success rate. "But if you're new here this evening, here's how tonight will go. The ladies will find their assigned seat and remain there for the duration. Gentlemen, you'll get three minutes with each gal. When the timer dings, move along to the next lucky lady. At the end of the night, you'll pick your favorite daters, and if you make a match, you'll be sent their contact information." She gives us all a warm, encouraging smile that sings of cookies and milk and after-school specials. "Let's get to it!"

I take a seat at table number five, attempting to make myself comfortable in my folding chair. I can't seem to stop fidgeting, and long before I'm ready, I'm faced with the first of my suitors.

"Hi, I'm David." His hand actually trembles as he reaches out to offer me a weak handshake.

I flash him a mostly genuine smile, taking some pity on him since he's clearly nervous. "Lana."

"What do you do, Lana?"

I try not to grimace, wondering how many times I'm going to have to answer the same standard questions tonight. "I'm a writer. How about you?"

"I work from home."

Working from home doesn't quite answer my question, but I don't want to be rude, so I don't press further. I attempt to think of something else to ask him, but he hasn't given me much to work with so far. "And do you like that? Working from home, I mean?"

"It's fun."

Okay. Really don't know where to go after that.

He spends the remainder of the three minutes staring at my chest and doesn't seem to hear the bell when it chimes, just as he seemed to be unable to hear any of my other pained attempts at conversation starters.

"Okay, nice to meet you, bye now!"

David moves along to the next poor woman and a new man takes his seat.

This one at least makes eye contact, but it's clear from the start that we have nothing in common. I guess the whole premise of speed dating means it's okay to make snap decisions about people, which is good, because I veto guys two through seven within the first thirty seconds.

Old Lana would've jumped at the chance to chat with ten men who cared enough about finding a partner that they'd put themselves through speed dating. Old Lana would've left this event with at least five phone numbers and possibly even a date that would quickly turn into a steady relationship. Old Lana wouldn't have cared about David's inappropriate staring or Suitor Three's bad breath or the way Suitor Five mentioned his "bros" four times in the first minute. Old Lana would've picked whoever seemed the most interested and would've vowed to make it work.

New Lana wants to go home and curl up in bed with a glass of wine and *Schitt's Creek*.

When I feel my phone vibrate during the middle of Suitor Eight's diatribe about gun rights, I don't even bother trying to be sly about it. I pull it out of my purse and check my messages.

Seth: So how's speed dating going? 😄

Suitor Eight isn't paying attention to me, so I swipe over to my camera and flip it in my direction. I point to my name tag, but mostly I let my get-me-the-fuck-out-of-here face do the talking for me; a selfie is worth a thousand words and all that jazz. I send him the photo.

Seth: 😄😄😄😄😄

Me: I hate you.

Seth: If it makes you feel any better, I had another therapy session today.

Me: I would kill to be in therapy right now. This task officially sucks.

Seth: I feel like you should probably not use the phrase "kill to be in therapy."

Me: Did I mention that I hate you?

Seth: 😄

Me: I only have a couple guys left but I'm tempted to pretend you're texting me with a family emergency and bail.

Seth: I'm going to pretend like you didn't just tell me you're thinking about quitting halfway through. That would be cheating, Parker.

Me: Please have some pity. I'm begging you!

Seth: Lol. You're almost done. Hang in there and then you never have to speed-date again.

Me: You're the worst.

Seth: You know you love me.

That stops my fingers in their tracks. The word *love* anywhere near Seth Carson sparks immediate warning bells. Especially after everything that went down in the bar the other night. Seth and I are still on shaky ground, and the last thing I need is a reminder of old feelings when I'm still not quite sure of my current ones. I shove my phone back in my purse and look up to find Suitor Eight has thankfully vacated the chair across from me. In his place is Suitor Nine, who is actually cute, in a very wholesome kind of way.

"Hi, I'm Tim." He holds out his hand and gives me a firm shake. "Sorry for just sitting here awkwardly, but I didn't want to interrupt whatever it was that was making you smile like that."

I don't feel the grin on my lips until he mentions it, surprised that a few snarky texts from Seth would make me smile.

"Boyfriend?" Tim asks, completely nonjudgmentally, all things considered.

"What? No." I immediately wipe the smile from my face. "Sorry. I'm Lana. Writer. Thirty. Been in LA for about twelve years."

Tim smiles, and it's genuine. "Tim. Thirty-five. Contractor. Born and raised."

A small laugh trickles out. "Is this your first time speed dating?"

"It is. I didn't really want to come, to be honest, but one of my buddies convinced me." He points his thumb over his shoulder in the vague direction of one of the other suitors. "How about you?"

"First time for me too." I don't mention I'm only here for an assignment.

"I take it it hasn't been going well?" He pairs his words with another teasing smile.

"They really should serve booze at these things, don't you think?"

This time he laughs, and it's what can only be described as hearty. "You're probably right about that."

The bell dings and Tim rises from his seat, and for the first time tonight, I wasn't actively counting down the seconds. He holds his hand out again, and this time when I offer mine in return, he wraps his fingers around my palm. "Maybe I'll see you again, Lana."

I wait for him to kiss my hand or something equally embarrassing, but he doesn't. Just gives my fingers a squeeze and heads on to the next lady.

For a second I think about cutting out early, because surely it doesn't get any better than Tim, who gave me lukewarm feelings, and I'm really not looking forward to the whole tell-us-which-guys-you-loved song and dance at the end. But I don't want to be rude and it's only a few more minutes.

I check my phone, but Seth hasn't texted me again, probably because I didn't respond to his last message. Because how the fuck am I supposed to respond to that. I raise my head with a soft sigh.

And a familiar pair of blue eyes meets mine from across the table, as if by my simply thinking about him, he miraculously appeared.

"Hi," I manage after thirty precious seconds have ticked by.

"Hi." His smile is soft and tentative.

"What are you doing here?" I try to surreptitiously take in a long breath, needing to calm my heart rate without making it obvious how much his mere presence has kicked it up.

"Natasha instructed me to come to this, but it felt like crossing some sort of line. I've been sitting in my car for the last twenty minutes, debating whether I should come in." He offers me an impish smile, but it's easy to see the nerves hiding underneath. "I almost turned around and went home, but then I got your texts and I guess I just wanted to see you. And talk to you in person."

The words are bare and honest and I don't want them to stop. I sit in silence, praying he'll keep going.

"Things got a little weird at the bar, and I know I shouldn't have been there in the first place." His fingers begin tapping an incessant rhythm on the table. "Look, you asked me before why I came here. Why LA." He takes in a long breath. "Clearly I came here for a reason and I'd be lying if I said that reason had nothing to do with you, Parker."

I cover his hand with mine, to stop the drumming, and also because I need to feel him.

His eyes look everywhere but at me. "I spent a lot of years on the road. Sleeping on couches and in run-down hotel rooms and a lot of the time not sleeping at all. I don't regret it because I loved the work that I did. It was important and fulfilling and I'll never be sorry for the stories I got to tell." He runs his free hand through his hair. "But it was so fucking lonely, Parker. I was never in one place long enough to make friends. I had colleagues and contacts and my family back home, but on those many occasions when I'd be by myself in some dingy hotel room, I just felt like I was drowning, like the loneliness was swallowing me up."

I remove my hand from his, but only so I can lace our

fingers together. Squeezing his hand tightly, I wait for him to speak whenever he's ready. I'm sure the final bell has dinged and people are probably leaving all around us, but I don't care. I will sit across this table from Seth Carson for as long as he needs me to.

He rubs his thumb over my knuckles. "I never really understood what it was like, feeling lonely. It—and the people I met and the things I saw—it changed me. Humbled me, hopefully." His grin is sheepish and so familiar I want to cry. He covers our intertwined fingers with his free hand and brings his gaze to mine. "When I decided to relocate and settle in one place, I didn't even have to think about where to go. I'm the spinning needle of a compass and you've always been my true north, Parker."

"Seth . . ." I blink away the tears that have sprung into my eyes, struggling to breathe. I don't know what to say. Words, which come so easily to me when I sit down in front of a computer, can't seem to find their way from my brain to my mouth. But I force myself to speak up. To not accept his explanation at face value, even if it would be easier. "If you've changed like you say you have, then why did you come here to try to take my job?"

His grip on my hand tightens. "That was never my intention. How could I have even imagined they'd pit us against each other? I wouldn't have agreed to the competition at all, but . . ."

"But . . . ?"

He shrugs, and it's sad, his shoulders settling and his head dropping. "But you didn't exactly seem happy to see me. I think your exact words were 'What the fuck are you doing here?'"

I settle back in my seat, clamping my lips shut so I don't immediately jump to my own defense. Because he's not wrong. I sit with the realization for a minute before I speak. "I'm sorry. I was thrown off, seeing you there. And I realize I wouldn't have been if I had responded to your message. So, I apologize."

He meets my eyes and something alarmingly like hope greets me.

And while we're confronting all the elephants in the room and demons from the past, I decide I might as well dive in. "And speaking of the bar"—which we definitely weren't, but I'm going for it—"what was up with that overprotective big brother act?"

His head tilts to the side, studying me. "You really don't know?"

"May seems to think it's because you were jealous." I study him back, watching for any flinch or flicker of emotion. "But I told her that couldn't be the case. Because you made it very clear two years ago just how much you no longer want me." I force myself to hold his eye contact.

His next breath is shuddering, like he's fighting to control his emotions. "I might not be as over that as I thought I was."

My hand goes cold in his. I control the volume of my voice, still somewhat aware of the room full of people. "You mean you thought you were over rejecting me? What did *you* have to get over, exactly? That night crushed me, Seth."

His hand releases mine. "Of course I wanted you. And of course watching you kiss another guy made me jealous." He pushes his chair back, just the slightest bit, but the intention is clear. "I rejected you at the reunion because you were clearly drunk, Parker. Not to mention the fact that you had a boyfriend at the time."

I don't bother blinking away the tears that have formed, letting them trickle down my cheeks. For once it's not anger that washes over me, but shame.

Seth sits further back in his chair, putting as much space between us as possible. "I waited ten years for a second chance with you, Lana. I thought about you constantly, I never stopped loving you. And when I finally found myself in the same room with you again, when I finally got to hear you say you wanted me again, it was because you were drunk, *and* still with someone else. What was I supposed to think? I could've reacted better, and I'm sorry for that, but it was devastating."

His tone is so measured and even, I would almost prefer if he yelled at me. I deserve it.

I reach for his hand again, and he lets me take it. "I'm sorry, Seth."

He lifts our hands to his lips, placing a soft kiss on my skin. "I think our three minutes are up." He gently sets my hand back on my side of the table and stands. "I'll see you around, Parker."

He strides out of the room before I can protest, but it takes less than a minute for me to shove back my own chair and rush after him, ignoring all the nice volunteers asking me to fill out their end-of-the-evening forms. I speed down the front steps of the church and into the parking lot, thankful it's mostly emptied out at this point.

Seth is practically racing toward his car, so I do the only thing I can think of and sprint after him.

"Seth!" I look toward the sky as I continue running, sure that a freakish summer rain is about to start pouring down because it's the only thing that could make this whole situation more cinematic than it already is.

Luckily he slows his steps, turning to face me before coming to a stop in the middle of the parking lot.

By the time I reach him I'm out of breath and sweaty. I hold up a hand, silently asking him to give me a minute to collect myself.

He does, a small, bemused smile tugging on the corner of his lips. Jerk.

I lace my fingers together and rest my hands on the top of my head. "How can you tell me all of that and just leave?"

He shoves his hands in the pockets of his jeans. "I don't need any kind of response, I just wanted you to know how I feel."

"Seth, I . . ." I'm thankful for the wheezing breaths huffing out of me, disguising my total lack of brain function. Despite running out of the church like I had a response burning at the back of my throat, I still don't know what to say. I just know I don't want him to leave.

He wipes a bead of sweat from my brow, right before it drips in my eye. Which is both sweet and gross. "I appreciate you sprinting after me, Parker, but I don't need any sort of pity response."

"It's not pity. Trust me, I would not run for pity."

He huffs out a laugh.

I finally collect myself, dropping my hands. "I don't have an excuse for my behavior that night. No excuse would be good enough anyway because I was out of line and I shouldn't have propositioned you like that." I can't believe I put him in that position, and that I came so close to cheating on Evan. I take a step closer, placing a tentative hand on his chest, feeling his heartbeat thump under my palm. "But despite my less-than-ideal way of going about it, nothing I said that night was because I was drunk."

"You had a boyfriend at the time, Parker. A serious one, one you later considered marrying." He doesn't remove my hand, but he also makes no move to reciprocate the touch.

I drop my head, unable to look him in the eyes. "I know. And that was unfair. To you and to him."

We're quiet for a minute.

"Did you really come here for me?" I ask when I can't stand the silence any longer.

That familiar smirk tugs on his lips. "Maybe. Partly." His hand reaches out, grasping my hip and pulling me just a bit closer.

My other hand drifts up, almost of its own accord, tracing the stubble along his jaw. "I'm so sorry you've been lonely, Seth."

His other hand snakes around my waist, tugging me in even tighter, removing the final inch of space separating us. "Whenever I was lonely, I thought of you. And it helped."

I stop thinking, stop fighting the attraction and the memories and all the reasons this can't happen. Cupping Seth's cheek in my hand, I bring my lips to his. The kiss is a soft press, a fleeting second, and I pull away before it overwhelms me and I lose myself in him.

Seth freezes, eyes wide, like if he moves it will disrupt the timeline and make us both fade away and disappear.

"I'm sorry I hurt you, Seth. And I'm really glad you're here." I give him a small smile before turning and heading for my car.

He doesn't say anything, doesn't try to stop me. I don't turn around and I don't look back, just shut myself in my car and drive home, wondering if there will ever come a time when we stop walking away.

18

There are few things worse in life than finding out your ex is seeing someone new.

—Lana Parker, "You Were Too Good for Them Anyway"

#LANAVSSETH

COREY: **@Rob**, where are this week's scores? This is way more important than whatever dumb sportsball thing is happening!

ROB: Sheesh. It's been two days. Chill out.

Seth: 153 Lana: 149

COREY: Yes, girl! Get those points!

TESSA: What are you two writing for this week?

LANA: I'm working on my speed-dating recap.

COREY: Ooooooooo, give me all the deets please!

LANA: What is the point of me writing the article if I tell you everything it's going to say first?

COREY: You're no fun.

@Seth, give me some hot goss. I'm bored.

SETH: Not much hot goss to be had, I'm afraid.

My article this week will be about deleting Tinder and my booty-call phone numbers.

ROB: Pour one out for the loss of the booty calls.

JAMES: Yeah, I actually feel your pain on that one.

SETH: Thanks, guys, I appreciate the support.

LANA: 🙄

SETH: Though I do have a second date planned for this week. Might even convince her to go on date three.

LANA: You have a date this week?

SETH: Yes?

LANA: After speed dating, you made a date?

SETH: Yes?

LANA: With Jessica?

SETH: Do you actually want to be having this conversation right now?

COREY: What happened at speed dating?

LANA: Nothing.

SETH: Nothing.

LANA: Just a little surprised you're going on a date.

SETH: Three dates with one person is on my list, correct?

JAMES: Normally this would be the time when I'd tell you to get a room, but I'm popping the popcorn so please keep this conversation going.

AS I PROOFREAD the post I just finished for my blog—a list of my favorite second-chance romances—my stomach turns. Compiling lists of my favorite romance tropes isn't unusual—I feature them on my blog frequently—but this particular trope is maybe not the best one to be dwelling on given the circumstances. And that's when I realize I might be a little more upset about Seth's upcoming second date with Jessica than I should be. I don't know what I expected to happen after our parking-lot confessional, but it definitely wasn't his turning around and going on a date with someone else. Even if I'm the one who wrote the damn task.

I swipe open my phone and pull up my texts with May.

Me: Is it weird that I'm jealous Seth is going on dates?

May: Is that a question you want an actual response to or just a one-word confirmation?

Me: Let's start with one word.

May: No.

Me: Okay, you're right. I need more explanation than that.

May: Of course it's not weird that you're jealous your ex whom you totally still have feelings for is going on a date.

Me: I don't have feelings for him. Seth and I are just friends. And we're barely even that.

May: Lie to yourself all you want, but don't try that shit with me.

Me: Okay fine. It doesn't matter if I have feelings for him or not—which I will neither confirm nor deny. Right now is about me. Finding myself and eat-pray-loving and shit.

May: Love the sentiment.

Me: Meaning?

May: It means, I fully support you eat-pray-loving and shit, but I also know you can't just dismiss your feelings for him like that.

I sit with that one for a minute before I respond.

Me: I know. I'm not dismissing them. I'm putting them on hold. Giving us time to reconnect as friends while I figure my shit out.

May: You going to tell him that?

Me: Fuck no.

May: Good. Happy hour today?

Me: Fuck yes.

THREE DAYS LATER, I plant myself at a work desk with a direct sight line to the *ATF* office's main entrance. My legs are crossed, foot swinging gleefully in time with the tap-tap-tapping of my pen on the Lucite work surface.

I haven't seen Seth in person since he told me I'm his true north and I kissed him in the parking lot. We haven't spoken at all since he revealed his big date-number-two plans in the Slack. I've been avoiding going into the office because I know things are going to be the very definition of awkward when I do see him. Fortunately, during some light Instagram stalking yesterday, I stumbled upon the perfect icebreaker, a legit reason to talk to him that has nothing to do with the breathless kiss I've replayed in my head a thousand times. Today is deadline day, and I know he'll be coming into the office. He still likes to hand-deliver his final drafts like it's the 1940s.

Seth rolls in about half an hour after I started my stakeout, which is really good timing, as I was just about to lose interest.

"Ha!" I shout the moment I see him. I jump out of my seat, which is a terrible idea as my foot has fallen asleep. I stumble a little but manage to right myself and thrust a triumphant finger in Seth's general direction.

Seth has frozen in the doorway, travel mug of coffee halfway to his lips.

"You!" Despite sitting and plotting for the past thirty minutes, working out every detail of my gotcha speech, I seem to have forgotten how to speak more than one word at a time.

"I just got here, what could I have possibly done?" Seth shuffle-sidesteps, moving in the general direction of away from me.

I grab my phone from my desk and wave it over my head. "You cheated is what you did." I should probably lower my voice, but Corey and James are the only other writers in the office right now, and I know they're probably already in the kitchen grabbing snacks and gearing up for a showdown.

"And what's worse," I continue, my voice growing louder as I remember the bulletproof takedown I have mentally prepared, "is you were stupid enough to put the evidence on Instagram."

Seth drops his stuff at a workspace across the room from mine before slowly making his way over to me. "Parker, I honestly have no idea what you're talking about."

Out of the corner of my eye, I see Corey exit the kitchen and start to creep closer to us, before she finally perches her tiny butt on the desk right behind mine. James is nowhere to be seen, but I'm sure he's well within hearing distance.

I type in my passcode and bring up my photos. "Corey, please remind me of Seth's task involving a pet."

"He has to get one and care for it for the duration of the challenge." Her voice is chipper and I know she's loving every minute of this.

"And is he allowed to replace his original pet should something happen to it due to negligence on his part as caretaker?"

"Um, no?"

"That's right!" I spin around, gesturing to the mostly empty room like I'm Elle Woods making my closing argument. "And yet, here I have the hard evidence that one Seth Carson has replaced his original pet—according to his own words, a blue delta guppy—with a brand-new specimen." I shove my phone under Corey's nose. "What color is this fish, ma'am?"

"Ooh, is this like one of those social media what-color-do-you-think-the-dress-is things?" She grabs the phone from me, examining the screen from all angles.

"No. Just tell me what color the fish is."

"It's red." She passes my phone back with a sweet smile.

I turn back around to find Seth watching me with his arms crossed over his chest, a bemused expression on his face. I falter a little because he doesn't look nearly as scared or guilty as I thought he would, being caught red-handed and all. "The prosecution rests."

Corey applauds my performance before turning to Seth. "Defense, you may present your case."

Seth saunters over to her, his own phone already in his hand. He shows her the screen.

She giggles. "Oh. I rule in favor of the defense."

"What?" My screech echoes around the open floor plan. "I object!"

Corey hands me Seth's phone, which is open to a photo of Seth's fish tank. Where there swims a red fish. And a blue fish. Not one fish, but two fish. I just got Seussed.

Corey hops off the desk and heads back to the office kitchen. "That wasn't nearly as entertaining as I thought it was going to be."

Sinking into my chair, I gently toss Seth's phone onto my desk. "You got a second fish?"

He shrugs, hands in his pockets, casual AF. "I didn't want Harry to get lonely."

The declaration would've been adorable on its own, but knowing what I now know about Seth's own loneliness, it's downright heart-melting. "What's its name?"

"Her name is Sally."

Of course it is.

Seth reaches across me to grab his phone, planting himself in what seems to be his favorite position: butt leaning against my workspace, right in my line of vision. "So . . . ?"

There are a billion different directions in which that question could go. *So how about that kiss? So did we basically declare we still have feelings for each other? So what should I wear on my next date?*

I refuse to play this game with him. Here I was thinking he was breaking the rules and about to be disqualified—putting an end to this whole fiasco—and instead I come to find out he bought his pet fish a companion so he doesn't get lonely. Which might be the cutest fucking thing I've ever heard.

I cross my arms over my chest and snap back, "So what?"

He mirrors my pose and pierces me with a gaze that sees a bit too much. "Jeez, Parker, are you seriously that upset that I didn't kill my fish?"

"Yes." I realize how evil that makes me sound and try to school my face into something less hostile. "I mean, no." Tugging on the end of my ponytail, I shift my eyes away from his. "I guess I just thought that if you couldn't complete the task, then we could call off this whole thing. It would be over."

He scoots closer to me, so our knees are pressed together. His voice softens and it suddenly feels like we're the only two people in the room. "Why do you want the competition to be over?"

"So I can win and get the column, of course." I push the words out in a rush before any other answer can make its way from my brain to my mouth.

He grasps my chin in his hand, turning my head so I'm forced to meet his gaze. "Is that the only reason?"

And I know what he's really asking. Just like he knows what I'm really saying. If we called off the competition right now, there would be nothing left standing between us. Nothing except the past and the walls we've each built. Walls we're slowly knocking down.

But as much as I want to give him an honest answer, I know I can't. Not yet.

"Yes, that's the only reason." I gently remove myself from his hold. "I might complain about it, but I really am learning a lot about myself as I go through these assignments, Seth. Like at speed dating."

His shoulders hunch over a little, like that wasn't the answer he wanted to hear. "And what did you learn?"

"That I shouldn't accept the attention of a man I'm not interested in just because I want attention." The declaration comes out much more succinct and confident than I would've anticipated given the whirlpool of emotions swirling around in my chest. But it's true.

"Oh." Seth straightens a little, offering me a sad smile. It crinkles his eyes just a tad. "I think that's probably an important lesson."

"And that sometimes it's about meeting the right person

at the right time. Something I haven't managed to do just yet." It's a bit of a dig, but it's also a truth I think we both need to accept.

Seth's smile fades, only to be replaced half a second later with one of his cocky grins. "Right. Well, I'll let you get back to work."

And he saunters off without another word or a backward glance.

And I'm left to wonder why that stings, just a little.

19

God, I need therapy.

—Lana Parker, in conversation with her friends, more than once

"HOW ARE THINGS GOING WITH THE ARTICLE SERIES?" Dr. Lawson asks almost the second I sink onto her couch for my latest session. "Are you still feeling comfortable with the competition element? How have the assignments been?"

I want to laugh, but I'm afraid if I do it will quickly turn into tears. "I'm not really sure how to answer that."

"How about honestly?"

I sigh, not even dithering before I pick up the throw pillow and hold it tight to my chest. "I guess the good news is that the series seems to be popular with readers. Clicks are up, which means ad dollars are up. Natasha is happy."

Dr. Lawson's ever-present pen is poised on her notebook. "Is that an important goal for you during this? That Natasha be happy?"

"She's my boss, so yes, I'd like her to be happy with the

work I'm doing." It's more than that, and we both know it, but she doesn't push the issue for now.

"And do you feel like you've had some worthwhile experiences?"

I nod, telling her all about the boxing class and speed dating, leaving out the conversation with Seth. I even mention the idea I've had of starting to take my blog more seriously. "And Natasha signed us up for a volunteering event that I think will be good for me."

"Natasha set it up for you?"

I nod, playing with the tassels on the corners of the pillow. "It's with some kids who want to be writers. Someone probably reached out to her to see if she had anyone who was interested."

"Has she been involved in any of the other tasks?"

I frown a little, catching the hidden insinuation there. "Sort of? Mostly peripherally though. She's set up some of the activities Seth and I have been doing together, but nothing major. She's done that before for some of my other pieces."

"Natasha has been sending you and Seth on these excursions together?"

"Yeah, but that was always part of the deal." I gently toss the pillow back to the corner of the love seat.

Dr. Lawson taps her chin with her pen. "Lana, have you ever felt like Natasha overstepped with you? Maybe she got too involved or asked too many personal questions? Is she overly interested in your life outside of work?"

Given how uncomfortable just hearing the question makes me, it shouldn't be hard to realize that the answer to all of those is yes, though I've never had cause to doubt Natasha's motivations. Sure, she's always taken an interest in my personal life, but that's only because she cares about me as a person. She's known me for nearly a decade. I clasp my hands together in my lap. "Maybe."

"Do you think Natasha knows you see her as a mother figure?"

"Most likely."

"And do you think she ever takes advantage of that?"

"*Advantage* is a strong word. I don't think Natasha does that intentionally. She just pushes me to do my best because she knows what I'm capable of." I know I sound defensive, and that this defensiveness is itself a sign, but I don't think I like where this line of questioning is going. I didn't come in here today looking to talk about Natasha. Honestly, Natasha feels like the very least of my problems at the moment.

Dr. Lawson nods, and I know she's picked up on my discomfort. She'll let the subject rest. For now. "Okay. Is there anything else you want to talk about today?"

I know there was, but all of a sudden I can't recall it. "No, I think I'm good." I stand, waving on my way out the door, my current priority being putting some space between me and this topic of conversation. "Thanks, Dr. Lawson."

I replay Dr. Lawson's questions in my mind for the twenty-minute drive home, and instead of flopping on the couch like I usually do, I head directly into my office.

I don't spend a ton of time working in my home office, even though I've spent countless hours meticulously decorating and arranging it. I usually choose to work at the *ATF* office or coffee shops, or even in my backyard, because frankly, sometimes being in this haven of a space, one I created for myself, just makes me sad.

Because this is the office of someone who is passionate about books and the arts. Not the office of someone who doles out dating advice for a living. Every time I sit down at my desk, I feel a wave of resentment. For Natasha and *ATF*, but also for myself. For not going after the job I really want. For settling for the relationship column because it allowed me to stay at the place where I'm comfortable. My relationship with *ATF* is perhaps a little too similar to my relationship with relationships.

I sit down at my desk, open my computer, and pull up my blog. When I created this website a few years ago, I intended it to be a personal outlet, a space just for me, to write about the things that really mattered to me. I never promoted it or attached my name to it, and the plan was always to keep it private. But maybe it's time to rethink that plan. Which means it's time to rework the site. I spend the next few hours redoing the design, making the text clean and sharp and the colors pop. I organize my existing blog posts and put links to my social media on the home page. It still needs work, and I'm still not a hundred percent sure I'll ever put this out there for the masses. But it's a start.

#LANAVSSETH

ROB: I know this isn't related to the competition, but since everyone is already in the chat, who's coming to the Dodgers game tonight?

LANA: I am! Looking forward to drinking beer and not having to worry about this stupid competition for one damn night.

SETH: Ouch. Should I be offended?

I'm also going.

COREY: As much as I enjoy men in tight pants, I've got plans.

JAMES: As much as I also enjoy men in tight pants, I have a restaurant opening I have to go to.

COREY: Oooh, do you need a plus-one?

LANA: You literally just said you already had plans.

COREY: Plans can change for a restaurant opening.

LANA: But not a baseball game with your most favorite coworkers?

COREY: Not for that, no 😘

TESSA: I'm going. Should we carpool?

LANA: You are on the west side, my friend, so we absolutely should not.

Wait, Rob, aren't you also on the west side? You guys could go together.

ROB: That works. And you and Seth are both on the east side so you'll carpool too?

Lana is typing.

SETH: That would be great, especially since I have no idea how to get to the stadium. I'll pick you up, Parker, if you don't mind my still-mediocre driving.

LANA: Sure. Great. Just what I was going to suggest.

20

Baseball games are a great date night!

—Lana Parker, "Twenty Unique Date Night Ideas"

MY DOORBELL RINGS EXACTLY WHEN SETH PROMISED to be at my place, and I once again curse Rob for turning my matchmaking tendencies against me. Rude.

Also, why the hell is Seth ringing the doorbell instead of texting me to say he's outside like a normal human being?

I open the front door with clear purse and sweatshirt already in hand, not wanting to let Seth take a peek inside. For some reason, the idea of seeing him in my home makes my stomach spin, and not in a fun, riding-the-teacups-at-Disneyland way. "Hi," I say, pushing my way past him out onto the front stoop, turning and locking the door behind me. "You didn't have to come up." Marching down the front path, I don't stop to see if he follows me.

Thankfully, I quickly hear the thud of his footsteps on

the concrete behind me. "I was kind of hoping to scope out your place."

"Oh, well, we don't want to be late." I throw the words over my shoulder, not bothering to turn around. "Parking at the stadium is a bitch." Which is totally the truth and a very valid reason for not giving him the grand tour.

He beeps the doors of a Prius, older than mine but still in good condition.

For a moment, I almost expect him to open the door for me, the way he always used to, but he walks straight to the driver's-side door and climbs in.

I direct Seth to the stadium, and even though the game doesn't start for another hour, it takes us almost as long to get through the line of cars waiting to park. By the time we get in, grab a round of beers, and find our seats, the first batter is already at the plate.

"Neither of you is from LA and yet you still roll in late like you were born here." Rob shoots us a judgmental look from underneath the brim of his Dodgers hat.

"Not everyone feels the need to be here for batting practice." I slip into the seat next to Tessa, leaving Seth the aisle seat since he hates having his long legs bunched up between the tight rows.

Tessa leans over under the guise of giving me a hug. "I've never been so bored in my life. What is one supposed to do while watching batting practice?"

"Rate the tight butts on a scale from *meh* to *I'd like to bite that*?" I hold up my beer, waiting for her to reciprocate so we can clink our plastic cups together.

She laughs before taking a swig of beer. "Something tells me present company wouldn't have enjoyed that." She cocks her head in Rob's direction, trying to look exasperated when instead pure adoration shines in her eyes.

Not that Rob notices, since his own eyes are glued firmly to the lush green field in front of us.

Seth adjusts his position in the seat next to me, drawing my attention away from my real-life OTP. Even with the added aisle space, his legs are still squished and intruding into my space. "Sorry," he mutters as he shifts again, trying to separate us from constant contact.

Like we didn't just have our legs permanently cemented together on the tourist bus. Like he didn't wrap his fingers around mine at speed dating. Like I didn't brush my lips against his in the parking lot.

But I guess some things have changed since then.

"It's fine." My words are as stiff as my posture.

Tessa shoots me a questioning look, but I shake my head, hopefully imperceptibly to anyone but her.

We make for an awkward foursome. Rob and Tessa clearly have feelings for each other but for whatever reason can't seem to find a way to admit it. Seth and I were a big ball of awkward from day one, and when you add in recent events, that ball of awkward has ballooned to the size of the moon.

Tessa and I keep up a stream of innocuous conversation, but Rob's attention stays firmly planted on the game before us, and Seth doesn't say much of anything.

In the middle of the fifth inning, the crowd-pleasing,

energizing music is replaced by a soft love song and a collective *awwww* echoes around the stadium.

I groan when I see the Kiss Cam pop up on the huge screen over left field. It's a known fact that the Kiss Cam is the absolute worst. Still, it doesn't stop me from subtly nudging Tessa closer to Rob. She shoots me a knowing look and I innocently smile.

Seth clears his throat, and I realize that in the process of pushing Tessa into Rob's space, I've inadvertently moved myself into Seth's. To the average viewer—and to any wandering cameraperson—I'm sure it looks like we're cuddled up close together.

"Sorry," I mutter. I turn my head, but all it does is bring our lips close enough that should we show up on-screen, it'd take only the slightest movement for our kiss to connect. "We should . . ." We should move, we should separate ourselves, we should do anything but sit here like this. But I can't seem to find the will.

Seth's fingers curl around my elbow, which is perched on the slim armrest between us, stroking the thin skin on the back of my arm. "Lana, I . . ."

I lean in an inch closer, because this close, the sense of him overwhelms me. The fear of a looming camera is all but forgotten.

He gently squeezes my arm. Then his fingers drop from my skin and he pulls away. "I can't do this, Parker."

My breath flutters in my chest and I want to ask what *this* is, but words don't seem to be coming to me. I yank my arm from the armrest like it burned me and scoot closer to

Tessa. My phone buzzes and I'm so happy for something to distract me, I don't even care that my boss is texting me during nonworking hours.

Natasha: Please make sure you take a selfie tonight and post it to our Stories before the game is over.
Me: How did you know we're at the game?
Natasha: I made sure Rob got enough tickets so you could all go together.

I pause for a minute before responding. On the surface, it makes sense that our sports reporter would regularly get tickets to local sporting events. It even makes sense that his boss would be the one to facilitate said tickets. But get enough for all of us? This outing isn't part of the competition, it's not one of our tasks. Seth and I certainly don't need to be here.

Pursing my lips, I swipe open to my camera and pull Tessa into a side embrace, snapping a quick photo of the two of us and uploading it to Instagram.

My phone chirps again a minute later.

Natasha: Cute pic, but post one of the whole group please.
Me: Sure.
Natasha: Also, I just emailed you and Seth the details about the upcoming writers' workshop for teens. Can you make sure he sees it?
Me: Fine.

I shove my phone back in my pocket. The nachos I scarfed down in the third inning churn in my stomach.

Before I can say anything to him, Seth nudges my arm. "Did you see this email from Natasha?"

"She just texted me about it."

"I guess we have an end date now. At least for our joint activities, it seems." He shifts his foot and it brushes up against mine.

Glancing in his direction, I try to read his expression to see how he feels about it.

Not that I know how I feel about it.

If I'm being honest with myself, I like having Seth back in my life. In the moments when we've been able to let go and have fun, it's felt like I had one of my best friends back. Rehashing the reunion mishap was awkward and painful, but I know it was necessary to clear the air, and for me to apologize. But some of his comments, "true north" in particular, still haunt me, and his oversized reaction to my stranger's kiss didn't exactly scream "just friends."

And if I dive into the depths of *true* self-honesty, the way it felt seeing him on a date with someone else wasn't exactly driving the highway to Friendsville either.

In so many ways, it would be so easy to let myself fall back in love with Seth Carson. Hell, I don't think I ever really fell completely out of love with Seth Carson, though the man sitting next to me is certainly not the teenager I grew up with. But despite everything, I want to see this competition through to the end. Not just for the chance at the column—though that certainly doesn't hurt—but because

I'm genuinely learning things about myself. I'm enjoying not just the assignments themselves, but how it feels to complete them.

I turn fully toward Seth. "It might be good for us to get some space, yeah?"

He doesn't answer me right away, a little crease forming at the center of his forehead. I fight back the urge to smooth it away. He clears his throat. "Yeah. Some space might be good."

It isn't until after the game, when Seth has dropped me back at home, after I've showered and changed into my pajamas and tucked myself into bed, that I realize I never posted the group photo Natasha asked for. It was mostly an oversight—I truly did forget about it once I put my phone away—but it also might be the first time I explicitly didn't do something Natasha asked me to do. A couple of weeks ago, the stress of it would've kept me awake all night, but tonight, I drift right off, not concerned in the slightest.

#LANAVSSETH

ROB: Current standings as of week six, Seth: 188 Lana: 184. The gap is slim, but Seth maintains his lead.

TESSA: Can you believe you guys are more than halfway through? Time is flying!

COREY: **@Lana**, thank you for holding back on speed-dating details in the group chat because that article was a wild ride and I am here. for. it.

LANA: Thanks! The pickings out there, they are slim.

JAMES: **@Seth**, how are you holding up after the loss of Tinder?

SETH: It's been strangely freeing.

ROB: Oh shit, does that mean you've already defeated the final boss? Did you find someone with long-term potential?

SETH: It's a little early, but things are going well, and I can see this one going the distance.

LANA: You've been spending that much time with Jessica? With everything else that's happened?

TESSA: Maybe that's a conversation that should be had in private.

COREY: Yeah, we don't want to hear about long-term potential, we want to hear more about Harry and Sally, the cutest fish on the planet.

SETH: I just wrote a whole article about them.

LANA: I still say a fish is cheating.

SETH: It's not my fault you weren't specific.

As a writer, you should know how important words are, and yours were ambiguous.

LANA: Maybe it has nothing to do with my words and everything to do with you looking for the easy way out. You've done it before.

SETH: Easy way out? Is that some kind of joke?

LANA: Come on, Seth, you've always gotten everything you wanted in life. You're the golden boy.

SETH: That's rich coming from you. I've never had anything handed to me.

LANA: Wow, you're really going to throw my mother in my face right now?

JAMES: Whoa. Guys.

SETH: I would never do that.

And I can't believe you would even think I would.

COREY: In the words of **@James**, I think it's time to get a room.

21

So imagine my surprise and shock and terror when I came home one day to find my houseplant, whom I have been lovingly caring for, completely wilted and dead. Luckily, after a little research, I realized this particular species just needs lots of love and attention. Like more attention than any girlfriend I've ever had. God help me.

—Seth Carson, "It's a Jungle Out There"

Seth: Please tell me you were not serious about that.

Lana: What am I supposed to think when you basically call me a spoiled brat?

Seth: That's not what I said and definitely not what I meant.

Seth: YOU accused me of taking the easy way out.

Seth: You have no idea what the past twelve years of my life have looked like, and the work I've done.

Lana: . . .

Lana: . . .

Lana: It does sometimes feel like you've always gotten everything I wanted.

Seth: It does sometimes feel like you assume that because I have supportive parents, my life must be a walk in the park.

Seth: And it hasn't been.

Lana: You're right. I'm sorry.

Lana: You've worked really hard to get where you are. I know that. And I really admire that about you.

Seth: Thank you.

Seth: I know how hard you work too. And I know you'd never rely on anyone to take care of you. Especially not your mom.

Lana: Do you really think that?

Seth: Of course I do.

Seth: It will be a really good day when you can finally see yourself the way the rest of us see you.

Seth: And a *really* good day when you stop trying to pick a fight with me every five minutes.

Lana: Well, that's never going to happen.

Seth: Good night, Parker.

Lana: Good night, Seth.

"I CANNOT BELIEVE that poor girl is still interested in going out with him after everything that went down at Cabo Cantina." May skims through Seth's booty-call article, which, even though it focuses on deleting his dating apps, still mentions going on a second date. May somehow manages to roll her eyes and read at the same time.

I pull down the brim of my Dodgers hat, shielding my

eyes from the sun and her words. We're sitting in my backyard enjoying the summer warmth. Or at least, I was enjoying it until the topic of Seth came up. Again. As it seems to do in every conversation these days.

May still can't believe I sort of kissed him on speed-dating night. And she refuses to believe that I have no feelings about the situation.

She's right to be suspicious of that part. Of course I have feelings about the situation, how could I not? They're just feelings that change practically from minute to minute, depending on who I'm with and what I'm thinking about at any given moment.

May lets us sit in the quiet for several seconds, reveling in the gentle sound of birds chirping and the rustle of the palm leaves as the breeze picks up.

"You never really told me about the breakup, you know."

I feign ignorance. "With Evan? I mean, you were practically there when it happened, I didn't think I needed to give the details."

"You know that's not who I meant."

I pull at the loose strings at the hem of my cutoff jean shorts. "It was a long time ago."

"Feels like it's pretty relevant to the present situation, my friend."

It's been hard not talking about my messy, muddy feelings with May, and if I have any hope of even articulating what's currently going on in my mind, she probably should know how the whole thing started. And while I don't wish to relive the details, maybe talking it out will bring some much-needed clarity. Letting my head fall back against the cushion of the chaise longue, I take a deep breath. "Seth and I started dating toward the beginning of high school. We'd known each other practically our entire lives, had been friends since we were kids, but I never thought he would like me like that. He was always the popular kid, so smart and hot and cool."

May scoffs. "As are you."

I smile at her immediate defense. "One night, we were hanging out and watching movies in his basement, and he just turned and kissed me and I . . . I don't even know how to explain it really. It was this strange combination of excitement and butterflies and exhilaration, and at the same time, just this overwhelming feeling of peace."

"Shit. My first kiss was a wet slop in the smelly gym at a junior high dance."

This gets a laugh out of me. "Kissing Seth was perfect. It was everything."

"Did you do it on his basement couch?"

"We were fourteen! No, we did not do it on his basement couch." I give her a playful shove. "Not that night anyway."

"Okay, I like where this is going." May shifts in her seat, angling her body in my direction, prepped for more salacious details.

"From that moment on, our lives were intertwined. I had already spent a lot of time at his house, but once we officially started dating, his parents practically adopted me. His mom knew mine wasn't around much, so she always included me in family gatherings, and trips, and holidays. It was like every part of my life was somehow connected to his." Looking back with an adult's perspective, I can see how that maybe wasn't the healthiest, especially considering Seth was my first-ever boyfriend. But at the time, I felt safe and accepted and wanted, and I hadn't ever really felt that before.

"Ah." May brushes a stray strand of hair from her eyes, squinting a little as she studies me. "That explains a lot."

"Yeah." The pattern is easy to see now. I latched on to Seth not just because of who he was, but because of what his family meant to me and the sense of security they brought.

"So what happened?" she prods after giving me a minute of quiet.

I sigh, not looking forward to this part of the story. "By the time we got to senior year, it was just expected that we would be together forever. I know most people scoff at high school sweethearts, but no one ever doubted us. Even my mom loved Seth, although the feeling wasn't mutual. We both wanted to be writers and we both wanted to move to LA, so we applied to all the same schools and made plans for our future."

"And he didn't get in?"

I shake my head, fingers still threading through the loose strings of my shorts. "No, he did. We both got into USC, but he didn't get the financial aid he was expecting. His parents couldn't afford to send him. So I did something I had never done before and haven't done since."

May raises her eyebrows.

"I asked my mom for money. I asked for her to pay for Seth to go to college."

She lets out a low whistle. "Damn, girl. You really loved him."

I give her a nod of confirmation as my lips turn down.

"And your mom said no?"

"She said yes. Of course she did. Education is her whole life's mission." I wait for May to interject, but she's too shocked to speak. "We made our plans to come to California together. It was going to be perfect. We'd live in the dorms for a year, then get an apartment off campus. He probably would've proposed at graduation and we'd have been married by twenty-three."

"Given our very single thirty-year-old asses sitting here, that obviously didn't happen."

I shake my head. "I moved out here a week early, mostly to avoid having to do the sappy goodbye thing with my mom. Seth would've come with me, but he had to stay for his sister's birthday. The night before he was meant to fly out, he called me and told me he couldn't do it. He couldn't take the money from my mom." The memory of total abandonment washes over me along with the words. "Even though my mom really liked Seth, he always harbored a lot of resentment toward her. He was there, and his parents were there, all the times she couldn't be bothered to show up. Seth couldn't stand the idea of being indebted to her, and rather than swallow his pride and accept her scholarship, he decided not to go away to school. And he waited until I'd already left to tell me."

"Shit, LP. That's awful."

"I would've stayed," I say quietly. "I would've stayed at home with him, gone to a state school, continued to live with my mom, even if by that point I was already pretty much living on my own."

"But he didn't want that for you." May already knows him better than she thinks.

Shaking my head, I purse my lips tightly. "He told me to stay in LA, that we'd find a way to make it work long-distance. He told me our love for each other was strong enough and real enough to overcome anything. A few thousand miles was nothing in the face of our feelings."

"That's quite poetic for a high school boy."

"He always had a way with words."

"When we first met, you never mentioned having a boyfriend."

I turn away from her, facing directly into the overhead sun so I have an excuse to close my eyes. "I was mad at him for not coming, for turning down our perfect future, for putting his own pride before me. But we still talked and texted constantly. And I started to think he was right; we could make it work. We spoke so often I hardly had a chance to miss him."

May makes a face, and I know what she's thinking. Who wants to move across the country to go to college only to spend the whole time talking on the phone to your long-distance high school boyfriend?

Apparently, Seth felt the same way.

"By the end of the third week, he called me and told me it wasn't working. That he had thought he could handle the distance, but it was just too hard." I swallow the thick lump of tears that's lodged itself in my throat. "He didn't even make it a month before throwing away four years together. And he never would've had to if he could've just gotten over himself and taken what was offered to him."

"I had no idea. I mean, you definitely were quiet those first couple of weeks, but I just assumed you were shy. And then, what was it? A month or two later you were dating Joey and it got serious so fast."

I grimace a little, thinking about my college boyfriend. We didn't have much in common, but he asked me out after we were paired up on an English lit project and he seemed nice enough. When I learned he had a huge family who lived nearby, I kept agreeing to date after date. Before I knew what had happened, we were exclusive and it didn't really matter if I didn't love him like I loved Seth because he was a companion, and he came along with a whole family for me to hang on to.

May clears her throat, drawing my attention to her face, which is fixed in an *I'm going to say something you're not going to like* expression.

"What?" I ask with trepidation.

"I know that the way he went about it led to heartbreak and tears and some serious relationship issues for you down the line, but did you ever stop to think about the deeper reasons why Seth broke up with you?"

I give a half-hearted shrug. "I mean, he told me why. He couldn't handle the distance. I didn't really get much more info than that, and I never really wanted to."

She clasps her hands together under her chin. "Did you

never consider that maybe he thought he was doing the right thing by ending it? That you needed a push to go out on your own and live your best college life without feeling as if you were tied down to someone thousands of miles away?"

"Are you telling me you think Seth dumped me for my own good?" The moment I say the words, I can't help but consider their possibility. It's exactly the kind of thing Seth would do. But it doesn't soothe away any leftover stings. For starters, it's too late for that. It's also a decision I should've been able to make for myself.

May shrugs. "I don't know him like you do, but I'm just saying it's possible. Yeah?"

"I guess anything is possible."

"And if he didn't really want to break up with you, but he did it for your own good, and then years down the road decided to move to the same city as you and find a job connected to the website you write for, then maybe there *are* some lingering feelings there?" Her voice rises to an almost hopeful pitch, which is maybe the most disconcerting revelation of the day, that May would be hopeful about lingering romantic feelings.

This time my laughter is forced and fake. "I don't think we need to go that far. Besides, he had the perfect opportunity to act on those 'lingering feelings' two years ago and he most definitely did not partake."

May knows enough to not go down that path, but her stern look does plenty to convey her thoughts on the subject of the reunion. "And what about your feelings, LP?"

"A part of me will always love Seth."

"Then wouldn't it be fair to assume a part of him will always love you?"

I can't even consider the idea. "He's dating someone else now. And regardless, he rejected me—twice. Besides, weren't you the one telling me to enjoy being single?"

She gives me another one of her patented looks. This time it says I'm completely full of shit. "Would I ever stand in the path of true love?"

"Yes. Absolutely."

She looks around for something to throw at me but, coming up empty, punches me in the shoulder instead. "You are my best friend and I want you to be happy, bitch."

I grab her punching arm and pull her into an awkward hug. "Same. And I am happy, promise."

It's not a total lie, though certainly not a complete truth.

22

In the words of the great Cher Horowitz, "'Tis a far, far better thing doing stuff for other people."

—Lana Parker, "Feeling Down? Share the Love!"

I'M NOT REALLY SURE WHAT TO EXPECT WHEN I CHECK in at the small arts center in Eagle Rock, reporting for my volunteering duty. All I was told is I'd be talking with some teenagers about writing, that I should dress comfortably, and to bring a pen and some paper. I'd be lying if I said I was 100 percent excited for this. In theory, I'm looking forward to volunteering, but I've never done anything like this before and my nerves are roiling. Public speaking has never been my forte; I much prefer the chance to write down my thoughts and process them before putting them out into the world. And something tells me a group of teenagers isn't going to be the easiest of audiences to open up to.

I adjust my Ripped Bodice bookstore tote bag on my shoulder and give the woman at the front desk my name and a smile. She informs me my "counterpart" is already inside and directs me to a small classroom down the hallway.

Seth is indeed already waiting inside, wearing fitted jeans and one of the button-down shirts we bought during our shopping trip. This being LA, it's warm outside and only fractionally cooler inside the old building, so he's rolled up the sleeves. Of course he has. He's talking with a man who looks to be in his midfifties, tall and tan with salt-and-pepper hair.

Seth meets my eyes when I enter the room, giving me a timid smile. "Here she is."

I wave awkwardly, as if stepping foot inside a classroom automatically sends me back to my teenage days, when I was always shy and a little weird. "Hi."

The man comes over to shake my hand, introducing himself as Frank. "I was just telling Seth about the plan for today. We have a group of teens coming in who have all expressed interest in pursuing some sort of writing-related career field. We asked them to bring a sample of their work, and the two of you can decide how you want to utilize your time together."

"Wow. Okay. Great." I don't know why the thought of being in charge of a room full of teenagers is the scariest thing I have maybe ever faced, but I was hoping for something with a bit more structure. Someone to tell me exactly what to do and what to say.

Seth jumps in, noticing my discomfort. "I was thinking we could split them into smaller groups, have them share their work, and give one another feedback. And then maybe we can do a Q and A at the end if we have time."

I let out a small sigh of relief. "Yes, that sounds great."

Frank gives us both a wide smile. "Perfect. I'll let you

two get settled, the kids should be arriving in a few minutes. Let me know if you need anything." And with a salute, he heads out of the room, closing the door behind him.

And then it's just me and Seth. Alone in a classroom. Oof, the flashbacks. The press of Seth's arm against mine as he leaned across our shared table in science. Holding my hand across the aisle when we had a movie day in history and our teacher wasn't paying attention. Stolen kisses as we edited the school newspaper, staying hours after class ended with just our work and laughter and junk food from the vending machines to keep us company.

A wave of warmth cascades over me, washing away any lingering tension or anger, leaving behind only the fuzzy nostalgia of what was. And maybe a hint of what could be.

Seth clears his throat. "So we're almost to the end of this thing."

I blink away the memories and I wonder if he notices the flush in my cheeks. I'm instantly curious about whether he had the same kind of flashbacks, if he's ever thought about the two of us and any kind of future. I set my bag down on one of the student desks, riffling through it so I have an excuse not to look at him. "Just a few more tasks left." I hope he notices how I conveniently don't address my plans for what's remaining, since even I've been avoiding them. Mainly the one-night stand, which has been looming over my head since day one and is my own damn fault for insisting it be on the list. "How's Jessica?"

"Jessica?"

I look up just enough to catch a confused frown on his face.

Which he quickly schools into something more smirk, less frown. "Oh yeah, she's great. We're great."

"Great."

Seth perches on the edge of the teacher's table at the front of the room, his pen tapping against his thigh.

I look everywhere but at him, inspecting the linoleum floor and the various posters on the walls with such intensity they might as well be shirtless photos of Sebastian Stan. I can't help but replay my conversation with May, can't stop myself from wondering if she's right about Seth's motives for breaking up with me all those years ago. But even if she is right, does it matter at this point? Because yes, Seth is here. Yes, there might be lingering feelings. And yes, there's definitely still attraction. But he's with someone else, and I, for once in my life, am figuring out what it means to be on my own. Figuring out who I am without a man, and I'm actually liking what I'm finding.

I force myself to look at Seth. Not just at the physical attractiveness on the outside but at everything underneath. My ex-boyfriend, my first love. The things he was, but also the things he is now. A colleague, and a friend.

His eyes meet mine and he holds my gaze, almost as if he can see everything happening inside my brain. And maybe he can. Maybe he still knows me well enough so that we don't need words.

The door to the classroom opens and Seth and I both swivel our heads toward the sound, and our first student.

"Is this the room for the writing class?" a young girl asks with more than a hint of trepidation.

I give her a warm smile, or at least I hope it's warm, given the total black hole of my feelings at the moment. "You're in the right spot, come on in."

Over the next ten minutes, a group of fifteen teens trickles into the room. Some of them clearly already know each other, and the room fills with the sounds of laughter and gossip, and that general lightheartedness and excitement that comes from being a young person experiencing something new.

Once they've all found their seats, Seth looks at me for a nod of confirmation. He's always been better at public speaking than I am, so I let him take the lead.

"Hi, everyone, welcome. My name is Seth Carson, and this is Lana Parker. I'll let Parker introduce herself, but we're both writers, and we're really excited to be here today." He gestures for me to take the metaphorical stage.

I join Seth at the front of the room and give another one of my awkward waves. "Hi. Like Seth said, I'm Lana Parker, though most people just go with Lana."

"She always used to hate it when I called her Parker," he interjects like we're some slapstick comedy duo.

I roll my eyes but pair it with a smile. "I write for *Always Take Fountain*, which is a lifestyle website dedicated to all things LA culture. I grew up in Connecticut, and I've loved writing ever since I was a kid. In high school, I wrote for the school newspaper and had a couple pieces published in the literary magazine."

"She was the editor of the lit mag, and coeditor in chief of the newspaper, actually." Seth nudges me with his elbow.

"Though really I did most of the work, since this guy

was my partner." I don't mean to fall prey to Seth's schtick, but the habit comes back too easily. "Anyway. I moved out to LA for college and graduated from USC with a degree in journalism. I interned at *ATF* my junior and senior years, and luckily they hired me for a full-time job when I graduated. I've been a staff writer with them for the past eight years."

"It's a testament to how good of a writer she is, because she's pretty much the only person I know who found a full-time position that quickly and has been able to keep it." Seth smiles at me, nothing but pride in his eyes.

I think I actually blush from his praise.

"My career hasn't been as straightforward." Seth leans back against the teacher table, his arms crossed over his chest. "I went to community college after high school because, while I got into a number of renowned schools, I couldn't afford any of them." His eyes dart to mine for a half a second but give away nothing. "So, I stayed home, got a job, ultimately went to state school, and as soon as I graduated, I hit the road."

I listen intently, first noting how he glosses over the money he was offered and turned down, and second, realizing I don't really know much about Seth's life after I left home. Sure, I've read everything he's published, but he never really wrote personal pieces. Following his work mostly just allowed me to keep tabs on where he might have been living at any given time. It didn't give me a ton of hints as to what his life was actually like.

"I wanted to focus on more investigative pieces, so I found people who had interesting stories, and I explored those. I'd saved enough money by living at home and working through school that I was able to spend about six months on the road, meeting people, talking to people, writing their stories, before I really felt the pressure financially. Luckily, at the end of those six months, I was able to sell my first piece."

The group of teens is way more impressed by Seth's career trajectory than they are by mine. Not that it's a competition or anything. I'm a little bit in awe of him myself.

"It did well, and then I sold another, and another. Before I knew it, I had spent more than six years living on the road. Most of that time was in hotel rooms or short-term rentals, sometimes crashing with friends or colleagues if they were local." He grins, shifting on his feet a little. "I'm not going to lie, it was amazing. It was also awful. Living on the road is hard, not having a home base is hard. But I did some of my best work during those six years, and I don't regret any of it."

Our eyes meet once again and a shadow darkens the blue of his, like maybe there are *some* regrets somewhere in there. My chest squeezes and for a second, I can't seem to make my lungs function.

"Hold up, are you two dating or something?" a voice calls from the back of the room.

The rest of the group titters, and the laughter brings me back to my senses.

Seth looks to me to answer the question, the jerk. My cheeks heat and I'm sure they've turned a bubblegum pink. "Um, no, we're not dating. We did, in high school, but we haven't been together for a long time now."

Seth punches my arm like he's my older brother. "Now we just work together. And we're friends." His voice rises a bit on the word *friends*, like it's a question.

I nod. "Yes. We're friends."

"Uh-huh." The sarcastic muttered response comes from somewhere among the crowd.

"Anyway," I barrel on, determined to not let a bunch of teenagers make my life any more awkward than it already is. "For today's program, we were thinking we'd split into two groups. You could all then share what you wrote and do a workshop so that everyone can give some feedback and get some feedback. That sound good?"

I quickly realize my mistake when I'm met with fifteen uncertain stares.

Seth stands, shoving his hands in his pockets. "Look, sharing your work with other people is hard. We get that. But we're all going to take the plunge together, and this is a safe space. No judgment, no harsh critiques, no red pens circling your typos."

This earns him a small laugh and seems to relax the room just a tad.

"Parker, why don't you take the front of the room and I'll take the back. You're free to come to whichever group you feel most comfortable in. At the end, we'll all come back together for final thoughts." Seth claps his hands together in dismissal and heads toward the back of the room.

I find an empty desk and try not to freak out, low-key anxious that none of the kids will choose my group since Seth is obviously more personable—and much cooler—than

I am. Adjusting the desk so I can separate myself from the other group, I avoid looking at the room at large for as long as I can. When I finally do look up, I'm met with eight anxious faces. I breathe out a sigh of relief and gesture to the other desks around me. "Let's make a circle."

The teens comply, shifting around until we can all sit and face each other. It immediately brings back memories of every writing class I've ever taken, and I remember how nervous I always was to read my work in front of other people. It was maybe my least favorite part of writing classes but sometimes the most helpful.

I settle into my desk, noticing that Seth's own seat ended up positioned just behind me and a little to my left. If I shift in my chair I can see his profile, but his attention is solely focused on his students, and I turn mine to my own.

"Okay, I know you guys are going to hate me for this, but before we get started, let's go around the circle and introduce ourselves and tell everyone what you're reading right now." I clasp my hands in front of me on the desk. "I'll start. You already know I'm Lana Parker, and right now I'm rereading *Get a Life, Chloe Brown* by Talia Hibbert because it's one of my absolute favorites."

We go around the circle and I meet Izzy, Madison, Maddy, Addison, Mackenzie, Sophie, Finley, and Dylan. And I pray I can remember their names and keep them all straight. Once the intros are done, they all look at me expectantly.

"Okay, now let's get to reading." I paste on a self-deprecating smile when I hear a few groans. "It was always my least favorite thing to do too, after get-to-know-you icebreakers of course."

This earns me a couple of chuckles, probably out of pity.

"But I will say, reading your work out loud is a really helpful trick. It lets you know what parts of your writing are flowing well, where your voice is strong, where your descriptions are hitting. It's also the best way to catch typos and awkward sentences. Even though it feels mortifying, it's a good habit to get into." I look around the circle and see varying degrees of terror. "Does anyone want to be brave and volunteer?"

There's that expected moment of absolute silence, but then one of them, Izzy, the girl who arrived first, tentatively raises her hand.

I flash her an encouraging smile. "Awesome. Why don't you tell us what it is you brought, and then whenever you're ready, read it out loud to us."

She sucks in a big breath. "Okay. This is my college admissions personal essay. And I'm really hoping to get a scholarship, so I need it to be good."

I pick up my pen so I can make sure to jot down any feedback I have for her essay. But my hand freezes once she starts reading; I'm immediately drawn into her words. When she finishes, the group bursts into light applause. We go around telling Izzy all the things we loved about her essay. There's a little hesitation when I ask them to share anything they think Izzy can improve, but once they break the ice, the feedback flows, their ideas bouncing off one another like Ping-Pong balls. Izzy writes down all their suggestions, and by the time we wrap up, she's grinning from ear to ear and the next person volunteers without hesitation.

After the fourth reader has shared, I sit back in my seat,

watching as they all jump in with positive comments and constructive criticism without my having to prompt them. Obviously the majority of the credit here goes to the teens themselves, but I can't help but feel a small flicker of pride for my tiny role in the equation. It feels good.

I catch Seth's gaze in my peripheral vision, turning my head to watch him work with the teens in his group. His eyes briefly glance away from the student who's reading, meeting mine with a warm smile. A smile that perfectly encapsulates the same amount of pride and excitement I'm feeling in this moment. And oh, my heart. It feels like it just took a beating from Duke.

I force myself to look away, but the smile on my own face lingers. For the rest of the session, my eyes move of their own accord, finding his, and we exchange smiles. I watch him as he instructs his group with patience and enthusiasm, see how the cocky and charming first boy I ever loved has grown into a man who is kind and thoughtful and generous with both his time and his praise. My stomach starts fluttering and never seems to stop.

Our time with the teens comes to an end long before I want it to. I could sit and listen to their exchanging ideas for hours, and I don't want this closeness, both physically and emotionally, with Seth to end. I collect email addresses from my entire group and promise to be in touch to set up another workshop day soon. I take hugs and high fives from those who feel comfortable giving them and collect waves and smiles from the rest. We snap one big group photo, Seth and me in the middle surrounded by our smiling students.

I'm sure Natasha will wring every drop of publicity out of it that she can, but I dismiss the thought as quickly as it comes, not willing to let her ruin this day. The last student leaves and the door closes with an echo in the suddenly silent room.

Seth and I put the desks in order, working quickly and quietly, until we're back at the front of the room, facing each other, with nothing and everything left to say.

I want to cry. I want to hug him. I want to punch him. I want to kiss him. I want to open my mouth and tell him every emotion that's roiled through me since I first saw him in the *ATF* office. But I can't even manage to part my lips, let alone form the words.

"You want to go get a drink?"

I nod. "Yes."

23

All relationships, whether they be good or bad, leave a mark on our souls.

—Lana Parker, "It's Okay to Still Think About Your Ex"

WE WALK TO A BAR ACROSS THE STREET, CLAIMING A high-top table in an isolated corner and ordering a round of beers. Neither of us says anything until our drinks are delivered. Tension wraps around us, and it's heavier than it's been since the night in the parking lot. And this time it isn't angry or even sad. It's tingling and warm and dangerous.

"Cheers." Seth holds up his pint glass, his eyes meeting mine over the rim.

I clink mine against his. "Cheers." I pull my eyes from his the second we've finished our first sip. His gaze is dark and I'm scared to even question the emotions I'm seeing.

He studies me for a long second. "I'm really glad we did this together."

I take another quick drink, hoping the cold beer will

help cool the flush in my cheeks. "Yeah. Me too." Shifting a little on my chair, I attempt to put some more space between us at this tiny table. "I've never done anything like that before, but I'd love to do it again."

He crosses his arms, leaning on the table, closing the short distance I just put between us. "I haven't been able to do any workshops in a few years given all the traveling, but I tried to do some when I was still living at home. I feel like I learn as much as they do."

"For sure." I think about how fearless some of the kids were today, sharing their stories, possibly for the first time ever, and being totally open to hearing the feedback from their peers. Fearless and open: two things I'm trying hard to be in my life. Though I don't feel much of either at the moment. "You know, for a minute there earlier, I kind of understood my mother."

Seth raises his eyebrows, taking a long pull from his beer. "Really?"

"Yeah. I mean, I know the point of volunteering is to help others, but I never realized how gratifying it'd feel on my end. And this was just one small workshop; I can only imagine what it must be like to build a whole freaking school." I shrug, sitting back in my seat. The fact that I'm happy to shift the conversation to the topic of my mom shows me just how much I want to avoid thinking about Seth, about us. "Kind of makes sense why she's made it her life's work." It's the nicest thought I've had about her in a very long time.

"I don't think anyone would ever argue that your mom is a bad person, Parker. She does a lot of good for a lot of people." He hesitates, like we might not yet be back at the place where he can say whatever he wants to me.

"But . . . ?"

"But she was a shitty mom. And you deserved better."

"Your family showed me better." My voice is quiet, and I wonder if he can detect the trace of pain in my words.

He's silent for a long moment, then he reaches over and takes my hand. "We should've done better—no, I should've done better—with keeping in touch. Just because we didn't work out didn't mean you had to lose your relationship with them."

His words are kind and generous, but it's the skin-to-skin contact that flips my heart to stuttering. Suddenly all I can feel is my hand in his. All I can see is the fathomless blue of his eyes. "You didn't want to be with me anymore, Seth. I wouldn't have wanted to make things weird with your family. I know how much they mean to you."

His fingers tighten around mine. "Lana. It's not that I didn't want to be with you." His free hand rubs at his forehead, and I can hear the exasperation in his voice. "God, I really thought you would've known. I see now that it's on me for not being clearer back then. I should've made sure you really understood what I wanted and why. I never wanted you out of my life for good."

And I guess we're doing this now, whether I want to or not. Whether or not I'm ready to face the past. Whether or not I can admit just how very much my feelings for Seth are a part of my present.

"Seth, you called me on a random school night and

point-blank told me long-distance wasn't working and you didn't think you could do it. And that's after you completely torpedoed all our plans." Part of me is dying for our whole breakup to have been some kind of misunderstanding, while another part of me is annoyed he's taking a red pen to the pages of our history.

"Because I didn't want to hold you back. I wanted college to be everything you ever dreamed it would be. I didn't want you missing out on experiences or activities because you had to rush back to the dorm to call your loser high school boyfriend." His thumb traces the line of my knuckles and every nerve in my body is numb except for those he strokes, which have sparked like a firework in a California summer.

I take in a sharp breath. "You have never been a loser, Seth Carson. And please don't forget that you could've been right there with me. We could've had those experiences together."

"I know. And I'm sorry my pride got in the way of what could have been. I don't really have a good excuse, other than I was an eighteen-year-old boy and foolish and should have been more up front about not wanting the money from the start."

"Do you know how hard it was for me to ask her for that?" I force myself to look him straight in the eyes, so he can really see the truth I've held on to for all these years. "I asked my mom for money, Seth. You of all people should know how much it killed me to have to do that. But I did it for you. Because I'd do anything for you." I wipe away a tear that's just managed to squeeze through. "And you threw it all away."

He hands me a napkin and doesn't say anything for a minute. "There are a lot of things I'd change about how I handled the situation, but not taking the money isn't one of them. It would've created more problems than it solved, Parker. Sometimes—not often, but sometimes—I hated that you had the financial privilege I didn't, and being indebted to your mother only would've made it worse."

I tug a little on my hand, because it's basically the worst thing he could say in this moment, even though I know he's not wrong.

But he doesn't let me go. "I was an asshole in how I went about it. And I'm sorry, Parker. I've seen a lot over the course of the past few years. I didn't know how good I had it. How good I still have it."

"I would trade every penny she's ever given me for a family like yours."

"I know." He barrels on, voice low and bordering on rumbly, and I wonder how long he has been holding on to this. "I shouldn't have ever put you in that position. I'm sorry I took our relationship out of your hands. I was hoping to give you some space, and some freedom, and I always thought it would be just a temporary break." He flips my hand over, cradling it with his palm. "But then I saw that you started dating somebody new, not even two months after we had split up. I figured you had moved on." Hurt and heartbreak lace his words. He kisses the palm of my hand before setting it gently back on my side of the table.

I inhale a quick succession of short breaths, trying to steady myself. I don't know what's more disarming, his revelation or the press of his lips against my skin. I did break Seth's heart. Maybe not in the way he broke mine, but I hurt him all the same. Blinking back tears, I focus my attention on the wood grain of the table. "I had no idea you felt that way. I thought you were done with me."

"I never would have been done with you."

His words are carefully chosen. *I never would have been done with you*. Not *I've never been done with you*. He wouldn't have been done with me if I had given us some space, a little breathing room, some time to grow up. If I hadn't done what I did at the reunion, completely fucking up our possible second chance. If I hadn't allowed my pride and immaturity to get the better of me and turn this competition into an actual battle. But I didn't. And now he *is* done.

I don't know what the future holds for Seth and me. I don't know if I could ever see myself with him again, but I do know that his assertion that there isn't even a possibility stings more than I'd like to admit.

I lean all the way back in my seat, clasping my hands together in my lap, subtly trying to rub away the memory of his kiss, needing to put an end to this line of conversation. "If you don't win the competition and secure your spot at the *Chronicle*, what's your plan? Are you going to move back home?"

A half smile tugs on the corner of his lips, and I'm sure he catches the question as the deflection it is. "If I say yes, will you let me win?"

"I don't know." The honest answer flies out before I can stop it. I may not know much about the future, but I do know, suddenly and yet fervently, that I don't want him to leave LA.

His smile spreads across his face and it does something to my heart. Something that needs to stop.

"But I also really want to win." I spit the words out in a rush, before he can jump in. I want it to be clear to Seth—and to me—that I still plan on seeing this whole thing through. "I want that column. I've wanted off relationships and dating since nearly the minute I started at *ATF*, and Loki knows I'm not exactly qualified to be giving anyone romantic advice these days."

He drains the last of his beer. "So, full disclosure time, do you have plans for your remaining tasks? Since they're all ones I can't be there for."

He would never say as much, but I can't help but feel like there's one particular task he's interested in. But if he's going to dance around it, then so will I. "Not exactly. I still need to take a solo vacation. And I have to learn to be okay with being alone, which I'm planning on exploring last for obvious reasons, but at least I'm making some progress there." I take a long gulp of my own beer, holding the glass completely vertical to get every last drop. "And, of course, the one-night stand. What about you? What's left on your list?" I rush out the words before the mention of the one-night stand has a chance to register.

Seth's pupils expand just a tad, but he clears his throat and sits up straight. "Hmm, well, I have to make it to the end of the competition with no sex." He tugs a little on the collar of his shirt. "And I still need to do my last one too. Find someone to be happy with long-term."

I furrow my brow. "What about Jessica?"

"What about her?"

"Isn't she someone you could be happy with 'long-term'?" The words didn't sound sarcastic in my head, but they sure as hell do coming out of my mouth.

He presses his lips together in a straight line and I can tell he doesn't quite want to share what he's about to say. "She ended it after the third date, actually. Apparently, she only even went on date three because she felt bad for me and wanted to make sure I could complete the task."

"Ouch." I flag down the bartender and ask for the check. "Did she say why?"

He runs a hand through his hair. "Um, no. Just that she didn't think it was going to work."

It's definitely not the whole truth, but I decide to let it slide because I'm not a monster. I pay for our beers and we gather our stuff and head out.

The walk back to the arts center is short and quiet, both of us lost in our own private thoughts. Seth walks me over to my car and before I even know what's happening, he's wrapped me up in a giant hug.

I don't want it to feel as good as it does, but I can't stop myself from sinking into his embrace. His arms tighten around me and I press my cheek to his chest. He rests his chin on the top of my head and suddenly I'm seventeen again. All thoughts of a nonexistent future for us vaporize from my brain, as if the words *done with you* were never uttered. All it would take is a quick tilt up and our lips would meet, and I wouldn't cut it short this time. I wonder if he still tastes like spearmint. He smells like salt and sunshine and I fill my nose with it.

He cups the nape of my neck in his hand, and I pull back just the slightest bit, so our eyes can meet. His thumb traces my jaw, brushing over my bottom lip. I'm leaning in to close the final inch between us when the *Avengers* theme song blares out of my bag.

Seth's arms fall and he puts several steps between us, breaking whatever spell the embrace held us under.

"Sorry, that's May's ringtone," I mutter, digging through my bag to fish out my phone and let May know she has the worst timing ever. "Sorry," I say to Seth again, swiping to accept the call. "May? Is everything okay? If you're not dead, I'm going to kill you."

"Fuck yeah, better than okay. We're on the list for Warwick tomorrow night!" She's practically shouting in my ear.

Groaning out loud, I hold the phone away from my head to protect my hearing. "May, I don't know if I want to go to a club, like, ever. And this is definitely not an emergency."

"I didn't say it was an emergency. You're the one who picked up the phone." Her indignance is clear despite a fuzzy connection.

Granted, she's not wrong. She has no idea what she interrupted, but that doesn't mean I'm not annoyed as hell that she killed the moment. "Well. That doesn't change the fact that I don't want to go dancing."

"LP, Warwick is the perfect place to pick up a one-night stand. You're going. We're going. You know I'm right."

I groan again, because she *is* right. Even though I can

think of few things I want less right now than hooking up with a random guy, the fact of the matter is it's on my list, and I not only agreed to it, I insisted upon it. And we're quickly approaching the end date of this whole shebang. I might as well put the *bang* in *shebang*.

I sigh, loudly and dramatically so she knows how much I hate this plan. "Okay, fine. We'll go to Warwick and I will get my one-night stand."

It's only after I say it that I remember Seth is standing just a few feet away from me, listening to every word. Even though the night sky shadows most of his face, the emotion in his eyes is thick. Is he angry that I'm about to complete one of my toughest tasks, and maybe, potentially, push ahead in the rankings? Or is that hurt? Why would he be hurt?

New hurt, old hurt, so much hurt lies between us.

"May, I gotta go. I'll text you later." I hang up before she can say goodbye. "Sorry. I should've ignored that."

Seth shoves his hands in his pockets. "No big deal. Sounds like you have important plans."

"Well, I do need to complete the challenge."

"Yes, you do." His shoulders slump in defeat, like he doesn't realize that all I want from him is a little resistance.

"I did agree to have a one-night stand." I'm goading him, pushing him to see if he'll snap. I wait for him to say something, anything, to give me any sort of hint as to what's going on in his head. If he asked me not to go through with it, I honestly don't know what I'd say.

"That you did." He gives me a half wave and a stoic smile and crosses the parking lot to his car. "Good night, Parker."

It's getting harder and harder to watch him walk away

from me, but it seems to be our recurring pattern, and I'm more than ready to get off this carousel. I could never say I was excited about the prospect of picking up a man at a club for a little casual sex, but maybe it's exactly what I need. Maybe in order to get Seth out of my mind, I need to put another man in. My mind, that is.

24

I personally have never subscribed to the whole notion of getting over one person by getting under another, but if it works for you, have at it! (Use protection!)

—Lana Parker, "Tried and True Ways to Move On from a Breakup"

#NOBOYSALLOWED

LANA: Guys. I'm freaking out.

TESSA: What's going on?

LANA: I am attempting my one-night stand task tonight and I've literally never done anything like this before. I am freaking out.

COREY: You mentioned that ☺

TESSA: I'm afraid I'm not much help on this topic, but I totally understand why you're freaking out and it's okay to feel that way.

COREY: I on the other hand have plenty of experience with this topic so let me just say a couple things.

Use a condom!

Stay mostly sober!

Use this opportunity to practice asking for what you really want in the boudoir!

LANA: 1. Obviously.

2. Obviously.

3. Does anyone actually say boudoir anymore?

COREY: I'm serious! Having a one-night stand is the perfect time to practice asking for/instructing your partner on what works for you. It can be hard to do that when you really like the person, but if you know you'll never see them again, then you can say whatever you want without worrying about long-term embarrassment.

TESSA: Wow, that actually makes a lot of sense.

COREY: You should have a one-night stand too!

TESSA: No thanks.

LANA: Can I also say no thanks?

COREY: You put this task on the list, dude.

TESSA: You can do it!!!

COREY: Literally!

I CHECK THE time on my computer and do a little mental math. If I want to be ready for May's mandatory club outing, I need to leave the office ASAP. After a final read-through, I send my volunteering article to Natasha, pack up my stuff, and head for the door.

"Lana, can I see you quickly please?" Natasha's voice echoes across the room.

Rob gives me one of those *Ooooh, busted* faces. I roll my

eyes and punch his arm as I make my way over to Natasha's office.

She ushers me in and closes the door behind me, practically pushing me into a chair across from her desk.

"I don't want to be a pain, but I do need to be heading out soon. I have plans tonight." I hold my bag on my lap, wanting to keep up the appearance of someone who needs to jet sooner rather than later.

"Big night tonight?" She raises her eyebrows suggestively.

I probably would've never noticed before, but after my conversations with Dr. Lawson, it does seem a bit weird for my boss to be giving me waggling eyebrows. "Um, just going out with a friend."

She clasps her hands together under her chin. "Is tonight the night you complete your one-night stand?"

I shift a little in my seat, pulling down on the skirt of my cotton sundress. "Not sure, actually."

"Well, just in case it is, I'll make this quick so you can get to it."

My stomach starts to squirm a little bit as this conversation grows more and more uncomfortable. At least for me. Natasha doesn't seem to be suffering the same qualms.

"So, here's the long and short of it. This whole series is doing everything we needed it to do. We're bringing in new followers and lots of clicks, people are spending longer on the website, and we've seen a huge growth in ad revenue in just the past few weeks, exactly the impression I wanted to make on the new boss." Natasha lets her clasped hands drop to her desk.

"But . . . ?"

"But if we really want to drive this home, make the biggest splash possible, not to mention really get your name out there, I need something more salacious than volunteering at an arts center." She turns her laptop toward me, the article I just emailed displayed on the screen.

"Natasha, the volunteering was your idea. And honestly, of all the things I've done during this whole experiment, it was probably the one that benefited me the most."

"And I love that for you, really, I do." She pouts her bright-red lips. "But I'm going to need your one-night stand article to be juicy. The kind of piece that goes viral. Sex sells, Lana, and since Seth is supposed to be abstaining, it's on you to deliver."

My cheeks heat and I have to look away from her penetrating stare. And not ever think the word *penetrating* in her presence ever again. "I mean, I plan to complete the challenge, as expected, but I don't know how much of my sex life I'm willing to put out onto the internet that never forgets. I was planning on focusing more on what the experience teaches me, not the details itself."

She studies me for an uncomfortably long minute. "You do want your own column, don't you? The freedom to write whatever you want? You've been after this for years and I always told you that eventually it would be your turn. Once you paid your dues."

It's the first time in eight years she's blatantly acknowledged how much she's been dangling a promotion in front of me. And I'm not sure where the resolve comes from—maybe from the image of Duke, nodding proudly when I land a punch, or from Izzy, who drank in my every word about what it's like to work as a writer. Or maybe it comes from me. Whatever the source, that resolve is there.

"I've already paid my dues, Natasha." My voice is soft but strong. "And writing one article about sex isn't going to change the work that I've done over the past eight years. And it's not going to make me any more deserving of a job you already know I can do."

For a second, she seems surprised by my resistance, but she recovers quickly, shrugging off my words. "It might affect how the readers vote."

"I'm okay with that." I push out of my chair. "Anything else?"

She doesn't even deign to give me a response, just nods me out of the office without a word.

I'm not going to pretend like that rebuke doesn't sting, because of course it does. I've thought of Natasha as a pseudo mother figure since the moment I met her. But she's not my mother. She's not even really my friend. She's my boss. And yes, she has done a lot for me over the years, but I have also given so much because I didn't want to disappoint her. Natasha gave, and Natasha probably took advantage. Both things can be true.

And if this is the reaction I get when I put up a little bit of a fight, well, I don't know that it bodes well for the future.

I YANK DOWN on the hem of the sparkly silver dress May strapped me into—mostly unwillingly—earlier this evening, but it doesn't keep the thin fabric from riding halfway up my thigh the second I take two more steps.

"Stop fidgeting." May pulls on my arm, tucking it into the crook of her elbow.

"This dress is way too short. And tight. And glittery." And she vetoed my *Feminist Bitch* necklace, which was really just rude.

"Tonight is not about being subtle. Or comfortable, for that matter."

We stroll down the sidewalk, bypassing the line of people waiting outside Warwick. May gives her name to the doorman and we're immediately whisked inside. Thank Thor for friends with PR connections, because had I been forced to stand in that line and wait, I would've 100 percent chickened out. After volunteering yesterday, I was resolute in my mission to find a hottie and bow-chicka-wow-wow, but right now, my resolve is wavering.

"We're meeting some of my work friends, but we don't have to hang out with them for long if we don't want to." May leads the way through the still-early and not-quite-throbbing crowds, putting a vast amount of space between me and the exit.

Warwick is one of the typical LA places I'd never go to if it weren't for May, and even under the influence of May, I still avoid it like I avoid dude-bros at Comic-Con. It's on the small side as far as LA clubs go, and while I can appreciate the overall vibe—imagine if Gatsby's interior designer took over a hipster warehouse—it's not really my scene. Loud music and expensive (though delicious) cocktails have always taken a backseat to a night at the movies. Or the theater. Or being home alone in bed with a good book.

So yeah. Take the venue, plus the task at hand, plus the lingering weirdness from my conversation the day before with Seth, and it's a recipe for a cranky Lana.

We find May's coworkers and she exchanges a bunch of air kisses with the lot of them. Luckily the volume of the music means I don't have to do more than smile and wave and accept a cocktail poured from the bottle service spread across the table.

"You only get one of these." May hands me my drink and a stern look. "If you're going to have a hookup tonight, it's going to be a fully consensual hookup."

Oh fuck. The reality hits me as I down my drink. I'm here to find a one-night stand. A one-night stand I will be totally sober for. Here I was last night thinking this whole experiment might be just what the doctor ordered to help me gain some clarity on my not-feelings for Seth. Instead, I already hate everything about this.

May loops her arm through mine again, pulling me away from the table and into the crowd. "Let's do a lap and find some top contenders."

She guides me around the room, pointing to a couple of different guys who could be potential targets, as if sleeping with someone for one night only has become some sort of mission impossible.

It should come as no surprise that none of the chosen few pique my interest. There's nothing wrong with any of the men—at least not that can be discerned in dim club lighting—but none of them give me even a hint of the tingles previously derived from a mere swipe of Seth's thumb over my knuckles.

After I mentally eliminate the fourth contender—who's engaged in some sort of fist-pumping dance—I tell May I need to use the restroom. She starts to walk with me, but I shoo her back in the direction of her workmates, suggesting she help herself to another cocktail and have some fun. Sensing I need a break, she blows me a kiss, warns me not to try to sneak out the bathroom window, and sends me on my way.

Once I locate the restroom, I lock myself in a stall, relishing the simple peace and quiet of the tiny cubicle of space. The room at large is miraculously empty, which is nice, but it also means I'm left without any *Let's go to the bathroom to talk about our dates* gossip to distract me.

I take out my phone, planning to scroll through Instagram for a few minutes before forcing myself back into the jungle of men in too-tight pants, determined to find, if not a suitor, then at least one who passes as suitable.

The latest post on the *ATF* account pops up in my feed as soon as I open the app. And it punches me in the gut.

Seth has his arm around some girl—and by "some girl" I mean a totally knockout-gorgeous woman—a wide smile on his face as she looks up at him adoringly. I don't know who this woman is, but it definitely isn't Jessica. The caption is basic—*Putting myself out there*—but a particular hashtag catches my eye.

#LongTermPotential

I suck in a breath. It was only yesterday when Seth himself was telling me he hadn't found anyone with potential. So either he was lying or he went out and found someone *real* quick.

And both of those options suck.

Before I can truly process the strange feelings twisting my gut, my phone beeps with a text.

Speak of the devil.

Seth: I know you can't really send evidence of your *activities* tonight, but maybe snap a selfie at some point so I know you're not at home in your pajamas watching *Mean Girls* for the millionth time.

The first genuine smile of the evening tugs on my lips. I'd much rather be at home in my pajamas, and he knows it. Because he knows me.

I open up my camera and check to make sure it's not super obvious I'm in a bathroom stall before snapping a selfie and sending it off. Then I watch as the three little typing dots appear and fade and appear and fade and appear and fade. Because of course Seth continues to be maddening, even over text.

Finally, my phone beeps.

Seth: Wow. You look gorgeous. Not quite watching-a-movie-in-pajamas gorgeous, but pretty close.

Well, what the fuck am I supposed to do with that?

More blasted bubbles, and then finally another message.

Seth: Be safe tonight, Parker.

Me: I will.

Me: Are you out on a date?

I send the message before I can think about all the reasons why I shouldn't.

Seth: No, I'm home. Why?

Me: Just saw the photo of you and your #LongTermPotential on IG.

Seth: Oh.

Seth: Well, good luck tonight.

Me: Thanks.

I stare at my screen for a solid three minutes, waiting to see if he has anything more to say to me, anything more than "Oh." But no messages come through. No blinking dots appear.

And my stomach turns.

Because I want him to say something. I want him to tell me the photo was just for show, that he doesn't actually have feelings for anyone else. I want him to tell me to fuck all those other guys—figuratively, not literally—and come spend the night with him. I want him to want me. I want him to want to be the one-night stand, just so we can have one more night together.

And in a flash, it comes to me: I don't know that he doesn't. At least, not until I ask. Sure, he may have found a woman who he might have long-term potential with, but maybe he's in need of this closure as much as I am.

I swipe over to my notes app and open my list of assignments from Seth, plus my one small amendment.

Have a one-night stand.

It never said with whom. This isn't a kiss-a-stranger situation. I can sleep with whomever I want, as long as it's only for one night.

The only path forward becomes ridiculously clear. For the chance at my dream job, I need to complete this task. I also need closure. And in order to be truly okay with being alone, I need to put Seth firmly in my past.

I take thirty seconds to wash my hands and check my appearance in the mirror before I push through the bathroom door and head straight for the exit. I wait until I'm in the back of my Lyft before I text May, telling her I'm heading out. She responds with an eye-roll emoji.

May: Be safe, you ballsack. This is not the end of this.

Me: Did you just call me a ballsack?

May: I was going to say pussy, but pussies are strong and beautiful. Ballsacks are weak and fragile. Like your commitment to getting laid!

Me: 😄

Me: Who said I'm not going to get laid?

May: Oh fuck. Please tell me you're not going where I think you're going.

Me: This is the perfect solution, May. I check off my task and I can finally close the door on Seth Carson.

May: Sounds more like you plan on opening a giant-ass can of worms, my friend.

Me: This is the only way I can stamp out the attraction between us. It's the last thing standing in the way of us being well and truly done.

May: I hope you know what you're doing.

Me: I do.

May: Okay. Good luck. Love you. Talk to you tomorrow.

Me: Love you too.

I tuck my phone away and keep my eyes locked on the driver's GPS, counting down the minutes until we arrive at Seth's, refusing to let May's concerns niggle at my mind. This is the best solution, the only solution, really. Seth and I have had all the talks, we've hashed out the past, the only thing left to do is put this lingering sexual tension to bed. Literally.

Crossing my fingers, I make a quick list of all the things I wish for tonight: Seth really is home. Seth is alone. Seth agrees to sleep with me. And somehow, some way, I wake up tomorrow ready to fully let go of Seth Carson.

25

I've always firmly believed that when you find "the one" you just know it, deep down in your bones.

—Seth Carson, "Am I Doing Dating Right?"

MY FINGERS KNOT THEMSELVES TOGETHER AFTER I knock on Seth's front door. I use the age-old "inhale for five, exhale for five" trick so I don't hyperventilate and pass out on his porch. That would not be hot.

The door swings open, and Seth's face registers confusion that immediately turns to concern. "Parker?"

It should be simple to confirm, yes, that's me, that is my name, but I seem to have lost all power of speech.

He's wearing gray sweatpants.

He's wearing only gray sweatpants.

And they're slung low on his hips, highlighting that blasted V and the trail of dark hair that leads down to the waistband of said sweatpants.

Seth pushes opens his door and gestures for me to come in. "Are you okay? Did something happen? Did someone hurt you?" His eyes search my face as if it can provide the answers my mouth seems unable to form.

Finally, I manage to shake my head. Pulling my eyes from his abs and directing them to the floor, where they won't be distracted, I clear my throat. "No, nothing happened. I'm fine."

His bare feet move into my line of vision. "If you're fine, what are you doing here?"

It should be another simple question to answer. *I want to fuck you.* Surely this is a thing most guys are happy to hear, right? Yet I can't seem to manage to spit out those five little words.

Seth's fingers find my chin, raising it so I have to make eye contact. "Parker. Why are you here?" His voice is commanding yet laced with concern.

I open my mouth and decide to go for the long-winded approach. "Well, I was at the club with May and things were going okay. We got in and got some drinks, but then when we started looking around for potential hookups I just couldn't seem to find anyone I was interested in so I hid in the bathroom for a bit and I saw that you texted and then I got to thinking that my list doesn't actually have any requirements about who I sleep with and so I figured rather than risk going home with some stranger, I'd much rather come here, because if I have to have a one-night stand with someone, well, why not you?" I rush out the last few words and then promptly clamp my teeth down on my lower lip so I don't spew anything else out and make it even worse.

Seth takes a tiny step back, his expression unreadable.

"You came here to sleep with me? You want me to be the one-night stand?"

I nod, not trusting myself not to release more word vomit.

He runs a hand through his hair, and I'm pretty sure if I'd had the foresight to record this moment—Seth standing here in front of me with nothing but gray sweatpants on, hand ruffling his gorgeous dark hair, biceps flexing—I'd never need to watch porn ever again.

"Are you sure that's a good idea?" he finally asks, somehow managing to keep all emotion out of his voice.

And, not gonna lie, this is not the enthusiastic response I was hoping for. He doesn't have to sound so indifferent about it.

I take my own small step away from him. "Not if you don't want to, of course. And no pressure, obviously, if you're not into it. If you're not interested. If you don't want me like that. Anymore. It's totally fine. I can just . . . go. I should probably just go." I spin on my heel to turn toward the front door, but his hand catches my elbow before I can take a step.

"I didn't say I wasn't interested." He gives me a gentle tug and any space left between us disappears. "I just want to make sure this is something you really want. Something you've thought about."

I bite back a laugh. Um, yeah, I've thought about it.

"I have. And I want it to be you. I need it to be you." I dig my teeth into my lip since I seem to have managed a coherent and succinct statement for the first time since I arrived and I don't want to ruin it.

"One night only?" His blue eyes are absolutely blazing, searing into mine.

I nod, trying not to be offended by his insinuation that one night won't be enough for me, that I won't be able to control my feelings after a night of passionate sex with Seth Carson. Because I totally will.

"I have one condition." He wraps one arm around my waist, pressing his hand flat against the small of my back, and any hint of offense slips away with the heat of his palm. "I get you for the whole night." He leans in closer. "Agreed?"

I nod again, every one of my senses completely filled with him. His touch burns my skin and I can't catch my breath.

Seth dips his head, sucking my lower lip free from my teeth. He traces the tip of his tongue over the worried skin and I gasp into his mouth. He takes advantage of the opening, and all of a sudden we're kissing. Really kissing. And oh god. I almost forgot the head-spinning sensation of kissing Seth Carson. His hand tightens on my back, pulling me into him, while the other hand cups the side of my neck, his fingers threading into my hair, his thumb grazing the line of my jaw. My hands travel from the bare skin of his chest up and around his shoulders, tightening around his neck, using the support to pull myself even closer into him because suddenly being pressed this close together isn't nearly close enough.

The thin fabric of May's dress, which I cursed earlier, allows me to feel every inch of him. His body is all hard planes and heat and I want to kiss every inch of it.

He starts to walk me backward, heading I don't know

where. I don't care where we go as long as he continues to kiss me as if it's the only way we can breathe. His lips switch effortlessly from teasing and light and sweet to plundering and urgent and desperate.

My back hits a wall and I use the leverage to tug on his hips. He finally breaks the kiss with a groan as his hard length thrusts against my belly. But I'm not done kissing him yet, pulling him back to me while my fingers dance along the cut ridges of his abs, tracing along the waistband of his pants.

"Parker," he growls, his lips moving from my mouth to the edge of my jaw. His hand travels up from my lower back to skim my exposed cleavage.

I whimper a little and his eyes meet mine, his pupils so wide they almost obscure the clear blue.

"You still want this?" He pauses his movements, his hand cupping my breast.

"Hell yes." I take his hand, shoving aside the silver sparkly fabric of my dress and placing it directly on my skin.

His fingers scarcely brush my nipple before he pulls them away. "Turn around."

I hesitate for less than half a second before I obey, spinning to face away from him. My hands rest gently on the wall in front of me, my head turned slightly to the side because I don't know if I'm physically capable of taking my eyes off him.

He sweeps my long, loose waves over my shoulder, his fingers finding the zipper of my dress. I hold my breath as he lowers it at a maddeningly slow rate. When I feel his lips on my skin, following the path of the zipper down my spine, I let out a little gasp. He finally reaches the small of my back and his hands return to the straps of the dress, guiding them down my arms. I shimmy out of the dress, revealing just a lacy pair of black panties underneath.

He sucks in a breath and I ache for his hands to return to my heated skin. When they do a second later, he pulls me back into his embrace; his hardness nestles in the curve of my ass while he cups my breasts in his hands.

"Seth . . ." I'm practically panting already, the feel and the smell and the taste of him so overwhelming I can barely see straight, let alone think.

He spins me back around, putting a sliver of space between us so his eyes can trace my bared chest. "Jesus, Parker." His fingers return to my breasts, circling my nipples before tracing down my ribs. They stop on my tattoo.

Shit. I forgot he didn't know about it, hasn't ever seen the sunflower tattoo, an image he will no doubt recognize.

He bends over a little so he can see it better, his fingers outlining each petal. "When did you get this?" His voice is hoarse, choked with both emotion and arousal.

"Two days after I moved to LA." I don't say the obvious, that it was just before we broke up. During that brief period of bliss when I thought I could live my dream and keep Seth too.

He stands up straight and swallows thickly. Then a half grin tugs on his lips as he lowers his waistband on the left side, just an inch or two.

My eyes watch his every movement, but they definitely

aren't expecting to find sunflower-yellow petals tattooed onto Seth's hip. My fingers travel to his skin, completing their own tracing of the familiar shape.

"When?" I manage to choke out.

"The day you left for LA."

For a second, we just stand there in the middle of Seth's living room, practically naked in more ways than one, our eyes never leaving each other's.

And then his lips are on mine again, and my arms are cinched around his neck, and this time he hoists me up, wrapping my legs around his waist as he stumbles over to the couch. He sets me back on my feet, and the next instant his thumbs are hooked in the sides of my panties, dragging them down my legs before tossing them off to the side.

He comes in for another kiss, but I place a steadying hand on his chest.

"Wait."

Seth immediately stops, taking a step away from me.

I grasp his hand in mine, pulling him back into my bubble. "Not like that. Just wanted to make sure you have a condom. If you feel like you need one, I mean. I'm on the pill. And I got tested right after my breakup. All clear." I hold up the three-finger on-my-honor salute. I hesitate a second before asking my next question. "Are you? All clear, I mean?"

"I am." He kisses the tips of each of the fingers I'm holding up. "But I also have condoms if you would prefer."

"How long has it been? For you? I don't need the details or anything, just like a rough estimate." I'm cursing myself for not having this conversation before we got started with all the kissing and the touching and the naked time.

He cradles my cheek in his hand. "It's been a while for me, Parker. A long while." Tilting my head up just slightly, he places a soft kiss on my waiting lips. "What would make you most comfortable?"

My hand travels down, brushing through the hair on his stomach, over the waistband of his pants, until I'm cupping his cock in my palm, only the gray fabric separating us from skin-to-skin contact. "I want you, Seth. Just you. Yeah?"

He twitches in my hand. "Yeah."

And his lips are on mine once again. I forget that I'm completely naked until my body is pressed against the length of his. Seth gently pushes me back onto the couch and kneels in front of me. His palms slide up my calves and to my inner thighs, pressing me open so I'm completely bared to him.

We've done this before. We've done all of this before, and yet, it doesn't stem the tingles of anticipation as I watch him slowly lower his head, his lips trailing a path from the back of my knee up my thigh. When we were teenagers, I could never bring myself to watch as Seth pleasured me with his mouth, even though he was always a willing and enthusiastic participant. I wasn't comfortable enough with my body and my sexuality, and even though I was almost always able to orgasm, I could never fully let go.

But now I'm thirty, and while I'm still stumbling on the path of figuring out who the fuck I am, I do know this: I get Seth for one night. And I'm going to enjoy every damn second of it.

So this time I watch as his fingers open me up, and I watch as his tongue circles my clit. I watch as he slides one finger and then two inside of me. I watch as his lips and tongue devour me while those fingers thrust inside me. I watch my hips roll against his mouth.

And I see the equal amount of pleasure in his eyes when I tighten around him, crying out a release that rips through my entire body and leaves me breathless.

Seth plants a row of light kisses along my inner thigh before he stands, finally shucking those blessed gray sweats.

I won't pretend to know how anatomy really works, but I'd bet a million dollars he's bigger and thicker than when we were teens. I can't take my eyes off him.

He strokes himself slowly and I nearly come again. The knowing smile he gives me as he sits next to me on the couch, pulling me onto his lap, is both cute and cocky. Pun intended.

I straddle him, taking his face in my hands and kissing him deeply. "That was amazing."

He runs his hands down my spine, smug smile growing even wider. "I remember what you like."

I take him in my hand, guiding him to my entrance, hovering for a few drawn-out seconds before letting him sink fully inside me. He groans and I give him my own wicked smile. "So do I."

A part of me wants to take this slow, to enjoy every single second of being with Seth. Milk it for all it's worth, as it were. But once his hips start thrusting and his mouth lands on my nipple as he moves inside me, I can't hold back.

My entire body is racked with shivers and I'm skirting the precipice, frustratingly close to release but unable to fully fall over the edge.

"Seth," I groan.

He still knows me, knows my body. His hand slips between us, his fingers stroking me right where I need it. My fingers lace through his hair, pulling not so gently as I explode around him. His hands grasp my hips, thrusting into me until his own release takes him a second later.

And I collapse, my head falling to his chest, which is heaving with the same winded gasps as mine.

For few minutes, the only sound is our quickened breathing.

"Fuck me, Parker." His mouth is buried in my hair and the words tickle my neck.

"I'm pretty sure I just did."

He laughs, taking my hips in his hands once more to guide himself out of me.

I move to climb off his lap, but he pulls me down, his arms wrapping around my back, pressing me into his chest once again. We're both a little sweaty, but our breathing is returning to normal. He brushes my hair out of my face, and when his fingers comb through the strands, I let out a contented sigh.

"I almost forgot what that felt like." I'm too blissed out to process words, so they're just coming out of my mouth without a filter.

"What, sex with me?"

"No, orgasms. At least, orgasms at the hand—and mouth and dick—of someone other than me."

His hand in my hair stills and he leans back a little so he can look me in the eye. "Are you trying to tell me none of these boyfriends of yours were capable of giving you an orgasm?"

I shrug a little, my brain finally catching up and realizing this is a low-key-mortifying revelation to make, especially while naked and draped over my one-night stand/ex-boyfriend's lap. "I mean. They could. Sometimes."

"So they knew how and just didn't?"

"I don't think it was really their fault."

"Yes, it most certainly was." His hands resume stroking up and down my spine as if he wants to prove just how easy it is for me to get turned on.

"It's probably your fault actually, for giving them such a high bar to live up to." I trace the tip of my tongue over his nipple.

He growls, which was the exact reaction I was hoping for. A distraction reaction.

I sit up, putting some space between us. He's pinned beneath me and so I take advantage, circling my hips ever so slowly.

"Parker . . ."

"What?" I turn up the innocence, even as I let my hands slide over my belly and up toward my breasts. "You did say you wanted me for the entire night."

He chuckles, but his eyes never leave my hands, watching intently as I brush them over my nipples. "I'm not seventeen anymore. I need more than five minutes."

I pout playfully. "Fine." I push myself up off his lap. "Guess I'll just go take a shower then, while I wait." I head down the hallway, letting my ass sway like Jessica Rabbit's as I walk. And frankly, I don't know what the hell has come over me, but I do know that when Seth scoops me up in his arms a few seconds later, I smile wider than I have in a really long time.

26

Sex with an ex may seem like a good idea at the time,
but in reality, it just leads to more heartache.

—Lana Parker, "Refrain and Abstain: Why You Should Never Sleep with an Ex"

THE SUNLIGHT FRAMING SETH'S NAVY-BLUE CURTAINS is fuzzy when I wake up, and I can tell by the hints of pink and orange that it's barely sunrise. I'm not sure how much sleep we ended up getting, but it couldn't have been more than a couple hours. After our shower, where I went down on him and he returned the favor, we wound up in the kitchen, searching for sustenance, which we eventually got to eating. The leftover pizza left us both full and the multiple orgasms left us both sated, and we fell into Seth's bed at some ungodly hour and promptly drifted off to sleep.

My bladder is protesting, so I slip out from underneath the sheet and make my way to the bathroom. I'm absolutely wrecked. My hair is tangled so badly even rats wouldn't nest in it. Remnants of my smoky eye have trailed all the way down my cheeks, my lips are swollen, and my chin is covered in a pink rash courtesy of Seth's ever-present stubble.

But my eyes are clear, and those bee-stung lips are smiling. I pee and wash my face and find some mouthwash to swish around.

It's most definitely morning, and I know I should leave. I had my one-night stand. What I should really do is find my dress and my panties and head home before Seth wakes up and we have to have a super-awkward conversation.

But instead, I find myself back in his room, sliding in between the cool sheets. The movement stirs him out of his sleep.

His hazy eyes find me and he smiles. "You're still here."

"I can go, if you want."

His arm latches around my waist and pulls me into him. Neither of us bothered to put any clothing on before climbing into bed last night, so the movement brings us skin-to-skin. He's already half hard against my thigh and I know I should stop this before it starts—or starts again—but I don't want to.

Seth rolls over so he's on top of me, our bodies practically melting into one. His hand cups my cheek and he lowers his head; his kiss is soft and sweet, as if this is the first time. Or maybe the last.

Gone is the frantic passion from the night before. Gone is the urgency, the feeling that this all might slip away if we pause for even a second. It's morning, and everything feels slower. He takes his time, his mouth exploring every dip and curve of mine before it moves down to my neck. He kisses the hollow of my throat and nips at the line of my collarbone. My hands tangle in his hair, pulling his lips back to mine so I can do some exploring of my own.

His chest presses against mine, our heartbeats synced and pounding. My fingers trace the stubble of his cheeks and the defined line of his jaw before my hands set to roaming, needing to feel every inch of him.

He captures one of my hands in his, kissing my palm before lacing our fingers together. I take him in my free hand, guiding him to my entrance. His eyes find mine and don't let go as he pushes into me, so slowly I gasp when he's fully seated.

It's a fullness, and a completeness, that was somehow missing the night before.

He stays still inside of me, kissing me softly. When he does start to thrust, it's the barest of motions, our bodies never separating, our eyes never straying from each other.

I memorize every second. When his fingers tighten around mine. When his mouth brushes mine in the lightest of touches. When his forehead meets mine and we literally can't get any closer.

I know it will never be like this again. This is my last time with Seth; it's the closure we both need to fully move on. Seth needs to be open to a serious relationship, and I need to be comfortable being alone. But nothing else—no one else—is ever going to feel like this again. Like my whole body and my mind and my heart are on the verge of implosion. I'm aching and sated and exhilarated and devastated and cherished.

Tears start clouding my eyes and I bring his lips to mine in the hopes he won't see them. I use the press of his mouth to center me, to focus me on the here and now. He still moves achingly slowly inside of me, and I'm caught off guard when the tension begins to build. I'm not barreling toward release like I did so many times with him the night before, but the pressure is rising within me so steadily, I'm reaching for the explosion.

"Seth," I gasp.

"Oh god, Lana," he groans.

I'm not sure whose fingers clench or whose mouth crushes, but we tumble together, every inch of us intertwined and connected.

The soft kisses continue, neither of us wanting to separate or face the reality of what happens when we're no longer in this bed and wrapped up in each other.

But eventually we have to breathe.

When Seth slips from me, rolling to the side of the bed so as not to crush me, my heart empties, deflating like a week-old balloon.

I allow myself ten seconds to steady myself before I sit up and swing my legs to the edge of the bed, turning away from him.

His hand strokes down the length of my spine. "Lana..."

"I should go." The absolute last thing my body wants to do is stand, but I force myself into motion. My clothes are still in the living room, so I grab a blanket that was knocked to the floor, wrapping it around me. It's not like I need to hide my nudity from him at this point, but this shield of armor might help me make it to the front door.

"You don't have to go." He climbs from the bed, grabbing a pair of boxers from his dresser and stepping into them. "I don't want you to go."

Despite our being as physically close as two people could

possibly be for the last twelve hours, the sight of him still takes my breath away. As much as I want to, I can't let myself stay. Staying means finding myself back in another serious relationship, because being with Seth couldn't be anything but serious. And I don't want that; I've come too far to throw it all away now. I'm learning to stand on my own, and remaining here in Seth's house for even a minute longer has the power to totally derail all the progress I've made. Not to mention the fact it could cost me the biggest opportunity of my career.

"Our one night is over, Seth. I have to go." I start toward the door of his bedroom, needing to gather my clothes and my resolve and leave. "One night only, remember?"

He puts a gentle hand on my forearm, more than enough to stop me. "You don't actually think I only wanted you for one night."

I clutch the blanket closer to my chest. "That's what we agreed on. One night. No strings. Just sex. Closure."

His jaw clenches, his eyes piercing mine. "I know that, but you have to know that's not what I really want."

"I don't know what you want me to say, Seth. I came here to complete my task, have a one-night stand. That's all this was."

"That is not all *that* was." He points at the bed, his meaning clear. What happened there, just a few minutes ago, is not the same as what happened last night. "Don't try to tell me that didn't mean anything, because I know it did."

"It meant something because you will always mean something to me, but it was just sex, Seth."

"Not to me." He scrubs his face with both hands, and it flips some kind of switch. "I can't fucking believe you're doing this again. And I can't believe I fucking fell for it."

My fingers clench the blanket even tighter, as if it will protect me from Seth's angry words. "Again? What are you even talking about?"

He throws both arms wide open. "This is just like the fucking reunion, Parker. You're using me, using my feelings for you to get what you want, and then bailing when it doesn't go exactly as you planned."

Heat rises in my cheeks and I am not about to let him rewrite this story. "Absolutely fucking not, Seth Carson. Yes, I made a mistake that night—a mistake that I've apologized for, by the way—but that is not what's happening here. We laid the ground rules last night, you could've said no. You could've turned me away. You sure as fuck didn't have a problem rejecting me two years ago."

"It *killed* me to reject you. Not that you gave a shit about my feelings, not then and certainly not after."

"Oh, you want to talk about the 'after'? How about how humiliated I was by you turning me away, only for you to show up at my fucking job and try to steal it!" I step closer into his space, the spring of emotions I've been trying to hold in for the past few weeks finally gushing to the surface. "If I'm such a terrible person, if you're still so angry at me, why the hell would you even come here, Seth?"

"Because I still fucking love you, Parker! That's why. I fell in love with you when we were fourteen and I've never stopped. I turned down job offers everywhere—New York,

DC, San Francisco—because no matter what I fucking do, I can't seem to get over you." The frustration and anger come pouring out, clear in the tension and the volume of his voice, but underneath it, there's nothing but hurt.

The words bowl me over. His admission is everything I've longed to hear, said at the worst possible moment. Because this isn't just about him, it isn't just about us, it's about me. It's about my career and my future. "Seth, you know how much I have always cared about you, but it is not fair for you to lay this all on me. We talked about our boundaries, we agreed this was a one-night-only situation, what more do you want?"

"I want you." The words barely come out of his mouth, his jaw is so tightly wound.

"You had me."

He sucks in a breath at the double punch. "I never wanted to let you go."

"But you did." Somehow my voice holds steady. I sound calm and collected, like this night and morning with Seth actually provided me with the closure I've been so desperately seeking when I know once I've had time to process, the opposite will prove true.

He reaches for my hand and I let him take it. "I don't want to let you go again, Lana. Jesus, you had to know how I feel. I never stopped loving you."

I let myself be pulled into his embrace because it feels too good not to. I bury my face in his chest, his hands tangle in my hair, and I breathe in every inch of him.

He lowers his head to kiss me, and I pull away from the

warmth and safety and comfort of his arms before our lips can meet and I forget myself all over again.

I don't know when the tears started for both of us, but they pour down my cheeks and cloud his eyes.

He drags both hands through his hair. "So, this is it."

"I never stopped loving you either, Seth. And I know I never will. But I also know I'm not ready yet. I'm not okay on my own. I haven't figured out who I am without a man to define me." I know I shouldn't leave the door open, it's not fair to him or to me, but I also can't bring myself to close it fully just yet. "If we're ever going to do this, *really* do this, I need to take this time for myself."

His hands fall to his hips and he gives me a solemn nod. "Okay." He takes a few steps away from me, leaving the path to the hallway clear.

"Okay." If I don't walk away now, I never will. I'm halfway to the living room when his voice halts me in my tracks.

"But don't expect me to wait for you, Parker." A hint of anger laces through the warning.

I don't turn around. I don't want the last image I have of him in my head to be one of spite. Or hurt. I locate the two items of clothing I came with, shimmy into them, and leave without another word.

27

Living by yourself can be lonely at times, and so even though it was sometimes a challenge taking care of these living beings who depend on me for survival, I also found myself depending on them.

—Seth Carson, "When Harry Met Seth"

I PACK MY BAG AS SOON AS I GET HOME. IN ADDITION TO that last, seemingly insurmountable challenge of learning to be okay on my own, I still have one more task to complete, and the timing couldn't be better. I throw only the bare essentials into a weekender bag: a few bathing suits, some cotton dresses, shorts, and T-shirts. My laptop and a stack of books are my only luxuries. I make a quick last-minute reservation and am in my car within an hour.

I wait until I arrive in San Clemente and check into my rented beachside condo before I text May, letting her know I'm going to be out of town for a week and avoiding my phone as much as possible. I don't tell her that I slept with Seth. When I do fill her in, I want to have a better handle on how I feel about it, and that might take me the entire week to figure out. Fuck, I might need to extend my stay an extra month or two to figure it out.

It's too late in the afternoon to head out to the beach itself, so I hop in my car and drive to the grocery store, stocking up on all the necessities: carbs, ice cream, and wine. I also buy some frozen meals and some fruit so I don't, you know, die. As soon as I've unloaded all the goods, I pour a glass of wine and head out to the small balcony.

The condo is one street away from the beach itself, but I still have a perfect view of the water and the sunset. I sink into a chair, kicking my feet up on the railing.

And I sit.

And I breathe.

THE NEXT MORNING, I sleep in. When I finally roll out of bed, I put on my bathing suit and a cotton dress, grab a book from the top of my stack, and walk down to the coffee shop right across from the beach.

Taking my iced hazelnut latte, I find a spot at a picnic table overlooking the water. I sit and read for almost two hours, losing myself in the pages of my book, slipping off into a fantasy world that looks nothing like mine. And thank Thor for that.

On my second morning, I treat myself to another iced hazelnut latte, but this time, I take it along with a chair and a towel down to the beach. I find an isolated spot in the sand and sip my coffee while I watch the surfers. San Clemente is a popular surfing spot and my eyes wander from person to person, observing as they paddle out and catch a wave and fall down and paddle out and try again. Sometimes one of them will ride a wave all the way in, back to the sticky wet sand, shaking water droplets from their salty skin as they walk back up the beach. But just as many of them stay out in the ocean for hours, completing the cycle over and over again: paddle out, catch a wave, fall down, try again.

Eventually my eyes tire, and I doze for who knows how long because it doesn't really matter.

I wake up when a group of surfers strolls by me on their way to the parking lot. The beach is much more crowded now, with most of the empty spaces filled in with umbrellas and beach chairs and brightly colored towels. More swimmers are now in the ocean than surfers.

One of the surfers jogs out of the water and over to a towel to the left of mine. I'm glad I'm wearing sunglasses because he's beautiful, and I can't help but watch as he unzips his wetsuit, pulling the sleeves down and revealing tanned, ripped abs underneath. His hair is on the long side, golden blond and damp from the ocean.

He packs up his stuff and heads out, board tucked under his arm and a sparkling white smile wide on his face. He pauses near my chair. "Hi."

"Hi." I have to tilt my head up and shield my eyes in order to meet his, which are a striking green.

"You a local?"

I shake my head. "No, I'm from LA. Just here for the week."

He plants his board in the sand, tail end down, leaning

on it like he's posing for a calendar shoot. "Here all by yourself?"

I imagine he's probably asking so he can discern whether I'm single or taken, but the question hits a little differently for me now. "Yup. All by myself."

He grins, which somehow causes his abs to flex. "Maybe we could go grab a drink."

A vision of the future plays out in my mind like those little slides in a toy View-Master. Me and Surfer Guy falling in love over cocktails. Me and Surfer Guy walking hand in hand on the beach. Me learning everything there is to know about surfing. Me begging Natasha to let me work remotely so I can spend all my time at Surfer Guy's apartment, which in my mind is full of empty beer cans and carpeted with sand.

I give him what I hope is a warm smile. "I'd love to, but I'm not really dating right now. I'm spending some time focusing on myself."

I wait for him to needle me, try to convince me I'm making a huge mistake.

But he doesn't. "I get that. Self-care is essential." He hoists his board up, tucking it back under his arm, the ever-present smile never fading. "Take care of yourself."

"Yeah, you too."

And with a half wave and another killer grin, he's on his way.

On my third day, I head back to the beach, my eyes buried in a book instead of glued to the surfers in the ocean. That night, I shower and put on one of the cotton dresses I brought with me and drive to the small downtown strip, cluttered with restaurants and bars and small shops. I pick a Mexican place and head to the hostess stand.

"Table for two?"

"Just one, actually." I adjust the strap of my cross-body purse so I have something to do with my hands.

The hostess gives me a smile that has a good dose of pity in it, but I try not to focus on that. I take my seat and peruse the menu and order a margarita and chicken fajitas. I force myself to resist pulling out my phone, staying content with reading a book while I wait for my food to be delivered.

As I eat, I people-watch and eavesdrop and focus on enjoying the flavors of my meal. After I pay and head out, I walk around for a bit, exploring the shops that are still open. I find a used bookstore and make a mental note to come back tomorrow. I treat myself to more ice cream before I drive back to my rental condo. It's not that late, but being in the sun all day has made me tired, so I change and wash my face and climb into bed. Sleep comes easily at the beach.

On day four, I finally take my laptop out of its case, plug it in, and turn it on. Even though I'm technically on vacation, I still have a deadline to meet. My next column is due in three days, and I have no idea how I'm supposed to write about my one-night encounter with Seth and make it suitable for the intended audience.

I also have no idea how to write about what happened with Seth without bringing our history and all our baggage into it. Something tells me I can't get away with simply saying that I had mind-blowing sex with my ex-boyfriend and now I'm miraculously cured of all my serial-monogamist tendencies. Natasha wants details, which I'm not willing to give. But I also can't go with my original plan of focusing on the lesson learned, because, frankly, I still don't know what I learned from that night. Other than that we still have the kind of sex that curls my toes, and that we still have the power to hurt each other in a way that scares me a little bit. A lot of bit.

I stare at my computer screen for an hour, the cursor blinking at me, the page as blank as my mind. Deciding I need a mental break, I head out to pick up a coffee and a snack, but even after sucking down twenty ounces of caffeine, I still can't manage to make the words come.

Bribery is usually a good motivator, so I promise myself a trip to the used bookstore if I make some progress, write just one measly sentence. But even the thought of new-to-me books doesn't budge my fingers.

I pull out my phone and text Dr. Lawson, letting her know I'm out of town but could use a little help. She texts back an hour later and we set up a video chat for the next day.

As a last resort, I close my laptop and take out a notebook and a pen. If I can't write words fit for public consumption, then maybe I can write some words just for me. Maybe that will help me clarify what it is I need and want to say in this next article.

I start by writing down some of the things I've learned about myself so far as I've completed the tasks set before me.

Boxing with Duke taught me I'm stronger than I think. And that sometimes it just feels good to hit something.

Going on a blind date and speed dating both taught me

that there are plenty of men out there that I could connect with. I don't need to settle for the first one who shows interest, because there will always be other options out there. And timing does matter. Meeting the right guy at the wrong time means he's not the right guy. If it's meant to be, he'll show up again someday.

Kissing a stranger taught me that I'm braver than I think, and that sometimes a kiss is just a kiss.

Volunteering taught me that I have something to offer others that has nothing to do with being in a relationship. It taught me that helping people feels amazing. It helped me understand my mother.

Therapy taught me to look under the surface, to examine not just my feelings about something but how I react in certain situations. What kind of patterns exist in my life and why. That I cannot control the actions of others, only how I react to them.

Spending the day exploring Los Angeles taught me that there is still so much out there in the world left to see, and sometimes I need to try new things and be open to new experiences.

I fill the page before my pen comes to a halt. But I don't want to overthink it, so I set the pen in motion again and I don't let it stop as the pages keep turning.

Sleeping with Seth taught me what it feels like to be completely in sync with another person. It taught me what it feels like to be truly loved, inside and out and all the corners in between. It taught me that it's never too late for second chances. And that sometimes, a kiss is way more than just a kiss.

Sleeping with Seth made me realize that I am still in love with him.

But I need to be whole before I can tell him those words and possibly give us another shot. If he'll still have me.

I leave the notebook open on the table when I go to bed. I don't know that I'm any closer to having all the answers, but I do know that I'm ready to find them.

***

I SPILL ALL the details to Dr. Lawson the moment our video call connects on day five, and surprisingly, instead of going in for the kill with the Seth revelation, she turns her focus to my work. I shouldn't really be surprised given how our last session went, but still, I figured sleeping with Seth was much more of a psychological conundrum than my conversation with Natasha.

"Would you say that in the past, Natasha has asked you to do things she knew you didn't want to do?"

I shrug, sipping from a glass of ice water. I figured I should attempt to hydrate myself at some point—woman cannot live on coffee alone. "I mean, yeah, but isn't that kind of what bosses are supposed to do? It's her job to give me assignments and tell me what to write about."

Dr. Lawson nods, her expression completely neutral. "Sure. However, does she ask you to do things you don't want to do because she knows you won't say no?"

I ponder that one for a minute. "I guess, maybe. To be honest, other than not getting to write the column I wanted to write, I've never felt like I was being pushed into doing things I didn't want to do."

"Isn't writing the entire description of your job? By continually asking you to write a section you don't enjoy, isn't she by nature asking you to do something you don't want to do?"

I purse my lips, forcing myself not to jump to Natasha's defense. "I suppose."

"Don't you find it a little troubling that she has been promising you the opportunity to advance for eight years but has never delivered? That is, until she can offer it as some sort of prize in a competition, one that was not your idea in the first place?" Her tone has grown sharper and sharper as the conversation has gone on, though I don't get the feeling she is upset with me.

I stare down at my fingers, tapping on the edge of my laptop. "Yes."

Her voice softens. "Why do you think you've allowed yourself to be treated that way?"

"You know why."

This time she gives me a small smile. "I know I know, I'd like to know if you know."

"Because I see my relationship with Natasha as a kind of do-over relationship with my mother. And unlike my mother, Natasha gives me what I seek: attention and, occasionally, praise. I feel like she needs me and that she actually likes having me around. So I do whatever I can to keep her happy because the last thing I want is to disappoint another mother." I raise one eyebrow. "Nailed it?"

"Nailed it."

I sit back in my chair with a sigh, not saying anything for a minute, just letting the words sift through my brain.

"I think I should maybe call my mom," I finally say.

This time Dr. Lawson's smile is proud. "I think that's a good idea."

We spend the remainder of our time together prepping me for the call. What I should say and how I should frame it, and strategies for me to remember that I can't control her words, only my reaction to them.

It's still early in the day when we end our session, so I gather up my beach supplies and head back out to the sand, the sun, and the clear ocean air.

28

Can all of our issues with relationships really be traced back to our relationships with our parents? The answer is probably yes.

—Lana Parker, "Parents Just Don't Understand"

Lana: Hi, guys.

Corey: She's alive!!!!

Lana: Haha.

Lana: Sorry I disappeared, I just needed some time to get my head together.

Tessa: That's okay! We understand.

May: Now would you like to fill us in on what sent you running for the hills? Or the beach, as it were?

Lana: . . . I slept with Seth.

Corey: HO-LY

May: Shit.

May: You actually did it.

Tessa: Are you okay?

Lana: No?

Lana: I don't know?

Corey: How was it?

Tessa: C, there are bigger problems right now.

Corey: If it was crap, then in the long run, it doesn't really matter that they slept together.

Lana: It was not crap . . .

Lana: It was amazing.

May: Of course it was.

Corey: So then why are you now in San Clemente all by your lonesome?

Lana: Because it meant something different to him than it did to me.

May: Did it?

Lana: He thought it meant we were getting back together.

Tessa: And why aren't you?

Lana: You mean besides the fact that we're currently embroiled in a competition for the one job I've wanted my entire adult life? A major part of which is that I have to stay single?

Lana: Not to mention he's already broken my heart before. Why should I think he won't do it again?

May: A lot has changed since you broke up the first time, LP.

Tessa: Yeah, neither of you is the person you were back in high school.

Lana: But is that enough?

May: The running away makes a lot more sense now.

Lana: Yeah.

Tessa: We love you, and we're here. Anytime.

Corey: Yes, this. All of this.

May: And remember, you are loved and you deserve love. And we're proud of you.

Lana: Thank you, guys. I love you back.

THE NEXT MORNING, I take care of business first thing. And by that, I mean I order not one but two iced hazelnut lattes and take them back to the condo. Before I call my mother, I extend my stay in San Clemente for another day. Something tells me this conversation is going to increase my need for peaceful beach time.

I dawdle for as long as I can, but I know it's better to just rip the Band-Aid off and get it over with. So, with a little hesitation and a healthy dose of courage, I pull up my mom's contact information on my phone and hit *Call*.

I halfway expect her not to pick up, and almost entirely hope she sends me to voicemail.

But her voice comes over the line after the second ring. "Lana? Is everything okay?"

I promptly burst into tears.

I'm not sure how long I cry, but when my heaving sobs finally die down, I'm surprised to find her still on the line.

"Why don't you get yourself a tissue and blow your nose and then we'll talk." It's the most motherly advice she's offered me in years, maybe ever.

And I take it, running to the bathroom for a few minutes to wipe my nose and splash some water on my face.

"You still there?"

"Of course."

"I'm really angry at you, Mom." I don't make a conscious decision to put it out there like that, but I guess it's not the worst way to start a conversation. It's honest, if nothing else.

Her sigh trickles through the phone. "That's fair."

"I grew up feeling like you didn't want me. Like you'd rather be halfway around the world than with your own daughter. It's brought me a lot of problems in my adult life. Evan dumped me because he claimed I have mommy issues, and I'm not sure he was wrong. I'm thirty years old and I still don't know who I am, Mom." My voice wavers slightly at the end, but overall, I think Dr. Lawson would be proud.

"Oh, Lana." There's a long pause. "I don't think *sorry* is going to cut it in this situation, is it?"

"Are you? Sorry, I mean?" The amount of hope in my chest at this slightest possible admission of wrongdoing is obscene.

"I'm sorry I hurt you. And I'm sorry if you ever felt like I abandoned you or didn't want to be with you."

It's a weak statement and a blanket apology, but it's already more than I expected to get from her. "Why did you leave me on my own so much?"

She sighs again, like she is the one being put out here. "You're an adult, Lana, so I'm just going to say this bluntly. Some people are not cut out to be parents, and I was one of them. I never felt like a good mom, I always felt like I was screwing it up, so I figured why not leave you in the hands of people who knew what they were doing."

"All the nannies?"

"Yes. But then later on, the Carsons. I could tell how happy you were when you were with them, as a family, and so I figured since you had them, you didn't really need me anymore." If I didn't know any better, I might think there was a tinge of resentment in her voice.

"Yes, well, I did have the Carsons, and they did show me what a family looked like. And then they left me too." The tears start up again, but I manage to keep them silent.

"I'm not going to lie, that one definitely surprised me a bit. I always thought you and Seth had what it took to be together in the long run."

Yeah. Me too. "He's here. In LA, I mean. Seth moved to LA." I didn't intend to share that, but once the words are out, I hold my breath for her reaction. As if she can be the one to tell me what to do despite barely knowing a thing about my life.

"Oh?" I can almost see the smile on her face. "Well then maybe you two have what it takes after all."

"You don't think I need to focus on me? Focus on being single and standing on my own two feet?" I don't know why her opinion on the subject suddenly matters, but it does.

"Oh, honey, you've been standing on your own two feet for almost your entire life."

It's a simple statement, but the truth of it punches me in the gut. She's right. I've been taking care of myself for a really long time, and whatever my relationship status is doesn't change that fact. I had to learn how to fend for myself and how to be alone long before I ever sought constant companionship from whoever was willing to hand it to me.

We sit in the silence for a couple of minutes.

"I should go, I have a meeting with the contractors soon." And just like that, everything goes back to the way it always was.

"Okay. I guess I'll talk to you later."

"Lana, I hope you know that you can call me anytime. I will always pick up for you. And I have always, and will always, love you."

"Thanks, Mom. I love you too."

"I'll call you soon." The phone clicks and the other end goes silent.

And I open my laptop and I write.

29

Feel free to bring a buffer date with you when you know you're going to see your ex at a party, but please don't try that fake-dating trope. It only works in romance novels.

—Lana Parker, "How to Survive That First Run-in with Your Ex"

NATASHA SENDS ME AN EMAIL ASKING ME TO COME INTO the office the day I return from San Clemente. The fact that she's emailing instead of texting is alarming enough on its own, but when I knock on her office door and find Seth already sitting in front of her desk, I almost pass out.

Natasha greets me with what she probably thinks is a warm smile but borders on a grimace. "There she is! Come on in and have a seat."

It takes a second for my brain to kick in and for my feet to move. I don't look at Seth as I perch myself on the edge of one of Natasha's blue velvet chairs, positioning myself as far away from him as possible. I don't need to look at him to feel the surge of anger and hurt radiating from him. "What's going on?"

Natasha clasps her hands together and looks at us both as if she's the proud parent and we're her all-star children. It's a look that would've once made me glow with pride. Now it makes my stomach turn.

"So. As you know, our competition comes to an end next week, and it's perfect timing. The *Chronicle* wants to host a small party to celebrate the acquisition. They're really pleased with how this little experiment has paid off. I'm planning on making a short speech, during which I'll introduce the two of you, give a recap of the standings, and officially announce the kickoff of the reader vote."

Seth shifts in his seat, the subtle creak the only sound in the room.

"Does this mean you'll need us to be at the party?" I finally ask when the silence becomes too thick.

"Yes, well, of course I need you there." She looks back and forth between us, as if she is just now picking up on the fact that we haven't so much as glanced at each other. "But more than that, I want you two to do something special for this event, really make it something that brings *ATF* attention. Something to go viral."

"Just spit it out, Natasha." The words fly out of my mouth, and I don't know who's more surprised, her or me. "I mean, what is it that you want us to do?"

She shoots me a silencing look. "In conjunction with the end of the competition, I also want you to announce your relationship. That you both were able to learn and grow so much on this journey, and you finally realized at the end of all this that you were meant to be together. You're going to be our golden couple."

Just when I thought the silence couldn't get any more oppressive.

"But we're not dating . . . ," I say slowly, still trying to force my brain to process what's happening here.

Natasha waves her hand like she's swatting a bug. "Who cares. The people don't need to know that, they just want a happy ending to the story."

"So you want us to pretend? Natasha, I don't think—"

"No."

It's the first word Seth has spoken, and it's quiet yet firm.

"Excuse me?"

"I said no." He pushes up from his chair. "I'm not doing that, and honestly, it's completely out of line that you would even ask."

Natasha bristles. "Look, Seth, I'm not sure how things work out in the freelance world, but here at *ATF*—and at the *Chronicle*, I might add—it's important to work as a team. Sometimes we have to do things we don't want to do for the betterment of the site as a whole."

"That's bullshit. And my feelings for Lana will not be fodder for your little publicity stunt. So once again, my answer is no." He turns and heads toward the door.

"You do know that with one phone call I can put an end to your position at the *Chronicle*."

I suck in a breath at Natasha's threat. Shifting slightly in my seat so I can catch Seth's reaction, I expect to find him shooting daggers Natasha's way.

Instead his eyes are locked on me. When our gazes meet, it knocks the wind out of me.

"Do what you have to do."

I'm not sure who the words are truly meant for, but it's the last thing he says before he pushes out of the office, slamming the door behind him.

Natasha studies me for a second, her piercing glare seeing more than I want her to, I'm sure. "Is there any way you could convince him to change his mind?"

Of all the responses I expected from her, that was not one of them. "I think he made himself pretty clear there." I sit up a little straighter, channeling Dr. Lawson. "And honestly, Natasha, I don't want any part of this either. I'm not going to lie about a relationship just to get some extra clicks on the site."

She sighs as if her favorite coffee shop ran out of oat milk and she has to settle for soy. "You know, before Seth Carson came to town, you were a team player."

I stand, pulling myself up to my full height. "This doesn't have anything to do with Seth. I have been a team player for the past eight years. And look where it's gotten me." I gesture helplessly into the empty space. "We're not doing it, Natasha. And you shouldn't have asked in the first place."

I spin on my heel and head right for the door, not waiting for a reply. I'm not sure I can hold my ground if she threatens me like she did Seth. I pull the door shut gently behind me, tempted to slam it but not ready to go quite that far.

"You okay?"

The voice, and the question, startle me.

Seth is leaning against the wall, arms crossed and brow furrowed.

"I . . ."

I'm sorry.

I want you.

I love you.

I'm in love with you.

Every possible answer runs through my mind and I want to say them all.

"I'm fine," is what comes out.

For a moment, we just stand there, inches away from one another, eyes locked and hearts broken.

"Seth, I . . ."

He shakes his head. "We don't need to do that right now, Parker. I just wanted to make sure you were okay."

He passes by me on his way out and for a half a second, our fingers brush. He's gone before I have the chance to reach out and take his hand.

30

Be careful who you spill your breakup woes to;
not everyone is truly on your side.

—Lana Parker, "Who to Turn to with a Broken Heart"

I LET MAY TAKE OVER MY APPEARANCE FOR THE NIGHT of the *Chronicle* party. She styles my hair and slathers my face in makeup and is in charge of my outfit. I was worried for a second she would put me in one of her short, tight numbers like she did for Warwick, but instead, she riffles through my own closet, pulling out a pink tea-length tulle skirt. She pairs it with a black silk corseted top that I must have used for a cosplay at some point because I can't imagine ever wearing it on its own. At first I'm hesitant, but combined, the pieces make me look both soft and sexy.

We drive to Ivanhoe in Silver Lake together, neither of us speaking much. I told her everything once I landed back in town, including all the drama with Natasha, and she had just the response I needed: wrapping me in a big hug and telling me how proud she was.

Handing off the car to the valet, we both pause on the sidewalk in front of the restaurant.

"You ready for this?" she asks.

"Fuck no."

She gives my hand a quick squeeze. "You know I got your back."

I squeeze back. "I know."

My eyes find Seth the second we cross over into the outdoor courtyard; I'm as drawn to him now as I was when I was a teenager. And he looks good. Of course he looks good. He's wearing the suit we bought on our shopping trip, sans the sunflower-yellow tie. And thank Loki for small favors, because I don't know what I would've done if I'd seen him in that tie.

He glances my way and I swear I can see heat in his gaze, despite the physical distance between us. After giving me a short nod of acknowledgment, he turns back to James and continues their conversation.

"That could've gone worse." May loops her arm through mine and drags me over to the bar, ordering us each a glass of champagne.

I clink my glass against hers. "Thank you for being here with me, and for putting up with my black hole of drama the past few weeks."

She sips from her own glass, not leaving even a smidge of red lipstick behind, which is just unfair. "I haven't had to watch reality TV in months. Your life is better than the Housewives."

"I wouldn't go that far."

Tessa and Corey come join our little circle after grabbing

drinks of their own. Corey holds her glass up to the center. "Here's to Lana. May she kick some serious ass, win this vote, and finally get the job of her dreams."

I barely get a clink and a sip in before Natasha approaches. She's dressed in a black suit that fits her like a glove, hair sharp and makeup perfectly applied.

She places a hand on my shoulder and gives the girls a fake smile. "Hope you don't mind if I steal this one for a bit, she is my little superstar after all."

All three of them shoot her different variations of dirty looks, and I'm pretty sure May flips her off as soon as her back is turned.

Natasha guides me to the center of the patio area, near the fireplace. "This is where I want you to stand until I come get you for my speech. Talk to everyone. Smile. Say the words *Always Take Fountain* as many times as you possibly can." She's off before I can protest.

I don't have it in me to argue with her. At least not tonight, not in public. So I paste on a fake smile and prepare to chat with all the other journalists and bloggers and influencers who were invited here to give us some "free" press.

Two minutes later, Natasha deposits Seth a few feet to my right, basically setting up a receiving line for the guests as they enter the patio. Plenty of space separates us, but I'm aware of every single move he makes, every twitch of his hand, every shuffle of his feet.

I want to pull him aside and tell him everything about my week away. I want to let him know all that I've figured out about who I am and what I want. I want to tell him I just need a little bit more time, but I'm going to get there. I want to pull him into the tiny single-stall bathroom by the kitchen and let him fuck me up against the wall.

But I don't do any of those things. Obviously. Especially not that last one.

Instead I focus all my energy on mingling. It's exhausting, but I remind myself that these are some of the people who will have a say in who wins, and despite everything, I do still want to win. I think.

Either I get my dream job and Seth probably moves away, or I'm stuck with this dead-end column and Seth gets to stay. I don't even know which option is better at this point.

Either way, it's something of a relief when Natasha comes to collect us both, guiding us over to the makeshift stage created in one of the corners of the patio. Lining us up shoulder to shoulder, she gives us a little wink, like we're both in on the joke. She takes a microphone from the DJ and turns to face the party at large.

"Hello, everyone, and welcome!" Her smile is wider than I've ever seen before but it doesn't mask the insincerity in her voice. "On behalf of everyone at *Always Take Fountain*, thank you so much for joining us this evening to celebrate our new partnership with the *Los Angeles Chronicle*. I know I speak for everyone at *ATF* when I say how excited we are for this new chapter to begin!"

A small ripple of applause travels through the crowd, though from the looks of it, most of the party guests have already lost interest in her speech and probably just want more free booze.

Natasha turns to me. "I'm sure these two faces are familiar to all of you. When I first met Lana Parker, she was a bright young college student with the world at her feet. She had everything: talent, looks, brains—and terrible taste in men." She pauses for the crowd to laugh, and they do. "I watched Lana go from bad relationship to bad relationship, and I knew she desperately needed my guidance, not just as her boss, but as her just barely older and yet much wiser friend."

I bite my lip to hold back a scream. My cheeks are flaming. My eyes glue themselves to the ground, so I don't have to watch a party full of strangers literally laughing at my love life, as Natasha continues to tell my private stories to the crowd. My intense studying of the wooden-planked floor means I have the perfect view of Seth's foot as it gently taps against mine in some sort of subtle sign of solidarity. It's our first real physical contact since, well, our extreme physical contact two weeks ago. Somehow it affects me almost as much.

"And when I found out Seth and Lana had a history together, and that that history had led them down opposite romantic paths, I knew we had a blockbuster series on our hands," Natasha continues on, oblivious to my embarrassment. Or maybe she just doesn't care. "But even I couldn't have predicted just how much these two would capture your hearts."

Seth leans into me, ever so slightly, our shoulders pressed together. It helps soothe the sting of Natasha's words but does nothing to calm my heart, which has been racing at 5G speeds. I want to slip my hand into his, but I don't know how he would react. And like it or not, the eyes of the crowd are on us.

"It almost pains me to have to pit these two against each other in a final vote, but a deal is a deal and we do need to determine a winner. Now, remember, you're not voting for the person who wrote the best columns but the person you feel did the best job with the challenges presented. Who showed the most growth and made a real change." Natasha grins as she comes to her favorite part. "Voting is going to be open on the *Always Take Fountain* website—that's AlwaysTakeFountain.com—as soon as the final columns are posted on Friday, so make sure you vote early and vote often!"

At that the crowd begins to perk up. People love an arbitrary vote. Shit. This whole thing is going to bring a ton of traffic to the site. I can practically see the dollar signs cha-chinging in Natasha's eyes.

Suddenly, Seth shifts next to me and his arm reaches toward Natasha. She thinks he's going in for a hug, but really, he's grabbing for the mic.

He steps to the front of the faux stage and clears his throat. "I just have one quick thing I need to say."

My breath catches in my chest as I mentally run through all the possible things that could come out of Seth's mouth. The one-night stand. The breakup. The reunion.

How he's still in love with me.

How I'm still in love with him.

Except, he doesn't know that last part yet.

I search for May in the crowd. Her eyes are as wide as mine, but she looks excited too, like this is going to be the beginning of some rom-com-level grand gesture.

Seth clears his throat again, directly into the mic, causing the sound to echo around the patio. "As many of you probably know, one of the bigger tasks I was assigned during this whole series was abstinence."

My stomach drops right into my butt.

"And unfortunately, at least in terms of the competition, I did not follow through." He shoves a hand in his pocket and I know it's to hide his clenched fist. "I had sex when I wasn't supposed to, and therefore, in good faith, I cannot say I completed the assignment."

Natasha's face is stricken. She's scrambling, and I know she's about to brush Seth's slight off, tell him it doesn't matter and the readers can still vote. She needs those clicks more than she needs to have a fair competition.

But Seth doesn't give her the chance. "I didn't follow the rules, and because of that I forfeit the contest." He turns to look at me. "Congratulations, Parker. You win." He drops the microphone into Natasha's outstretched hand, gives me the smallest of smiles, and turns away, pushing through the crowd and making his way to the exit.

The silence is deafening until the DJ attempts to defuse the situation by restarting the playlist. It somewhat works, with the crowd dispersing, most heading for the bar or the servers who are tray-passing cocktails.

Natasha looks at me, and her eyes could cut glass. "Did you know he was going to do that?"

I purse my lips and shake my head. "I haven't spoken to him since that day in your office."

She grits her teeth and I can practically see her calculating all she's lost. All Seth cost her by dropping out. "Well, I guess congratulations are in order then. As soon as the *Chronicle* has an opening for a columnist, it's yours."

The champagne I guzzled when I got here fizzes in my stomach. "What do you mean as soon as there's an opening? I thought the whole point of the competition was that there *was* an opening."

She shrugs, the move barely wrinkling her impeccable suit. "Openings come up frequently, I'm sure there will be something soon."

"And in the meantime?" I clench my fists at my sides, fully aware that we are still very much in public and punching my boss would probably be a bad look.

"In the meantime, you'll remain on relationships and dating." She turns to walk away from me.

"And if I say no?"

She doesn't even bother to look my way, barely throwing her response over her shoulder. "You won't. A boxing class and a volunteer gig haven't changed who you are deep down, Lana. You're a people pleaser. You always will be." And with that, she walks away from me, circulating back into the crowd, smiling like her entire evening's gone to plan and her ploy for clicks didn't just blow up in her face.

I slump into a chair at a table in the corner of the patio, partially hidden by an umbrella.

"Well that went about as well as Fyre Fest." Corey plops into the seat across from me.

Tessa and May take the other two open seats at the table, Tessa handing me a fresh glass of champagne.

"Should we even bother asking if you're okay?" Tessa gently rubs my shoulder like I'm a scared puppy.

"She's not going to give me the column." I down the entire glass of champagne, hoping it might erase the conversation from my memory. "I'm pretty sure she was going to declare Seth the winner whether he got the votes or not."

Corey twists her gorgeous face into an ugly grimace. "Of course. Then she gets exactly what she wants. Seth was always going to move to the *Chronicle* at some point, and at least now he did her some good while he was here."

"And you're still stuck writing the same bullshit love stuff you've been doing for years." May crosses her arms over her chest. "Want me to go punch her?"

"I'm perfectly capable of punching her myself." Over the past several weeks, I've been back to Duke's a few times and my arms only hurt for a day or two after each session now. I consider it progress.

"Fuck yeah, you are." Corey holds up her hand for a high five.

When I fail to respond, she turns to Tessa, who weakly taps her palm.

"What are you going to do?" Tessa asks softly.

I shrug. "I don't know."

It's not a total lie, but it's also not the full truth. I have a few ideas, but I need to think about it, and write about it, before I make any rash decisions.

I push my chair back and stand. "I think I'm ready to go."

ONCE I'M BACK at home, face scrubbed clean, fancy outfit hanging in the closet, I climb into bed and open up my phone. I don't know what to say to Seth just yet, but I know I can't say nothing.

Me: You didn't have to do that.

Me: I would've been okay with you winning.

Me: Are you still going to get the spot at the Chronicle?

Seth: It's okay.

Seth: I don't know. I'm not sure I even want it anymore.

I bite my lip, tapping my fingers on the edge of my phone case.

Me: Are you going to stay in LA?

I hold my breath as the little dots pop up, blinking at me like some kind of evil serial killer clown.

Seth: I don't know.

Seth: Good night, Parker.

Well, I guess that's the end of that.

Me: Good night, Seth.

I put my phone on Do Not Disturb, plugging it in to charge, and bury myself underneath my comforter. I don't sleep much. But when I wake up the next morning, at the very least I have the beginnings of a plan.

31

Is there anything scarier than professing your love for someone? And is there anything more wonderful than learning your feelings are reciprocated?

—Lana Parker, "Should You Say the L Word First?"

AS SOON AS I COLLECT MY ICED HAZELNUT LATTE FROM the barista at Constellation Coffee, I hunker down at a table in the back of the café, prepared to settle in for most of the day.

I have a column to write.

And a grand gesture to pull off.

Well, to be totally honest, I'm not sure it really counts as a grand gesture. It's not running through the airport or interrupting a press conference or holding a boom box over my head. But I am determined to get the truth, my truth, out there for the world to see.

After a long sip of my coffee, I flip open my notebook, the one I had with me in San Clemente. I read over my notes, and even though they're just my stream-of-consciousness thoughts, I decide to use them as is. I add another note about what I learned on my solo vacation—that I am enough on my own, that eating in public by yourself isn't that hard, and that when you have the resolve to turn down a hot surfer's advances, you might actually be cured of your quick-fire relationship tendencies.

And then I think of my conversation with my mom. Strangely enough, she was right: I have always been capable of standing on my own two feet, even if didn't realize that I was. I'm ready to share with my readers, and admit to myself, that my mom did, in her mind, what she thought was best for me. And that if I accept my mother for who she is instead of being angry at her for who she's not, we might actually be able to have a real relationship.

I sit back in my seat and stretch my arms. I've already hit my word limit and I haven't even gotten to the most important part. I know this isn't what Natasha's expecting from me, but I know she'll publish it regardless. If she can't get her clicks from the voting, then she needs something big. And this could be it.

> *My fabulous readers, I have come to the end of my journey. My final task feels like a somewhat arbitrary one. How do you know when you're okay being alone? I checked off the other boxes. I even accomplished some things that weren't on my original list (did I mention how hot the surfer was?). But that isn't how I know I'm okay with being alone, that I'm ready to be alone.*
>
> *I know it because I'm about to confess something*

that could cost me everything. And it's scary. Of course it is. Putting yourself out there, especially on the internet, is always scary. But I know I have to do it. If it all blows up in my face and I'm left alone and destitute, I will be okay. Because I've always been okay. I just needed a little push to realize it.

I know, I know, get to the juicy confession already, Lana, please. No one cares about your self-help bullshit.

Ready?

Here goes.

A few days ago, Seth Carson told the whole world (or a group of LA's fifty top influencers and a few fellow journalists) that he didn't complete his task and therefore forfeited the competition, declaring me the winner.

Well, I didn't complete all my tasks either.

At least, not in the spirit in which they were given.

Because I didn't actually have a one-night stand. I slept with someone. Yes, it was just the one night, but I couldn't ever dare to call it a one-night stand.

Because I love this person. I have loved this person since I was fourteen years old, and I have never stopped loving him. I don't think I ever will.

And I'm pretty sure he loves me too. But I also know how badly I hurt him. For that, I could not be more sorry. I can only hope he can find it in his heart to forgive me, but if he doesn't, that's okay. I will hold on to that love and I will find a way to be okay.

(But seriously, you know who you are, and I'm so sorry and I'm so in love with you so please forgive me.)

I proofread the piece once before emailing it to Natasha, worried I might change my mind if I think on this for too long. All I get in response is a one-word email: *Received*.

Great.

While I have my computer open and coffee at hand, I send a few outreach emails, mostly to people I've met at networking events over the years, but also to editors at a couple of sites I admire. I'm tired of writing about things I don't care about, and if Natasha isn't going to fulfill her promise, then I don't see why I should plan on sticking around. *ATF* has always felt like a family, but just like a family can be, it's also been a little bit toxic and a whole lotta manipulative. I love my colleagues, but Natasha is meant to be my boss, not my friend. She's the one who blurred those lines; I will be the one to remove myself from the situation.

Once she publishes my final piece, that is. If I quit before it goes live, I can easily see her refusing to run the column, just to spite me. Inspired by my own proactive job-hunting though, there's one more thing I need to do. I log on to my blog site. Now that I've redesigned it, it looks and feels like a site people might want to read. The final step is to let folks know that it exists. I copy the URL link and navigate over to Twitter. Taking in a steadying breath, I paste the link and add a brief intro and hit *Tweet*. I know if I actually want to drive readers to the site there's a lot more I'll need to do, but it's a good first step. It's not a career and it likely won't make me any money, but it's something for me. And I'm proud of it. It will give me something to focus on while I wait to hear back about potential job prospects and make other plans for the future.

Hopefully these new plans will also include Seth, though that remains to be seen. But even if he does decide to move on, I'm grateful for the time we had together and for the lessons I've learned over the past couple months.

Look at me, evolved as fuck.

BECAUSE I'VE BEEN avoiding the office and all communications from Natasha, I don't know exactly when, or even if, my lay-it-all-on-the-table article will go live. It could be its normal Friday time slot, or maybe, because she just wants to be done with us, Natasha could decide to publish it early. Turns out, my gut is right and Natasha sends me a terse email Wednesday night, letting me know our final pieces will be published at eight a.m. the following morning.

Luckily, it's still early enough in the evening that I have time to run to the grocery store to stock up on the wine and Ben & Jerry's I know I'll need to survive the next day. Halfway through my shopping trip I put the wine back and grab some bubbly and orange juice instead. If I'm going to be day drinking, I might as well be classy about it.

I get into bed early, knowing full well there will be no sleep happening. As I hunker down and turn on *Ted Lasso* for my hundredth rewatch, I do the best I can to at least rest, pausing every so often to respond to the steady stream of texts coming in throughout the night.

May: Are you sure you don't want me to come over? I have no problem lending you my tit as a pillow.

Me: Wow. That is so thoughtful?

Me: But I'm good. Thank you though.

May: I got your back, boo.

May: Let me know if you need me to shank someone.

Tessa: Do you want me to come over tomorrow morning? I can pick up coffee and be there by eight!

Me: You really are the sweetest, but honestly, I think I just want to be alone.

Me: Look at that progress!

Tessa: If you change your mind you can text me anytime. I can be there in 15 minutes.

Me: Thank you, friend.

Corey: Did you already stock up on booze? I've got plenty of champs here and I can totally swing by the market and pick up some OJ!

Corey: Day drinking but keep it classy!

Corey: I also make really good bloody marys.

Me: Lol. Already ahead of you and have my classy day-drinking supplies on standby.

Me: . . . But I may take a rain check on the bloody mary.

Corey: Hell yeah! Anytime!

IT'S CLOSE TO midnight and my phone has been silent for over an hour when it chirps again. I groan, tempted to turn it on Do Not Disturb and ignore it for the next century, but

I don't want to worry my friends. At least, not any more than they already are.

I punch in my passcode, expecting to see more words of encouragement/threats of violence toward Natasha from May, but the text isn't from her.

Seth: Did you see the final articles are going live tomorrow morning?

I sit up in my bed, shoving aside in the blanket cocoon I've built. We haven't talked since the night of the party. I may or may not have been stalking his social media the last few days to see if there was any hint of a relocation on the horizon, but he hasn't posted anything. And since I've been avoiding the office, there haven't been any chance run-ins. This single stupid text message feels like a lifeline, an olive branch. I don't want to fuck it up.

Me: Yeah, Natasha told me.
Me: Did you write a final piece? I kind of thought after your bottom-of-the-ninth walk-off you might have opted out of the assignment.
Seth: Considered it. But I do enjoy this thing called getting paid.
Me: It does come in handy.

Neither of us says anything for a few minutes. I wonder if he's staring at his phone screen like I am, willing it to beep, or if he has more patience than I do. I think I've kept it pretty light and breezy and haven't said anything to scare him off. But maybe he's said all he needs to say.

Finally, I get a notification.

Seth: I look forward to reading your article tomorrow.

Me: Yeah. Same.

Me: I mean, I look forward to reading yours.

Seth: I know what you meant.

Seth: Good night, Parker.

Me: Good night, Seth.

I have the sudden urge to email Natasha and beg her not to publish my piece. But I know that a) she wouldn't care, and b) the words need to be out there, even if I'm scared shitless. Seth needs to hear them. Or read them, as it were. And I need them to be read.

I turn my attention back to Roy and Keeley and let them lull me into thinking true love is possible.

Miraculously, after all that, I manage to fall asleep.

32

THE ONE

By Seth Carson

Well, friends. Here we are. The end of the road. Cue the Boyz II Men. If you saw the recap of our ATF/Chronicle *party posted earlier this week, then you know I've already withdrawn myself from the competition. I didn't complete the tasks as assigned to me and have forfeited, making Lana Parker the undisputed champion of whatever the hell you want to call this whole fiasco.*

And, not going to lie to you, readers, there were a lot of moments over the past several weeks that felt like a disaster. At least to me. Because throughout this whole experience, I've been lying to everyone. To you, to my colleagues, to Parker, and to myself.

I told myself I was moving to Los Angeles to pursue new writing opportunities. I wanted to settle down, and living and writing in LA has always been a dream of mine. All of that is true, at least partially. But there's really only one reason I chose to move to LA, instead of New York or Chicago or London, and it has nothing to do with the weather.

It has to do with love.

The woman I love is here in LA, and she has been for the past twelve years, ever since we broke up. Ever since I made the biggest mistake of my life in letting her go. But that's selfish of me to say because it was my biggest mistake. But I don't necessarily know that it was a mistake for her.

This woman, she has always been remarkable. Strong. Independent. Smart as fuck. Talented. Gorgeous. Kind. She was all those things when I fell for her at fourteen, she was all those things while we were together. And she was all those things when she flew across the country to pursue her dreams, promising we would find a way to make it work. We didn't. Because of me. Maybe we would have grown apart on our own; maybe I would have moved to LA a lot sooner; maybe we'd be married with a couple of kids right now. All those were possible paths for us, if I hadn't decided I knew what was best for her, without asking for her input.

And yet somehow, in the space of the twelve years we were apart, all of those traits that she embodied have multiplied by a million. Because she's still strong and independent and smart and talented and gorgeous and kind, but now she's also confident, and comfortable in her own skin, and knows who she is. She may not think she does, but she does.

I'm so proud of the woman she's become, and maybe we needed to be apart in order for her to become that person. Again, I had no place in making that decision for her, but the results are undeniable. She's simply magnificent and I count myself lucky to even know her.

But, readers, I don't just know her. I love her. I'm in love with her. I always have been, and I probably always will be. I hurt her, both in the distant past and in the recent past. That kills me. I'm so sorry for any and all of the pain I have ever caused her. I hope she can forgive me.

The final task required of me was to find someone I could be happy with in the long term. I knew back on day one that this would be the easiest on the list. Because I already found that person. I know who I am supposed to be with, not just long-term, but forever.

And to that person, you know who you are, I'm sorry, and I love you.

I READ SETH'S column with a bleary gaze. It's just barely eight a.m. and my morning-crusted eyes are already clouded with tears.

Our articles are published as one post, with one of the photos of us from our tourist day positioned between our stories. In case anyone out there didn't realize who these mysterious people we each spoke of were.

By eight fifteen my phone is chirping and beeping like R2-D2 is having a full-scale meltdown. I turn it off without checking any of the messages, needing to sit with this on my own for a little while. I read Seth's words a second time, and then a third. By round four, I hop out of bed, throwing on the first clean items of clothing I can find.

I think I finally understand what Billy Crystal meant at the end of *When Harry Met Sally*. Because I know who I want to spend the rest of my life with, and I want the rest of my life to start right now.

I pull my hair into a ponytail but take the time for a full teeth brushing. There's going to be a lot of kissing on the other side of this and I want to be ready.

Once I'm halfway presentable, I grab my car keys and my still-turned-off phone and throw open the front door. And stop in my tracks.

"Hi." His smile is sheepish, his clothes as rumpled as mine.

"Hi." My smile is bright, my greeting as breathless as his.

He hands me a single sunflower.

I want to cry, but I'm too happy for tears. I gesture for him to come inside, closing the door behind him.

I take a glass from a kitchen cabinet and fill it with water before placing the flower in.

As soon as I've turned back to him, Seth's arms are around me, pulling me into him. His lips find mine and the kiss is everything. Soft and sweet and so full of love.

We part after a minute, both of us struggling to breathe.

His forehead falls to mine. "I love you, Lana. I'm so in love with you. I've been in love with you for half of my life. Part of me is so mad at myself for all the years I wasted, but the other part of me is so fucking proud of you that I know it's all been worth it."

I press my lips to his again, hungry for him, so bolstered by his admission I feel like I might actually burst. "I love you too, Seth. And I know the past, our past, is important, but it doesn't mean nearly as much as our future. And I want a future with you. I'm so in love with you it hurts."

He takes my face in his hands and kisses me like it's the first time and the last time. I sink into him, and my hands latch on to his hips, pulling him as close to me as possible.

We stumble our way down the hall, shedding items of clothing as we walk. We're both down to our underwear by the time we fall onto my bed, lying on our sides, face-to-face.

I have to stop kissing him because my smile is too big, and so I pull away, taking the opportunity to truly look at him. My finger traces a path down the slope of his nose, across his brow, around the edge of his jaw.

"Do you even know how beautiful you are?" I finish up my exploration, brushing the tip of my finger over his lips.

He kisses the pad of it. "I think that's supposed to be my line."

I place my palm flat over his chest, feeling the pounding of his heart through the heat of his skin. "Did you really move to LA just for me?"

His bright-blue eyes twinkle. "You know I did. And I meant what I said about always wanting to live here and finding a place to settle down."

His fingers begin their own path of exploration, tracing the curves of my breasts before traveling down to my nipples. He brushes over them with the lightest of touches and I shiver, pressing closer to him.

"I never stopped loving you." I cover his hand with mine, guiding it down my stomach to the edge of my panties.

His fingers slip into the waistband, not dipping down nearly as low as I want them to. "And I never stopped loving you."

I tilt his head up so our gazes lock. "We're doing this for real."

He gives me a wicked grin. "Which 'this' are you referring to?"

I pinch his hip. "You know which 'this,' and if you want *that* you better take this seriously."

His hand slides up to my neck, lacing into my hair and pulling my lips to his. "We're doing this for real," he mumbles against my skin.

Any response I would've made gets swallowed by his kiss. It's slow and perfect and I can't believe I get to kiss this man for the rest of my life.

I shimmy out of my panties and he shucks his boxers. My fingers wrap around his thick length and his fingers slip inside me. Our mouths never part. I cry out my release and he swallows my gasps. He rolls me on top of him, our bodies connected at every possible point, until I sit up, straddling him, guiding him into me.

He watches me move on top of him, heat blaring from the depths of his eyes. "I love you, Lana."

"I love you, Seth."

His free hand snakes in between our bodies, stroking me right where I need it. A minute later I tighten around him, and the orgasm is so strong I can't even make a sound.

Seth's hands move to my hips, grasping me as he thrusts, finding his own release a minute later.

I collapse on his chest and his arms come around me, holding me tightly. Eventually we separate, but not by much. My head rests on his chest; his fingers work their way through my hair. It's the most at peace I've ever felt.

I'm almost overwhelmed by the absolute certainty that this is how we are meant to be. And it doesn't really matter how we got here, it just matters that we did.

SETH FORCES US out of bed at some point, citing some outlandish theory that we need to eat and hydrate if we want to be able to have more sex.

I don't have anything decent in my fridge, so we order Chinese food and pour some wine and find a seat on my couch. I tuck my feet under me, taking a large sip of wine because it feels like something important is coming.

Seth sits facing me, his arm draped along the back of the sofa, his fingers gently grazing my shoulder. "I want to apologize, not just for all the miscommunication the past few years—back in college and even at the reunion—but for how I handled things the morning after we slept together."

I reach over, placing a hand on his knee. "You don't need to. You said everything you needed to in the article."

"But that isn't the same as saying it to your face. I'm sorry I hurt you. But I'm mostly sorry that I didn't trust you to make the best decision for yourself. You've always known what you wanted, and gone for it, and I should've trusted you when you said you could handle long-distance." His fingers wrap around a strand of my hair.

"I'm sorry about the way I acted the morning after also. I wasn't ready to acknowledge my feelings, even though you were right and it was already clearly more than just sex. I'm sorry I hurt you." I lean over and place a soft kiss on his lips.

"Open communication from now on, yeah?"

"Deal." I take another long sip of wine. "So now that your job at the *Chronicle* is off the table, do you think you still want to stay in LA?"

He purses his lips. "Well . . . the job at the *Chronicle* isn't exactly off the table."

I raise my eyebrows. "Oh?" I guess I shouldn't be surprised by this news since Seth's position was clearly secured long before the stupid competition even existed.

"They still want to bring me in, but I turned it down." He takes my hand in his, lacing our fingers together. "I don't think I could ever work for someone who talked about you the way Natasha did on that stage. And even if she wouldn't technically be my boss once I moved over to the *Chronicle*, I still couldn't stomach the thought of working for a company that lets that happen."

I set my wineglass down on the coffee table. "I've been thinking about exploring other career options myself."

"Oh yeah?"

"Yeah. Natasha told me after you left the party that I wasn't going to get the column. At least not until some unforeseeable spot just happens to open up, who knows when."

His fingers tighten, first around the stem of his wineglass and then around my fingers. "What a bitch."

"Yeah." I breathe in and out, attempting to clear my anger. "I let her take advantage of me for a long time. I was so desperate for any maternal attention that I stuck around there way longer than I should have."

"Have you started looking for jobs?"

"I have. And I started to publicize my blog a bit, though I don't expect much to come of it financially. I've had it for a few years and I figure now is the time to make it public. I only wanted to wait to give notice at *ATF* until my article went live. Didn't want to chance her not publishing it." I pick up our joined hands and kiss his. "What about you?"

"I've already been offered a new job, actually." He swirls his wine around in his glass before taking a sip.

"Oh? Where?" My stomach tightens just a tad, wondering where he could be off to next. I know it doesn't really matter, wherever it is we'll make it work, but we just got here, and I don't want to say goodbye yet. Or ever, really.

The corner of his lips curves up in a half smirk, half smile. "It's at the *LA Times*."

I punch him in the arm, not putting my full force into it since now my arms have some serious strength. "That's amazing, you jerk."

"You're going to find something amazing too. Something you really love."

"I really love you." I plant a loud smack on his cheek.

"You have mentioned that once or twice."

This time I go for the ticklish spot on his ribs, which he dodges, hopping up to collect our Chinese food delivery.

"Saved by the bell."

We eat our dinner sitting cross-legged on the couch. I'm sure there's something playing on the TV in front of us, but I couldn't tell you what it is. We drink more wine and gobble down Chinese and talk about the future. Our future.

I don't know exactly what it's going to look like, but I do know it's ours.

Epilogue

And they all lived happily ever after.

—Lana Parker, from a book review posted on *Lana's Loves*

I DUMP A BAG OF ICE INTO A SILVER TUB STOCKED WITH wine and champagne, double-checking to make sure we have enough booze for all our expected guests. Seth brings over another bag of ice, dumping it into a cooler stashed behind the rented bar.

He comes over, sliding his arm around my waist as I straighten the napkins and cups resting on the bar top. He nuzzles into my neck, gently pulling me a few steps away. "Everything looks great. It's going to be great." His lips nip at my pulse point.

I can't help but relax into him, my head falling back against his shoulder. "I just need everything tonight to be perfect."

He spins me around, dipping me back into a breathtaking kiss.

"On second thought, let's cancel and spend the night in bed." I loop my arms around his neck and jump into his arms.

He catches me easily, a sparkling grin on his gorgeous face. "There will be plenty of time for that later." He plants one more loud kiss on me before setting me back on the ground. "But first, we have an anniversary to celebrate."

Because we needed an excuse for a party, we're marking the one-year anniversary of my blog's going public, which is also conveniently one year since Seth and I got back together, officially.

After our final articles were published on the *Always Take Fountain* website, Seth and I both quit. He started his new job at the *Times* while I focused on growing my blog, doing a lot of freelance writing on the side to actually make money and pay the bills.

Seth moved into my house a month later. Honestly, I'm surprised we made it that long, but Seth wanted to finish up some work on the place he was renting before giving his notice. It took some time for it to feel more like *our* house than my house, but Seth had no problem making himself right at home, and I had no problem welcoming him into my humble abode.

Tonight's party is being hosted in our backyard. The whole space has been strung with fairy lights, and between them and the golden hour of sunset, the whole place is glowing. There are a few high-top cocktail tables scattered around, but overall the setup is pretty simple.

Our guests arrive in a few small clumps. The *ATF* crew, whom I still make a point of seeing as often as I can. Corey and Tessa and I meet up usually once a week, and the rest of the gang turns out for monthly trivia nights.

Seth's family has come into town for both the occasion and an LA vacation. We've spent the week showing them all the sights and low-key trying to convince all of them to make the move to the West Coast. Seth and I spent Christmas back home in Connecticut and the entire Carson family embraced me with open arms once again. Seth's mom, Linda, wraps me in a big hug the minute she arrives this evening, whispering in my ear how proud she is of me.

My mom walks in next. I haven't seen her in over two years, though we've been talking more regularly. It's still a work in progress, but now that I've accepted her for who she is, it's much easier for the two of us to communicate. I was afraid she wouldn't deign to travel for something as silly as a blog anniversary party, but when I told her it was important to me that she be here, she booked her travel plans right away.

May shows up last, a little breathless, pulling me away from the backyard gathering and into the kitchen. "Sorry I'm late."

"No problem, did you get the goods?"

She hands me a paper-wrapped bushel before gesturing to the fridge. "The cake is in there."

I pull her into a hug. "Thank you. Are you ready for this?"

"I think the better question is, are *you* ready for this?"

"You both better be ready for this." Seth wraps an arm around my waist while giving May a high five. "I think it's time."

May gives me a last hand squeeze before heading out to the backyard.

I remove the bouquet of sunflowers from its paper wrapping, taking Seth's hand and moving to the back door, where we can easily hear May's speech.

"I know you all thought you were coming here today to celebrate the success of Lana's blog. Which is well earned and certainly deserving of some festivity." May catches my eye through the window and grins. "But that's actually not what we're here to celebrate. This isn't a party." She pauses dramatically, milking the attention for all it's worth. "It's a wedding."

Her words take a second to sink in, but when they do, everyone freaks out, cheers and shrieks echoing all around my tiny yard.

May hits play on her phone and the soft chords of "Here Comes the Sun" pipe out of a small speaker.

Seth and I walk down the "aisle" together, hands linked, smiles wide. We take our places in front of May. I hand my flowers to Tessa, who's already crying, and turn to face Seth.

His blue eyes meet mine, sparkling in the thousands of lights strung up around us.

And I'm home.

Acknowledgments

So, like, a lot of people told me how hard it is to write your second book and I didn't believe them, and LOL. There were a lot of moments when I didn't think this book would ever be done. There were a lot of moments when I considered deleting the whole thing and starting from scratch. There were a lot of tears and a lot of stress, and I would not have made it to the finish line without a million people supporting me.

Gaby. I cannot even tell you how essential your guidance and support have been. The only reason my mental health and this book are intact is because of you. Thank you for talking me off the ledge like a lot of times, and for making sure I didn't actually delete the whole thing and try to start from scratch. Thank you for loving this book and these characters when I couldn't yet. You are amazing and I am so #blessed to have you in my corner.

To my agent, Kimberly Whalen, thank you for always having my back and being my fiercest advocate. I am so grateful for your endless support and encouragement.

Everyone at Putnam has been an absolute dream. I am so thrilled to get to work with each and every one of you, but especially Elora Weil, Brennin Cummings, and Samantha Bryant.

Thank you to Aja Pollock, Rachel Lapidow, and Erica Rose for catching my many mistakes and fixing all my commas.

Sanny Chiu, I don't know if you'll ever know how much this cover means to me. It helped me find a deeper love for this book, and I will forever be eternally grateful for your beautiful work.

Corey Planer, your ability to listen to me whine and complain is unmatched. Thank you for always shooting straight with me and for your endless feedback and support. Also thanks for letting me steal your name!

Haley Kral, thank you for reading my words and providing insightful feedback and more praise than is deserved.

Denise, Sarah, Rachel, and Suzanne, thank you for your beautiful words about *Lease on Love* and for all the love and support you showed me as a baby author. I'm so in awe of your incredible talent, and it meant so much to me that you took the time to read and praise my book. Courtney, Lacie, Ava, Emily, Austin, Denise (in here twice you rockstar!), thank you for reading and blurbing this book and shutting up my imposter syndrome for a hot second.

To my SCV gals—Katie, Alyssa, Nicole, Lisa, Stacy, Mandi, Kristen, and Brianna—thanks for always showing up for me even though I never respond to the group text.

Ashley, you have been there for me for so many years I don't want to think about it because it makes me feel old. I'm so grateful for your friendship and am seriously looking forward to our *Golden Girls* years.

Brianna, thank you for continuing to be my first call when I have a plot that needs talking out. Thanks for smiling and nodding through all my bananas ideas!

To my family, who always show up when it matters most. Thank you for years and years of love and support.

Thank you to my son, who is way too young to read these books, but who always celebrates with me and lets me have work time when I need it.

The biggest thanks to my husband, Matt, who really had no idea what he was signing up for when he married me. Every time I come up with a new, wild plan, you tell me to go for it and that means more than you could ever know. Thank you for giving me the space and support to be brave.

And to the readers, the bloggers, the Bookstagrammers, the librarians, the booksellers, the BookTokers. Seeing your love for *Lease on Love* was absolutely mind-blowing. I am truly honored that you read and shared and posted about my little book baby. It means the world, and I am forever grateful.

Discussion Guide

1. In *Just My Type*, Lana Parker has always defined herself by her relationships. Why do you think that is?

2. At the beginning of the novel, Lana reacts poorly to Seth's arrival at *Always Take Fountain*, having only seen him once since they broke up twelve years earlier. Have you ever had someone from your past reappear like that? How would you react in that situation?

3. What did you think of the competition idea? Did you have a favorite challenge from either Lana's or Seth's list?

4. While Lana has written the dating and relationships column for years, her real passion is writing about books, art, and culture. Do you think Lana should go after her dream? Have you ever found yourself in a similar position?

5. While *Just My Type* is told from Lana's POV, Seth also undergoes a major transformation of his own. How did you see Seth change over the course of the story? Do you think any particular challenges or circumstances impacted him more than others?

6. Lana surrounds herself with supportive friends, including May, Tessa, and Corey. What role do Lana's friends and coworkers play in the story? Did you have a favorite?

7. Talk about Lana's relationship with Natasha. Why have they always been so close? How do you think Lana handles Natasha's growing interference in her professional and her personal life?

8. Do you agree or disagree with Seth's original decision to break up with Lana when they were kids? Do you think Lana and Seth have learned from their past mistakes? Why or why not?

9. Although it's part of the competition, Lana's list of tasks also works as a way for her to rediscover herself. If you had to make a similar list, what are some things you would include? How would you go about completing them?

10. What do you think is next for Lana and Seth?

About the Author

Photograph of the author © Brianna Mowry

Falon Ballard is the author of *Lease on Love*. She loves to write about love and has an undying affection for exclamation points and isn't ashamed to admit it! When she's not writing fictional love stories, she's helping real-life couples celebrate, working as a wedding planner in Southern California. She has a deep ~~obsession~~ appreciation for the Marvel Cinematic Universe, is a Disneyland devotee, and is a reality TV aficionado. If she's not busy wrangling her eight-year-old, you can probably find her drinking wine and posting a pic on Instagram while simultaneously snarking on Twitter, because multitasking!

VISIT FALON BALLARD ONLINE

falonballard.com

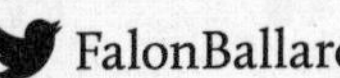